# BULL by the TALE

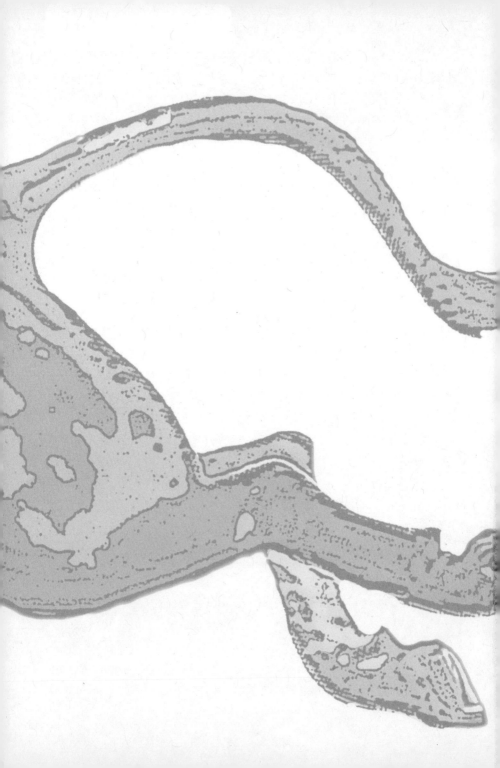

# BULL
## by the
# TALE

## JOHN DUNCKLEE

UNIVERSITY OF NEW MEXICO PRESS
ALBUQUERQUE

YEAR                                        PRINTING
10  09  08  07  06                          1  2  3  4  5


Library of Congress Cataloging-in-Publication Data

Duncklee, John, 1929–
  Bull by the tale / John Duncklee.
      p. cm.
  A collection of short stories about southern Arizona.
  ISBN-13: 978-0-8263-3889-1 (pbk. : alk. paper)
  ISBN-10: 0-8263-3889-5 (pbk. : alk. paper)
  1. Arizona—Fiction.  I. Title.
  PS3554.U46542B86 2006
  813'.54—dc22

                                        2006010481

Book design and composition by Damien Shay
Body type is Trump Mediaeval 9.5/14
Display is Vineta, Clarendon, and Adobe Garamond

To my loving and
gracious wife,
PENNY

# Contents

# The
# Developers

Jeff's collar-length salon-styled hair had started to turn salt and pepper during his junior year in high school. It had never bothered him until he reached thirty and he visited his hair stylist more frequently than before. Peggy Stack would have loved her husband even had he been bald, but Jeff's vanity was not for his wife's benefit, but for the younger women he became attracted to.

Peggy and Jeff plunged into marriage as soon as they had both graduated from college. Peggy's sorority sisters in the Chi Omega House, in spite of Jeff's background, had considered him a great catch. His widowed mother struggled to put her only son through college. But Jeff Stack had charm. It was that charm that attracted Peggy Donovan before she arranged to meet Jeff through her roommate. After one date she determined to make a husband out of him.

Peggy Donovan couldn't be called beautiful. However, she had a certain look about her that was intriguing. But her money attracted Jeff Stack more than her looks. Actually the money belonged to her father, "Big Jim" Donovan, who had founded one of Florida's most successful land development companies. He held the unofficial title of "Dean" of Florida real estate speculators with several million tucked safely away in Swiss bank accounts. "Big Jim" saw great potential in his prospective son-in-law, and as soon as Jeff and Peggy married there was no question where they would settle down after a lavish honeymoon in the Bahamas.

Jeff plunged into the business, and took advantage of his father-in-law's knowledge and experience. In five years he became "Big Jim's" most favored vice president. Peggy was happy with his advances in her father's business in spite of seeing less and less of her husband as he strived toward meeting the many demands of her "Daddy."

The absences didn't always relate to the real estate business because Jeff had never loved Peggy. He had only one thing in mind when he married her, money, and everything seemed to fit into his plan. He thought up easy business excuses to fly to eastern cities to enjoy clandestine affairs with the Yankee lovelies who frequented Florida's sun in winter.

Jeff's philandering didn't escape "Big Jim" Donovan. He saw his younger days mirrored by his son-in-law's errant behavior. But, as often happens, when a man like "Big Jim" has a daughter who is an only child, over-protection can jaundice an otherwise happy business relationship between the father and his daughter's husband. When "Big Jim" summoned Jeff into his spacious office, with walls plastered with aerial photographs of Florida, the promotion to vice president in the company wasn't the only topic of conversation. He admonished Jeff to stay closer to home.

Within a year Jeff announced that he had accepted an offer from Land Development International, "Big Jim's" closest rival. "Jesus, boy!" Donovan exclaimed in disappointment at Jeff's sudden resignation. "I know those bastards too well. Monahan, Bushnell, and all the rest. They're the biggest bunch of swamp-sellers in the business. Y'all are crazy to tie in with them!"

"They're goin' West," Jeff said firmly. "That's where the money is...West."

"Shit," Donovan said, biting the end off a long green cigar. He paused to clamp it between his tobacco-stained teeth and light it. His tone softened. "I think you're foolish, Jeff. Florida's been damn good to me, and there's a helluva lot of cake left. Y'all have heard the rumors about Disney figurin' to build another 'Disneyland' here. Hell's fire! We can tie everything up in options, and make a killin'. I'll give y'all the whole deal."

"I'm sorry, Jim, but I've already made the decision."

"What's Peg had to say?"

"This is my decision, not hers," Stack replied.

"What the hell do y'all mean, Jeff?" Donovan roared, as he rose from the large, leather, executive chair slamming his fist on the top of the large, walnut desk. "Y'all wouldn't be here if you weren't married to my daughter!"

"Maybe that's a good reason to leave," Jeff said calmly as he stood up, turned, and walked out of "Big Jim" Donovan's office.

"Stupid bastard," Donovan muttered as he picked up his phone to call Peggy. Yes, she knew about Jeff's decision. No, there was nothing she could think of to do to pound any sense into his head.

Within the week Jeff Stack, L.D.I.'s newest and youngest vice president, spoke from his hotel room in Los Angeles with Joe Bushnell at the Orlando headquarters. Jeff had learned where Disney Enterprises planned its destination project in Florida. By the time Jeff returned, L.D.I. bustled with activity as all the executives focused on "OO," Operation Option. It soon became known how Jeff had gleaned the important information from a pretty Disney secretary after dinner and a night in his hotel room. Bushnell dubbed him "Option Stud."

"Big Jim" Donovan discovered the information after L.D.I. had bought up most of the available options around the Disney site. He didn't make any moves of his own because he wondered why Disney Enterprises had not expanded their position with any other option buying of their own. "Big Jim" flew to Rome, and spent a month-long vacation cruising from port to port in the Mediterranean.

Being in the middle between her father and Jeff bothered Peggy Stack, especially since "Big Jim" had emphatically stated that Jeff was no longer welcome at his sprawling seaside estate. She had tried to discuss the situation with Jeff on several occasions, but gave up one evening after dinner at the Bushnells'. "It won't be long before I'll be able to buy and sell 'Big Jim' Donovan," Jeff bragged. At the same time Jeff told her that he would be leaving on a business trip out West, and might be away for a month.

He returned to Florida after three weeks. The trip took him to Arizona, and New York, and after landing in Orlando, he drove directly to L.D.I. headquarters. His colleagues gathered in the "War Room" to hear the details of L.D.I.'s latest purchase of the Dominguez Ranch near the Mexican border. "Fifty thousand acres for an entirely new community on an old Spanish land grant," Jeff explained. "I got it for three million, two million less than we figured. I found a way to discover the bottom line."

"Goddam, Jeff," Bushnell remarked. "If that thing of yours ever wears out, L.D.I. will go down the tubes."

"How much is usable?" Ernest Grayson, the chief engineer, asked.

"Damn near the whole enchilada," Jeff replied. "It sits in this beautiful Concepción River Valley between two mountain ranges. Helluva deal! While we're getting it all together we can lease the grazing to a rancher I met down there. Helluva deal!"

"I know we have discussed this before, but after this trip what are your latest ideas, Jeff?" Joe Bushnell asked.

"I still think our major market is California. There's a bunch of stuff in Arizona that seems to be attracting the prune pickers, but flyin' 'em in to look at our deal will make it fly. There are always the Texans too. They are always lookin' for a place to go to get out of Texas."

Ernie Monahan, L.D.I's president and chairman of the board, had listened to Jeff's ideas, both on the telephone and in the meeting. He had few doubts about the project's prospective, but he still wasn't acquainted with the West. "What about your projections for getting all the permits necessary to break ground, Jeff?"

"I spent a week checking that all out. I predict a year at most. That includes engineering, county, and state permits. If we get going right away it should be less. Those rubes out there won't know what hit 'em when we swoop down Florida style. The county planning director is about to retire, and he's all but given me approval after two dinners. He thinks we are the best thing to hit the tax rolls in Thunderhead County."

"Let's get going on it right away before he decides to hang it up," Monahan replied. "Y'all said closing is in two weeks, so we, all of us, better get out there and look around before then."

The board of directors made their tour, and all were impressed by the property and its potential. In spite of such a short period of research, Jeff Stack impressed them all with his knowledge of the entire region.

In the days that followed the master plan for Río Oro was formulated around the large, oval, pecan conference table in the "War Room" of L.D.I's headquarters in Orlando, Florida. The folks in La Flor, Arizona, stopped wondering about the sale of Rancho Dominguez when the six billboards appeared along the highway.

Monahan had sent Joe Bushnell and Jeff to hire a regional engineering firm, and acquire all the necessary permits from the state and county bureaucracies. Jeff and Joe were happy to report that not a single environmentalist had shown up at any of the meetings. Thunderhead County, Arizona, had little idea what it was in for.

The groundbreaking ceremony included three locations on the same day. The entire band of L.D.I. executives flew in for the occasion. First came the BIENVENIDO Building, near the river, where executives and salesmen would maintain their offices. The BIENVENIDO Building's main purpose at Río Oro stemmed from the need to impress prospective lot buyers that the planned community on the old Dominguez Ranch had integrity. Clients had to have something to look at besides the empty mountains, rolling foothills, and the cottonwood-studded floodplain of the Río Concepción. Land Development International may have been new to the valley, but their methods had proven lucrative in peddling swampland in Florida. L.D.I.'s executives pinned much hope on their venture in the West, and Jeff Stack was L.D.I.'s boy wonder.

Earth-moving machinery parked on a long mesa overlooking the valley waited to begin clearing mesquite, catclaw, and other brush for a hotel to accommodate prospective buyers. The last stop that day was across the river, and along Ochoa Creek, where an eighteen-hole golf course had been surveyed.

During the engineering phase two arguments arose between Ernie Grayson and the firm of Colter, Smith, and Marquez. Marquez wanted to locate the hotel beneath the crest of the mesa in the tradition of Frank Lloyd Wright, but Grayson following Jeff Stack's demand, insisted that it be located on top as a beacon for travelers along the highway leading to Mexico. Marquez also didn't approve of the close location to Ochoa Creek of the back nine holes of the golf course. He maintained that a hundred-year flood would take out half the course. Grayson believed in earth-moving machinery, and stubbornly held that a dike would prevent such a disaster.

"This is not Florida, Mr. Grayson," Marquez said.

"I've been engineerin' before you entered your so-called university, boy. We're keepin' the course as it is on the plat."

Antonio Marquez resigned his position, and moved to Colorado when his partners told him to go along with the Florida boys.

The BIENVENIDO Building took three months to complete by working two shifts. Joe Bushnell and Jeff Stack arrived for the final inspection, and to oversee the decoration of the interior. Joe had the responsibility of expediting the hotel and golf course construction. Jeff took on the advertising campaign and sales planning. Jeff's endeavors took him away from Río Oro for the most part. With Los Angeles the center of the prime sales target, he spent much of his time there, negotiating advertising rates, and trying to arrange air transportation to Arizona. After several attempts to do business with existing small airline companies, he came upon a man who owned four obsolete Lockheed Constellations, and would furnish pilots if L.D.I. signed a two-year lease on the aircraft.

Two weeks before the grand opening Jeff spent almost every hour working with the sales crew. They were instructed to follow the Río Oro formula that had proven effective in Florida. "Y'all need to know how to hard sell without it bein' obvious, 'cause when these people get here y'all have about eight hours to get 'em to sign."

The plan called for meeting the Constellations in Rinconada with chartered buses for the trip to Río Oro. The salesmen would rotate meeting the flights, and during the bus ride they were to describe the wonders of "The Planned Community For Western Living." They were also to stress the "investment potential" of the lots.

Chicago furnished the other sales target, but only for mail-order sales through full-page ads in the Sunday paper. Should Chicago prove to be a lucrative market Jeff planned an expansion to other major urban areas in the Midwest and East.

The grand opening drew many of the valley locals, mostly for the refreshments, but also out of curiosity. Three planeloads of potential buyers also arrived, and at the end of the welcoming sales talk by Jeff Stack, the first sale was made. The buyer, a plant by L.D.I., started things rolling, and by the end of the day sixty lots had been sold. The next day, as the first entourage of Los Angelenos boarded their buses for the ride back to Rinconada, Jeff happily reported to Ernie Monahan that the salesmen had a 50 percent success rate for the first go-round.

Monahan took Jeff by the arm, and they went into his office. "Jeff," he began. "You have done a helluva job here. A far better start than both of us figured, and I sure hope it continues half this good. I know you have worked your tail off on this, but I need you back in Orlando for a couple weeks to get the Disney stuff off the ground in case they make a formal announcement of their location. We've got two months left on our options. Joe Bushnell can handle things here until you get back."

"Sounds reasonable to me, Mr. Monahan," Jeff answered.

"By the way, Jeff," Monahan continued. "Why don't you route y'all's flight back through L.A., and snuggle up to that Disney secretary. See if you can get more specific information out of her."

Jeff smiled at the chairman of the board. "I'll do what I can."

Two weeks back in Orlando made Jeff restless to return to Río Oro. He had gone to L.A. and found that the Disney secretary had been fired. He tried to score her replacement, but the girl was married, and wouldn't give him the time of day. Sales at Río Oro, after the grand opening bunch, had slowed, and Jeff was sure it was because he wasn't there. He didn't know what to make of the Disney deal in Florida. Nobody else, including Monahan, did either. Monahan agreed that he might as well get back to the West, and stir things up.

Jeff Stack arrived at the BIENVENIDO Building at three in the afternoon after driving his rented LTD from the Rinconada airport.

The heavy, plate-glass door opened electronically at his approach, and upon passing into the spacious reception area his grayish blue eyes automatically zoomed to pretty Lucinda Sandoval seated at the desk. "Good afternoon, sir," she said. "Welcome to Río Oro. May I help you?"

"Hi, I'm Jeff Stack, Orlando headquarters. Joe Bushnell's expecting me." He met Lucinda's smile, and thought to himself, "she sure is an improvement over that old bag who used to be here."

Lucinda lifted the gold colored phone from its cradle on the multi-buttoned base, and pushed the intercom switch for the resident vice-president's line. "Mr. Stack is here for Mr. Bushnell," she said.

Jeff ran his eyes over Lucinda as he waited. His leering did not escape her soft brown eyes as she waited for an answer. "Mr. Bushnell will see you right away, Mr. Stack."

"Thank you, uh."

"Lucinda."

"Where did they find you?"

"I live near the mission."

"Fantastic," Stack replied. "Great gimmick!"

Lucinda wrinkled her brow quizzically at his remark.

"Nice meeting you, Lucinda," Stack said. "Y'all are a definite improvement for Río Oro."

"It's nice meeting you, Mr. Stack. Have a nice day."

Jeff walked over the polished, red, Mexican tile floor to the hallway flanked by sales and executive offices. Joe Bushnell had left his desk, and waited in the hall by his office door to greet his friend from Florida. "Jeff, good to see you," the ruddy-complected Bushnell said. "Welcome back to Río Oro."

Bushnell looked ready for eighteen holes of golf in his well-tailored, white sport shirt, and bright blue double-knit trousers.

"Thanks, Joe," Stack returned. "That's the second time I've been welcomed in five minutes. Where did you find Lucinda? What a doll!"

"You old son-of-a-bitch," Bushnell said. "Y'all never change."

"Son-of-a-bitch, maybe," Stack countered. "But never old."

They entered the office with its picture window view of the river and a major portion of the eastern part of the development. "Help yourself to a drink, Jeff," Bushnell said.

"Good idea, after that flight. Lots of bumpy air. One for you too?"

"Yeah," Bushnell said. "On the rocks. Walker Red."

"Well, ol' buddy," Jeff said. "What the hell's goin' on here?"

"I'll tell y'all, Jeff, I'm gettin' concerned about the sales. They're not up to where they should be."

"I agree," Jeff replied. "But what's the problem, the salesmen?"

"I don't really know. They seem to be workin' right. Maybe it's too far out in the boonies for these California cats to feel right about."

"I'm not sure either, Joe, but I'm thinkin' to get the sales force together and chew a little ass. Maybe that'll get things goin'."

"Worth a try," Bushnell said. "I'm kind of worried about that damn Disney deal back home too. Have y'all heard anything back there?"

"Not a damn thing. Monahan doesn't like it either."

"You can always go to L.A. and cuddle up to that secretary again," Bushnell said, and grinned.

"I already tried, and she's been fired. They put a new girl there who's married. Hell's fire, she wouldn't even go out for coffee."

Jeff and Joe called a meeting of the sales force before the next flight of Californians arrived.

"Y'all have got to convince these cats that they NEED a lot in Río Oro! That this is their last chance to own a hunk of this beauty here. Now, if y'all can't do that, I can damn sure find someone who can!"

"Mr. Stack," one of the salesmen said. "I think that a bridge over the river would help. I've heard comments in the buses that they are concerned about getting to the lots if there's water in the river."

"That's interesting. Thank you," Jeff replied. "Any of the rest of y'all have anything more to add?"

"That bus ride from Rinconada is too long," another man said. "By the time they arrive, they think they're out in the middle of nowhere. Maybe a shopping center would give the place a sense of community."

Jeff and Joe had thought about the comments before returning to Bushnell's office. "I think a bridge would help, Joe. That crossing with culverts looks all right to us, but for someone from the land of freeways, it might look inadequate."

"I think you might have something there," Bushnell said, leaning back in his chair. "I'll give Monahan a call right now, and see what he thinks about it. I know damn well he won't go for the shopping center yet. Who would shop in it?"

Jeff left the office and went to the huge map of the subdivision that dominated one wall of the reception area. Every lot was pictured, and when a lot sold, a tag in the shape of a cowboy hat was attached to that lot with a thumbtack. Jeff had added a hundred fake tags to the map to make it appear that Río Oro lots were selling like McDonald's hamburgers.

Bushnell reported happily, "Orlando thinks the bridge is a great idea." Joe called the engineers. They had already given thought to a bridge instead of the culvert crossing, so it wouldn't take long for them to bring down a complete drawing, ready for a contractor.

"What's goin' to happen to sales here when the pretty golden leaves fall off all the trees along the river, Joe?"

"Goddammed if I know, but you'll be here to find out. As I was talkin' about the bridge with Monahan, he said he had exercised the option on the Purcell parcel, and now Disney announced another delay. Monahan wants me back in Orlando, so Río Oro is your baby."

Jeff Stack sat in silence wondering about the Disney deal. He was concerned that Monahan had gone through with the option before there was definite word from Disney.

"By the way, Jeff, will Peggy be coming out to spend the winter with y'all?"

"No," Jeff replied casually still thinking about the options. "She doesn't want to take little Mike out of school. What's the story with Lucinda at the reception desk? She's a doll."

"She's lived in the valley all her life. I hired her after the grand opening while y'all were in Orlando. Lots of class for a local Mex, would y'all agree?"

"I had an idea out there as I was talkin' to her, Joe. She could bullshit the buyers that she can trace her ancestry back to Verdugo, the Spanish dude that rode through here to colonize up north. Might be a good gimmick to give this deal a more permanent image."

"I'm for anything that'll dump these lots as quick as possible," Bushnell replied. "I think the bridge will help. By the way, tell that salesman to come in here. Monahan wants to give him a little reward for his idea."

"I'm getting scared of that Disney outfit, Joe," Jeff said, changing the subject to his greatest concern. "That option exercise cost a bundle, and we've got several more due in a month or so."

"Everyone is concerned, Jeff. That's why I'm flyin' back on Friday."

At four o'clock Jeff left the office, and approached the reception desk. Lucinda was busily typing with her back to him. He stopped at the desk and cleared his throat to get her attention.

She turned around to face him. "Yes, Mr. Stack, can I help you?"

"I have an idea I'd like to talk over with y'all. How about joining me at the hotel for a drink?"

"Mr. Bushnell wanted these letters finished today."

"That's all right, I'll explain to Mr. Bushnell."

"My brother will be here to pick me up at five o'clock."

"That's easy to remedy," Jeff countered. "Call your brother, and tell him your boss will be driving you home."

"Well, I guess I could do that."

"Fine, I'll be back in five or ten minutes."

Joe Bushnell was staring at the river crossing through the picture window as Jeff returned. "I'm takin' Lucinda up to the hotel for a drink... How about that connection, ol' buddy?"

"Christ, I knew she wouldn't have a chance as soon as y'all saw her. Her brother's a big feisty Mex, Jeff, and meaner than a riled up gator when he's mad, I hear."

"Hell, she's out there callin' him off right now."

Bushnell turned to the window, and extended his arms. "Watch out women of the Concepción Valley, the gray stud's a roamin'!" He turned around and shared a laugh with his colleague.

Lucinda Sandoval enjoyed sitting with the charming man from Florida with the accent she was becoming used to. As to his proposal concerning her lineage, she found it amusing. Nevertheless she listened as Jeff Stack talked. Jeff, on the other hand, sensed that getting Lucinda into his bed might take more time and effort than he wished.

She accepted his invitation to dinner, and relaxed into easy conversation with her third margarita. "A beautiful girl like y'all must have dozens of boyfriends," Jeff said inquisitively. "I feel lucky just to be sittin' here with y'all."

"I'm afraid my father's strict, old-fashioned ways have scared most of the boys away," she replied openly. "I am twenty-one, and he still keeps me sheltered as if I were only sixteen. It is the way of the Mexicanos."

"Will you be in trouble having dinner with me?" Jeff asked.

"No," she replied. "You are my patrón. That makes it all right with my father."

"That's good. I don't want to see you get in trouble."

"What about you, Mr. Stack?" Lucinda asked. "Are you married?"

"No," Jeff lied. "I was once, but it was annulled." He made a mental note to make sure Bushnell wouldn't give him away before he left for Florida.

While they were eating dinner the Californians began drifting into the dining room. "I wonder how many of these prune pickers came over here for a free vacation from the smog with no intention of buying anything," Jeff said.

"I don't know, but the company seems to spend an awful lot of money getting them here," Lucinda said. She resented the land development basically, but the receptionist job paid better than anything she had done before, and Río Oro was not too far for her brother, Paco, to drive her back and forth to work. She also had a lingering resentment against most wealthy gringos in the valley, especially the Adamses, because her father now irrigated the fields that once belonged to her grandfather, José Sandoval.

After dinner Jeff and Lucinda returned to the lounge for after dinner drinks. When the four musicians arrived, she hoped Jeff Stack would ask her to dance. It took them a while to tune their instruments, and adjust the sound system. The first piece, an instrumental, sounded good to both Jeff and Lucinda, and when the braless vocalist took the microphone Jeff asked Lucinda to dance.

"I would like that, Mr. Stack."

"Let's make it Jeff, OK? 'Mr. Stack' is fine for the office, but we're not in the office right now."

"OK, Jeff," she said looking up into his eyes as he took her slender waist with his arm, pulled her in close, and began to dance. Lucinda hadn't expected such a beginning, and stiffened with surprise, but as Jeff guided her expertly she found herself relaxing against him. As she put her head against his chest, Jeff tightened his arm slightly, enjoying the feel of her breasts against him.

Lucinda felt comfortable with Jeff, even attracted to him. She had often thought that the only way to escape becoming a "broodmare" to one of the local Romeos, and raising his children on tortillas and frijoles while he went from one menial job to the next would be to find a man from elsewhere. That is basically why, at twenty-one, Lucinda Sandoval remained unmarried, still lived at home, and was guarded constantly by her overcautious father.

When Jeff kissed her goodnight in the mission parking lot before driving her to the old adobe home up the road, she felt completely under his control, but still reticent to encourage him further.

Jeff drove back to the hotel. There were still some of the lot-lookers drinking even though the musicians had packed up and left for the night. He sat down for a drink as he thought about the company situation and Lucinda Sandoval.

A fiftyish-looking red-faced man with a "Lakers" cap, and loud shirt expanded between the buttons by his round, protruding belly sat down next to Jeff at the bar. "Not a bad dinner they sprung for us, eh man?" he said, trying to strike up a conversation with Jeff.

"Helluva deal," Jeff answered. "What do you think of Río Oro?"

"Not bad," the man said slurring his words. "But it's a long way from everything. Havasu has shopping centers. I've been to a bunch of these deals."

"Y'all gonna buy a lot?" Jeff asked, suspecting the man used development excursions for a cheap holiday.

"Hell no, I'm just along for the ride...Only way I can get away from the old lady 'cause she don't like to fly." The soft, round belly jiggled up and down with his laughter.

"Go screw yourself, leech!" Jeff said as he rose from his seat, and left the bar.

The man stopped laughing abruptly, and with a quizzical stare, watched Jeff walk out of the lounge. "What's the matter with that jerk?" he asked the bartender. "Gimme another beer."

Joe Bushnell left the valley in the middle of a rainstorm. The winter storm front had moved in Thursday night, and by Friday morning the rain began gently falling over much of the lower Southwest. Jeff sat in the office looking out the window at the rain. The construction crew had left the bridge site, and gone home. "This rain will raise hell with sales," he thought to himself. He picked up his phone and pushed the intercom switch for Lucinda's desk. "Hi. Jeff. Have y'all seen any weather reports on how long this rain is going to last?"

"The morning weather on TV said it was a large cyclonic storm coming in from the Pacific, and it might hang around a few days. My father always watches the TV weather because he is an irrigator for the Adams Ranch."

"I reckon there's not much we can do about it anyway. How about dinner tonight?"

"OK," she replied. "I'll call Paco, and tell him not to pick me up."

They drove to the Mexican border town of Robles de Plata for dinner in a restaurant called La Gitana, "the gypsy," catering mostly to American tourists. Jeff had been there once before with his cronies from Orlando.

A long, old bar, made from native, black oak greeted patrons as they entered the plastered adobe building, stained from years in the weather without the benefit of paint. Behind the bar, a short wall divided two large dining rooms. A bevy of uniform-clad waiters and bus-boys stood around chatting idly on the rainy night with only a few diners eating by candlelight. Normally they would be scurrying about trying to keep ahead of the crowd of tourists.

Jeff took Lucinda by the arm, and led her into the bar. The Mariachi band slouched at the far end of the bar, but when Jeff and Lucinda took their seats, and ordered their drinks, they stood up slowly, picked up their instruments, and ambled over in hopes of a commission to play. Two violins, two acoustic guitars, and a bass guitar called a guitarón, began tuning as the trumpet player approached the couple. "Música?" he asked, looking at Jeff first, and then toward Lucinda.

"They want to know if you want them to play music," she explained.

"Sure," he said. "But y'all are gonna have to tell them."

"Sí, por favor," Lucinda said to the leader.

"What song do you want, Señorita?" the leader inquired impassively.

Lucinda hesitated momentarily as titles of Mexican songs passed through her mind. "First we want 'Guadalajara,' and then 'El Corrido del Caballo Blanco.'"

She had never been with anyone who could afford Mariachi, and the experience of making song requests thrilled her. "I hope you like the songs I requested," she said, leaning toward Jeff, as the musicians seemed to begin playing "Guadalajara" automatically.

Jeff ordered more drinks. He enjoyed the music, the atmosphere, and the company of Lucinda Sandoval. When they had finished "Caballo Blanco," Jeff told Lucinda to request another song. "'Malagueña Salerosa,' please," she said.

One of the violinists dropped his instrument to his side to sing with a beautiful baritone voice. Both Jeff and Lucinda sat mesmerized by the music. "Gracias," Jeff said to the Mariachi when the song ended.

The leader approached. "Twenty dollars," he said.

"What the hell do you mean, twenty dollars?" Jeff said, thinking he was about to get ripped off.

"For música...twenty dollars," the leader said calmly.

Lucinda put her hand on Jeff's. "You have to pay the musicians," she explained. "I'm sorry, Jeff, I thought you knew...I wouldn't have requested so many songs."

Jeff fished his wallet out of his pocket, and handed the leader a twenty-dollar bill. "Don't worry about it, sweetheart, it was worth it, if only to watch y'all listen. I thought the entertainment came with the place. I came over here with some of the guys from Orlando once, but we didn't know any songs to request."

"Poor gringo," she said, and laughed.

After dinner Jeff suggested they return to the hotel and dance. "Good," Lucinda said happily. "Let's dance!"

The rain had intensified by the time they had driven halfway back from Mexico. It no longer drizzled, and the lack of visibility made Jeff slow down. "I wish it would quit raining, dammit," he said. "We'll never sell any land in this weather. It's hard enough to sell when the sun is shining."

"It's been raining for three days," Lucinda commented. "My father said this morning the river will run if this keeps up much longer."

"That might be just what we need!" Jeff said. "Nothin' like runnin' water in the goddam desert to turn people on to buyin' land."

"As long as the river doesn't decide to take out the crossing," she said.

"Yeah," he said, and thought about the bridge, wishing it had been started at the same time as the rest of the construction.

They ran from the car to the entrance of the Río Oro Inn as the rain pelted down. Jeff forgot the problems confronting Land Development International as he held Lucinda close to him on the dance floor. "What are y'all thinkin' about sweetheart?" he whispered in her ear.

"I don't think I had better tell you that, Jeff."

Her initial embarrassment faded quickly once she was alone with Jeff in his room, and as his hands began unbuttoning her blouse she felt herself tingle with anticipation.

The rain continued throughout the night, and by the time Jeff sat down in the dining room by the window for breakfast, he could see a ribbon of water in the river.

It had taken three days of the gentle winter rain to fill the pores of the Río Concepción watershed to saturation. Then from the tops of the Sierra Diablo on the east, and the Sierra Cimarron to the west, tiny rivulets formed, trickling downward. As they progressed down slope they joined to form larger rivulets, and further on they began following the creases in the slopes formed by eons of natural erosion. In the creases other small streams from the ridges joined them. As the rain became more intense the volume increased. The entire watershed began to quicken its pace. The dry arroyos throughout the foothills soaked slowly, but as they too became saturated their courses filled with the excess, and eventually flowed into the river. It was another day before the sands of the deep sandy riverbed filled to capacity, and the ribbon of water began flowing downstream.

Jeff Stack watched as he ate his eggs and bacon. Luis Sandoval watched as he walked over the footbridge Bill Adams had paid for. Brian McTavish watched as he took his morning walk to the river under his slicker before the coffee drinkers arrived at his porch in La Flor. Sandoval and McTavish both knew that the ribbon of water could change to a raging, rushing, roaring flood if the storm front decided to stay around for another three days. McTavish had studied southwestern watersheds for years. Luis Sandoval drew his knowledge from listening to his grandfather and father as they described the changes in vegetation they had seen in their lifetimes. Both McTavish and Sandoval knew that too many cattle had been allowed to graze the fragile grassland, and the fuel for periodic fire had vanished, leaving room for brush to move in. Before, the fires would sweep through and kill the brush seedlings, and not harm the grasses, which have a different system in their roots, and stems that resist fire. The grasses once formed a sponge with their fibrous roots over the watershed, soaking up the rains so that the soil could absorb the water slowly, and eventually let it into the larger arroyos that carried it to the river. That was when the Río Concepción had a year-round stream-flow. Now the soil was bare between the clumps of brush, and nothing much was left of the grassy sponge. Now when the raindrops hit the bare ground the tiny silt particles rose to forge a film, and the rivulets formed quickly because there was nowhere else for the water to go except rapidly down over the surface instead of slowly through the soil. Flood.

Lucinda looked up and smiled as Jeff entered the BIEN-VENIDO Building. "Good morning, beautiful," he said as he arrived at her desk.

"Good morning, Jeff," she whispered.

"Y'all do good things to my heart, girl," he said before bending over to kiss her gently on the cheek.

"Mine too," she said, and smiled. "My father was right about the rain. Have you seen the river?"

"Yeah," he replied. "I just hope today's buyers like running streams."

The stream-flow increased steadily throughout the morning. The large concrete culverts of the crossing filled halfway with rapidly moving, muddy water by the time the first two busloads of lot lookers arrived. The drivers of the buses, instead of waiting outside for the passengers and salesmen to re-board after their indoctrination session in the BIENVENIDO Building, walked in, and asked Lucinda if the crossing was safe.

"The drivers want to know if the crossing is safe," Lucinda said, over the intercom to Stack.

"Tell them to get their asses in gear, and get those bastards over there to buy lots. Of course the crossing's safe, I can see it from here!"

Both drivers reluctantly proceeded over the crossing for the two-hour tour of Río Oro's lots, golf course, and countryside. Meanwhile the river swelled until the current became a rampage, filling the culverts. When the buses returned to carry the passengers to the hotel the river had risen further so that the crossing was no longer visible.

The buses stopped, and the drivers disembarked to view the situation. "I'm not driving over that son-of-a-bitch," the lead bus driver said emphatically.

"I'm with you, Bill," his companion seconded. "How long we'll have to wait for that river to go down is anyone's guess."

"Jesus Christ!" Jeff exclaimed as he saw the two buses stopped on the east side of the crossing. Quickly he walked out to the reception area. "Lucinda," he said. "Route your calls through Esther, and come with me!"

Lucinda pushed the re-route button on the console, and followed Stack outside. They drove hurriedly to the crossing, and parked. "Look at that current!" Jeff exclaimed. "I thought it looked bad from my office window!"

"The river can really be powerful. But, I don't ever remember seeing this much water in it."

"I just hope that crossing doesn't wash out," Jeff said.

Just as Jeff finished expressing his hope for the crossing they saw the first huge concrete culvert suddenly break through the surface of the wildly rushing torrent, and sink again as the current grabbed it from its place, and transported it easily downstream. They watched incredulously as the remaining culverts were lifted, and flung by the swift, tremendous force of the wild water until there remained no evidence that they had ever been installed. A bulldozer, left parked near the river by the bridge workers, suddenly flopped into the river as a huge section of the bank gave way, and joined the flow. "Holy shit!" Jeff yelled. "I never even noticed that dozer sittin' there until it went!"

"The crew left it because of the rain two days ago," Lucinda said. "They probably thought the rain would quit overnight."

"At least the dozer's their problem, not mine," Jeff
remarked. "Is there another way out somewhere?"

"There's a bridge near the crossroads, but they would
never get over Diablo Canyon."

"What about Ochoa Creek?" Jeff said. "They might get
through and get out on Camino del Río."

"I'll bet the Ochoa is high too," Lucinda said. She had
seen the dike that had been built to protect the golf course,
and wondered if it had held. She didn't express that thought
to Jeff, because it was obvious that he had enough to worry
about without wondering about Ochoa Creek.

Bob Cremin, the salesman in the first bus, walked out
as far as he dared, and beckoned to Jeff. Jeff stepped away
from the car and approached with caution. Cremin cupped
his hands around his mouth. "Any ideas, Jeff?"

"Just keep 'em happy, I'm goin' back to call the sheriff."

Cremin waved, and returned to the bus. Jeff and
Lucinda drove back to the BIENVENIDO Building. "Get
the sheriff on the line, sweetheart," Jeff said as they neared
the entrance.

The sheriff told Jeff the only advice he had was to wait
until the river went down. Jeff slammed the receiver down.
"Goddam dumb Mex son-of-a-bitch."

He looked out the window, and saw the rain begin to pelt
down again. "Lucinda, get me the state police on the line."

"Right away," Lucinda answered, and began pushing
buttons. She felt sorry for Jeff having to face so many problems in an area he knew so little about.

Jeff felt better after talking to the search and rescue
division chief who promised to send a helicopter as soon
as one became available. After hanging up he remembered
the incoming flight from L.A. He glanced at his wristwatch. "Jesus, they've already landed!" he said out loud,

still looking out the window. He almost had Lucinda call the airport to send the flight back to L.A., but remembered that he would need the two buses to take passengers from the stranded buses up to the hotel when the helicopter arrived. He sat down at his desk to try to puzzle out the best solutions to the problems he faced.

By mid-afternoon the helicopter had not yet arrived. He wondered why the buses from Rinconada hadn't arrived. Jeff paced in his office wondering if there could be some way to get food to the stranded people if the helicopter didn't show. He went out to the reception area. "Lucinda," he said. "Get search and rescue on the line again, and ask 'em what the hell happened to the helicopter."

Lucinda lifted the gold colored phone to her ear. "Jeff, I don't get a dial tone, the phone's out."

"Goddam, what next?"

The words had barely come from his mouth when all the lights in the reception room went out. "Oh shit," he said, with a tone of defeat in his voice.

Lucinda was accustomed to the frequent power failures during storms. She had always looked at it as part of the way of life in the valley. She decided to keep her thoughts to herself. Jeff walked outside to stand under the porch roof and heard the screeching sound of a siren from the highway. He wondered again about the overdue buses from Rinconada. As he turned to reenter the building the sound of the helicopter came thumping through the rain as the praying mantis–like aircraft circled near the stranded buses. Jeff opened the door and called to Lucinda. "Come out here, babe. If they try to dump them off here, tell them to go to the hotel. The putting green will make a perfect pad."

"OK, Jeff," she said, and went out to the porch as he ran to his car to drive to the hotel.

He raced up the hill and nosed the car into the loading zone. He reached the putting green just as the helicopter approached. He trotted to the center of the green, waved to the pilot, and retreated quickly to one side. Everyone in the hotel was gaping at the sight from the windows of the dining room.

In a rush of wind and rain the pilot eased the aircraft to a landing, and Jeff, ducking his head low, went to the door to help the passengers disembark. A crewman in fatigues opened the door, stepped out, and began helping the passengers. "Where'd y'all come from?" Jeff asked.

"We're army. State search and rescue are tied up, but we'll have your people over here pronto," the crewman informed Jeff.

"I damn sure appreciate y'all doing this," Jeff said.

"You bet."

The passengers had mixed feelings about the experience, but Jeff had little concern about that. He felt relieved to see them safely in the inn where almost all amenities were available except the telephone and power. He returned to the car, and drove back toward the BIENVENIDO Building. As he traveled the overpass crossing the highway he saw a state highway department truck parked with its circling yellow caution light on. Two men were erecting a roadblock on the northbound lane. Jeff stopped, stepped out of the car, and leaned over the railing. "What's goin' on?" He yelled.

One of the men looked up. "The river took the highway out this side of the mission," the man yelled back, and returned to his task.

Jeff returned to the car and continued to the BIENVENIDO Building.

"The highway's out this side of the mission," he informed Lucinda. "Looks like you'll be stayin' with me tonight, beautiful."

Lucinda smiled.

The sky cleared somewhat the following morning, but overnight the river had swollen considerably, and covered most of its floodplain. Mainly the raging Diablo Canyon charging into the river, exploding at its confluence, pushing the current west to undermine the bank beneath the roadbed, had caused the highway break south of the mission. The day before, the break was estimated at a hundred yards, but overnight the cresting river chewed out almost half a mile. Most of the huge cottonwood trees had been uprooted, toppled, and sent downstream. The first had taken Bill Adams's footbridge with it. The concrete ford that had cost him eight thousand dollars also disappeared. Bill and Nancy Adams were marooned in their spacious mansion on the east side of the river. They drove as close to the river as they dared to view their situation. "Goddam!" Bill said. "That's the last dime I'm spending on that goddam river."

"Well I hope the county comes and fixes things soon," Nancy said. "We have that dinner dance at the country club day after tomorrow."

"What the hell, Nance," Bill returned with impatience. "Look at the goddam river. We are going to be here for a helluva spell. How's the booze supply?"

"The booze is fine as long as there's no company, but we're almost out of Philadelphia Cream Cheese, and your special marmalade."

"As long as the booze holds out I don't give a damn. We ought to put the ranch on the market when the river goes down."

27

"I agree with that, dear," Nancy said. "The river makes me feel like a prisoner. Besides, if the ranch sells, the IRS might leave us alone."

For a change Nancy Adams felt happy about the flood if it would mean she could move to town.

The National Guard helicopter landed in the pasture of tufted fescue grass the following day with a cargo of emergency rations for those stranded by the floodwaters. Bill Adams left the house to see what was going on in his field. When the crewman informed him about the mission, Bill returned to the house to ask Nancy if she needed anything.

· "See if they can get us some smoked oysters, and some of that thin-sliced Russian rye bread that goes so well with cream cheese. Oh, I almost forgot, Bill, we are almost out of Philadelphia Cream Cheese."

"What the hell, Nance, that's an army helicopter, and they probably have C-rations!"

"Oh well, see if they have any Pall Malls, I only have a carton left."

"Good grief," Bill said as he returned to the helicopter to ask for some Pall Mall cigarettes. The crewman handed him a carton of Camels with no apology, and when Bill was clear the aircraft lifted off to fly to another location.

The few Hispanic families living on the east side of the river welcomed the C-rations and cigarettes. The ranch-owning gringos had freezers full of food. Most had portable generators in use during the power outage.

On the sixth day after the flood began, the stream flow had subsided enough that the highway department sent word that they would attempt to rig a tight line, and use a rowboat to help those who wanted to cross the next day. The ranch owners became excited with the prospect of escape, called each other with the telephones back in order, pooled their booze, and threw "the party to end all parties" at Margo Altman's place. Most had not been around during the days that partying had lasted for weeks, and even months on end, but they claimed the biggest party ever pitched in the valley.

Most, as usual during heavy rains, had left vehicles on the west side of the river. With the foot bridge washed away, the cars and trucks stood idle, except for one that had been parked too close to the river, and had been snatched away by the flood waters. Luis Sandoval rode the aluminum boat from the west bank to the east to report to work for Bill Adams.

For Lucinda, the days and nights with Jeff were full of pleasure. She enjoyed the freedom to spend all night with him, and wake up to join him for breakfast. She also felt that she was able to calm his nervous energy that was trying to solve all the problems of L.D.I. She didn't know whether to be happy or sad when the highway department took away the roadblock after blading out a one-lane detour away from where the river had taken the road.

The foreman of the bridge construction company arrived to discover his bulldozer missing, and Jeff told him about seeing it sink into the river. The company searched for days with metal detectors, and from the air. The machine was never found.

After the telephone service returned Lucinda received a call from Ernesto Maldonado, who worked on the golf course. Ernesto lived on the east side of the river, so when the storm ceased, he drove his old battered pickup truck to work. Ernesto informed Lucinda that Ochoa Creek had torn apart the dike, and much of the course behind it. Jeff nearly screamed when she told him about the call.

Jeff didn't enjoy having to sleep without Lucinda. After the first night alone he asked her to have dinner. She called her brother, and told him she would be home late. Jeff drove to Robles de Plata where they dined at La Gitana. Jeff drove her home at midnight.

The next morning when Jeff came in from breakfast he asked Lucinda to see what she could do about spending the night. "I don't know how I could explain it to my father. It was difficult enough trying to tell him I had to work late last night. I really must get back early today."

"OK," he said. "It's just tough to go to bed alone after taking you home."

"It's tough for me too, Jeff."

Lucinda went back to her typing. The telephone rang as she finished a letter. She picked up the receiver. "Good morning, Río Oro," she said.

"Mr. Stack, please," the voice on the line said.

"Who may I say is calling?"

"This is Mrs. Stack."

Lucinda was startled. She switched the call to Jeff's office, put the receiver back on the cradle in the console, and stared blankly, dazed, at nothing in particular. She didn't know whether to cry or scream. "Mrs. Stack," she thought. "What a liar!"

Jeff was upset with Peggy's phone call informing him that she had decided to fly out for a visit. He gave her a number of reasons why it would not be appropriate, but she accepted none of them. "I won't interfere with your busy schedule, dear. I'm sure there's much to see around there," she said. "I'll see you tomorrow, Jeff."

Jeff seethed with anger as he sat motionless at his desk, wondering how he would keep Peggy away from the BIEN-VENIDO Building and Lucinda. And how he would explain to Lucinda when he couldn't see her after working hours. He was also angry that she had called when there was no emergency. The rest of the day kept him busy trying to get the flights from L.A. and the buses coordinated so that Río Oro could start selling lots again.

Lucinda found it difficult to concentrate on her work, and felt relieved when Paco pulled up in front to drive her home. She had little to say at supper, and once in her bed she couldn't sleep for thinking about the big lie she had so innocently believed.

The drive back to Río Oro with Peggy made Jeff uncomfortable, but he covered his feelings with the expertise of the perennial philanderer. They had lunch at the hotel, and afterward Jeff suggested to Peggy that she get settled and take a nap. "Things here are all mixed up from the damn flood," he said. "I've got a lot of unscrambling to do, so I'll see you in the bar around five-thirty."

Jeff drove to the BIENVENIDO Building, anxious to get busy after his morning's absence meeting Peggy's flight. He wanted to find out the progress being made on the crossing repair since the stream flow had diminished enough so that new culverts could be installed. "Hi, Lucinda," he said as he walked toward his office. "Pretty dress."

"Thank you, Mr. Stack," she said coldly without looking up from her typing.

Jeff caught the icy tone in her voice, but dismissed it with the thought, "Probably having her period," and continued to his office. Esther came to his door. "Mr. Stack, there are several telephone calls for you to return. I put them on your desk."

"Thanks, I'll get to them right away."

"Mr. Bushnell seemed very anxious to talk to you," she said.

"OK, Esther, get back to him first for me, will you?"

Lucinda had considered staying home after a mostly sleepless night. She had also considered quitting her job, but after an early morning walk by the river she had put the situation into a perspective that put her anger toward Stack secondary to earning the better than average wage she made with the development company. She still felt taken in, and used by the handsome, suave Floridian, and remembered her grandfather's words: "The gringos own the valley now. It is our fault for selling our land to them. So we Mexicans had better learn to live next to them, not with them, if we are to remain here. It is truly a strange feeling to be working our land, which is no longer our land, and by continuing in this manner, we will never have the chance to buy our land back. We may remain in our valley, but so will they."

Jeff looked out the window after talking on the telephone most of the morning. He watched the one construction crew put the finishing touches on the crossing repairs as the other worked on the abutments for the bridge. He glanced at the clock, and decided to go for an early lunch at the hotel. "A couple of real dry martinis ought to settle my nerves," he thought. He had sent Peggy to Piedras Rojas for a shopping spree that would set him free of her for two days.

He stopped by Lucinda's desk on the way out. "Hey, sweetheart," he said. "Call your brother so we all can have dinner at the Gitana this evening."

"No thank you, Mr. Stack," she replied without looking up.

"What's goin' on, sweetheart? Why the ice?"

"Come now, Mr. Stack," she said after turning to look him straight in the eyes. "I really am not stupid. I have decided it is best not to go out with the boss when the boss is married!"

Jeff felt his face flush, and his stomach tighten to the point of pain. "I can explain everything, Lucinda."

"No explanations are needed or asked for, Mr. Stack," she said bluntly, and turned back to her typewriter.

Jeff left without another attempt. *How did she find out?* he thought. *"Damn, I should have told her to begin with. Jesus, no. She would never have gone out with me in the first place."*

The flood hadn't affected La Flor except for keeping the tourists away. Brian McTavish had driven his old Dodge pickup truck down to look at the river, and noticed that the old cottonwood grove still stood in spite of two feet of water, which had back-flooded into a large pool. Next, he had driven to the golf course, and decided to have a drink at the bar, and chat with his friend, Octavio Sotelo, who had been bartending there since the club opened. Octavio glanced away from the glass he was polishing as Brian sat on a stool at the empty bar. "What's happening, my friend?" Brian said in greeting.

"Not much," Octavio returned. He put the glass on the shelf, and walked over to Brian. The two shook hands across the bar.

"A lot of water, eh?" Brian said.

"Enough," Octavio said. "I get caught on this side of the washout in the highway. I don't go home for three nights, and the wife is all pissed off."

"That's like the old ladies," McTavish said, and grinned.

"That's the way they are," Sotelo said, and returned the grin. "What do you want to drink?"

"How about a Scotch?"

Octavio poured the drink, and placed it on the bar in front of McTavish. "What did the river do here?" Brian asked.

"Very bad," Octavio began. "They lose two of the greens, and four fairways are under water. Everybody is all pissed off."

"Build next to the river, and the river will take it," McTavish said.

"I try to tell them when they start all this. Nobody listens to a bartender."

McTavish finished his drink, and continued his observations of the flood by driving to view the bridge near the crossroads. The center part remained, and looked strange by itself in the middle of the swift current. There were no signs of the rest of the structure, but the raging river had widened the channel considerably when it worked to demolish the approaches. The flood, and all its consequences, were grist for his mill. "This should substantiate what I've been trying to write about," he thought.

He wondered how another writer in the valley was surviving being isolated across the river. Mike Moore and McTavish spent time together discussing many topics. Mike kept busy with his novel, and Brian worked most days on his ecological study of man's effects on southwestern grasslands. Brian had tried to call his friend, but the river had ripped out the line that serviced residents on the eastern side.

When Peggy Stack's flight to Miami was called, Jeff gave her a kiss good-bye, and left the terminal for the trip back to Río Oro. He felt relieved to have Peggy out of the way, because he wanted to take up with Lucinda again, if he could somehow smooth things over. He saw Esther at the reception desk when he entered the building. "Where's Lucinda?"

"Her brother came for her a little before noon, Mr. Stack. She wasn't feeling well, and went home."

"That's too bad," he said. "I hope she's not coming down with something. There's a lot of flu going around."

"She said she would probably be back to work in the morning."

"Any calls?"

"They're on your desk, Mr. Stack."

"Thanks, Esther."

The next morning Jeff saw Lucinda at her desk when he arrived for work. "Good morning," he said cheerily. "Feelin' better?"

"Yes, thank you," she said. "Mr. Stack...Jeff...I would like to talk to you in private."

"Well, sure," he said, wondering. "Come on back to my office, Lucinda."

She sat down in one of the chairs as Jeff took his place behind the desk. "What can I do for you?"

Lucinda hesitated, groping for words. "Jeff, I'm pregnant," she finally said as tears welled in her eyes.

"Good Jesus! Are you sure?"

"Yes, I'm sure," she said through her tears. "I went to the doctor yesterday."

Jeff Stack felt his stomach suddenly feel as if it was tying itself into a hundred knots. He got up from his chair, and stood looking out the picture window. Lucinda pulled a handkerchief out of the pocket in her blouse, and wiped the tears away. "What are you going to do about it?" he asked, still facing the window.

"What is there to do about it? I'm pregnant!"

"Get an abortion, Lucinda. I'll pay for it."

"I don't want an abortion, Jeff. I don't believe in that."

"Well we can't get married, Lucinda. I'm already married."

"I know that, Jeff. If I had known that from the beginning, I wouldn't be pregnant. I don't want to marry you anyway."

Jeff's thoughts were filled with confusion, guilt, and panic, and he felt his heart thumping through his temples. "What is it that you want from me, Lucinda?"

"Jeff, I need your help. I don't know what will happen when I tell my parents. They are very old-fashioned, and they might even turn me out of the house."

"In other words you are asking me to support you if that happens?"

"It's your child too, Jeff. I only ask that you support your child."

"Of course ... of course," Jeff answered, looking at the floor. "I wish this hadn't happened. I thought you must be on the pill."

"I don't believe in the pill either, Jeff."

Jeff pondered the dilemma, searching for something to say or do to solve the problem. "Your hospitalization insurance with the company will take care of your expenses."

"I really want to quit now, Jeff. I would feel better not to be here."

"If y'all quit, I don't know about the hospitalization coverage, I'll have to call Orlando."

Lucinda could feel herself turning to anger against Jeff Stack. *"He only thinks in terms of dollars, gringo bastard,"* she thought to herself. "You can call Orlando or whatever, I don't care, Jeff," she said with cold deliberation. "This is my last day. Will you please send my check to me in the mail."

Lucinda Sandoval stood up, and left the room.

Jeff felt relieved to have the office to himself. "Dumb broad, what did she think would happen without the pill?" he thought.

The intercom buzzed. "Yes, Esther."

"Mr. Bushnell is on two, Mr. Stack."

"Thanks." He pushed the button for the outside line. "Joe, how are things?"

"Not bad...not bad. Listen old buddy, when do the planes start flyin' again?"

"Should be startin' tomorrow. We've got the new culverts in, so we're ready for the buses."

"We've been with the auditors for a week, and the company's a bit shaky to tell you the truth. We could pull it out with some above average sales out your way."

"That might not be too easy since the flood got plastered all over national television."

"Yeah, what a bitch that was. Anyway I'll be there day after tomorrow to give y'all a hand."

"OK, Joe, before y'all hang up there's something I need to have y'all find out about the company health benefits. Can a girl who gets pregnant and quits, still draw benefits throughout the pregnancy?"

"She can't quit. She has to go on maternity leave. Who is it?"

"Lucinda Sandoval."

"Goddammit, Jeff."

"Jesus, Joe, how was I supposed to know she wasn't on the pill?"

"Write it up as maternity leave, Jeff...and good luck. See y'all in a couple days."

He pushed the intercom for Esther. "Esther, tell Lucinda to come back in here please."

Lucinda came to the door. "Yes," she said.

"Instead of quittin', put yourself on maternity leave. I just talked to Orlando. That way the insurance will pick up the hospital, and the doctor."

"Whatever you say, Jeff."

"Things are not going too well for the company right now, but I'll try and keep your check coming as long as I can."

"Thank you," she said coldly.

"Lucinda, why can't y'all understand that an abortion would solve everything?"

"Damn you, Jeff Stack. An abortion would solve your problem, not mine. I told you I don't believe in abortions, and besides it's my body we are talking about, not yours!"

Jeff stood, and watched her walk away. By the time he finished telephoning to get the buses and planes coordinated it was past five o'clock. When he left for the hotel, Lucinda Sandoval's reception desk was empty.

"All I can say is I'm sorry," Lucinda said through her tears. "I'm sorry I have brought disgrace to the family." Lucinda ran to her room.

Luis and Maria Sandoval remained silent. Luis, because he was sad and angry. Maria, because she would wait to speak to her daughter alone. Both stared at the candle flickering inside the red tumbler with its picture of the virgin of Guadalupe. "I have watched the gringos all my life," Luis said finally. "So did my father, and his father. They come to our valley because it is beautiful. They stay for a while, take from the valley, and then they leave. But while they are here they destroy part of the beauty. The beauty includes the people of the land."

"We have had a good life here, Luis," Maria mused.

"That is true," Luis replied with his eyes flashing in anger. "But this gringo with the fancy clothes has soiled our daughter. I will go to see this son of a bitch tomorrow."

Luis drove his old Chevy to Río Oro the following morning. Esther looked up as he walked into the reception room. "May I help you?"

"Señor Stack. I come to see Señor Stack."

"May I tell him your name?"

"Luis Sandoval."

"Are you Lucinda's father?"

"Yes, I am Lucinda's father. I come to see Señor Stack."

"One moment, Mr. Sandoval," Esther said as she picked up the phone, and selected the button for Jeff's office. "Mr. Stack, Mr. Sandoval, Lucinda's father, is here to see you."

"Christ, get rid of him somehow. Tell him I am in a meeting or something."

"Very well, Mr. Stack. Mr. Sandoval, Mr. Stack is in a meeting right now, and can't be disturbed. Can you come back another time?"

"No thank you, I'll wait," Luis replied stubbornly.

"Mr. Stack will be busy all day, Mr. Sandoval. May I give you an appointment for another day?"

"No...No thank you...no appointment," he said and left.

Luis Sandoval carried his anger with him to the county courthouse. Judge "Nacho" Ortega stood chatting with his secretary when Luis walked into the office of justice court. Ortega recognized Luis immediately. "How's it going, Don Luis?"

"Fine. Fine."

"What can we do for you, Don Luis?"

"I must talk to you in private," Luis said.

"Very well, Don Luis. Come on in to my chambers," the portly Ortega said.

Luis explained about Lucinda, and his unsuccessful attempt to see Jeff Stack. Ortega gave his full attention to Luis's account, and when it was finished, the justice of the peace of Thunderhead County leaned back in his chair. "You probably wouldn't gain anything by seeing that idiot anyway, Don Luis. This is a matter for the county attorney. I will see that something is done, and get word to you."

"Gracias, 'Nacho,'" Luis said. The words of Ortega made him feel confident that something would be done about the situation.

"Go home, and don't worry. I'll take care of the son-of-a-bitch."

Ignacio "Nacho" Ortega had been in office for fifteen years. His political base reached back further. He had established himself as the "Protector" of the Hispanic population in the county, and he had never lost an election, even against another Hispanic candidate. He bent, but never twisted the law to arrive at a unique fairness for both Anglos and Hispanics. "Nacho" Ortega had known both sides during his lifetime.

Two weeks went by before the process-server drove to the BIENVENIDO Building with a summons ordering Jeff Stack to appear before Judge Ortega in justice court. After the process-server left Jeff flew into a rage. "Goddam," he said to the picture window. "A goddam gringo doesn't have a snowball's chance in hell chance with these connivin' Mexican bastards!"

Ortega always took a calculated risk in paternity cases. Few errant fathers showed up in his court with attorneys. Very few of these cases had to be remanded to superior court because Francisco O'Malley had a reputation for stripping most fathers of most of their paycheck whether blessed by matrimony or not. The fathers preferred to take their chances with Ortega. Jeff Stack fell in with the norm, not wanting any more notoriety than necessary. He answered Ortega's summons alone.

The justice of the peace held the hearing in his chambers, where he could sit comfortably in his reclining chair. "Mr. Stack, these are serious charges against you," Ortega began. "I want you to understand the gravity of the situation." He enjoyed watching the dapper Florida land developer squirm in front of him. "What do you have to say for yourself?"

"Your honor," Jeff said with his voice wavering. "I really don't know why I'm here. I told the girl I would support the child...I even agreed to carry her on the payroll as maternity leave so the company health plan will pick up the tab."

"You studs just think in terms of dollars. You don't give a good goddam how all this affects the entire family. You think you can come here and screw around, pay the tab, as you refer to it, and leave. Mr. Stack, that is bullshit!"

Ortega reached for the manila folder on his desk, and opened it. His stubby fingers leafed through the legal-size papers until he found the one he wanted. He pulled it out, laid it on the desk in front of Jeff, and said, "Read it, and sign it."

Jeff read the document entitled "Agreement." It called for two hundred dollars a month child support, and a ten-thousand-dollar performance bond in favor of Lucinda Sandoval in case of default. "Goddam," Jeff thought as he read the conditions. "This bastard really means business. With this chicken-shit performance bond, I wouldn't escape anything if I split to Florida."

"Your honor," Jeff said. "These terms seem a bit severe to me. Are you sure this is ordinary procedure?"

"Mr. Stack, the performance bond is not ordinary procedure excepting that you are a resident of Florida, and I must insist on that security. Realize that I am not forcing you to sign anything."

"Suppose I choose not to sign?"

"I will remand you to Judge O'Malley, superior court. And Mr. Stack, let me give you some free advice. Judge O'Malley will nail your balls to the courtroom floor. You're getting off easy with me, because Lucinda Sandoval has already agreed to these terms."

"I guess you're right, judge," Jeff said. He took the pen, and signed the agreement.

"You have forty-eight hours to post the performance bond with this office, Mr. Stack," Ortega reminded him. "Court adjourned."

Jeff felt more comfortable when the formalities were over. "Where do I get this bond, judge?" he asked.

"That's up to you, Mr. Stack. Cash is cash, if you read the agreement."

"My God, I didn't realize it was cash," Jeff said. "That's a lot to raise in forty-eight hours!"

"That is your problem, Mr. Stack," Ortega returned. "Have a nice day...and uh, Mr. Stack, keep it in your pants."

Jeff turned crimson with embarrassment and rage. Ortega laughed at his own humor as he watched Jeff walk to his car.

"Give a connivin' Mexican a little power, and he thinks he's Pancho Villa," Jeff said aloud as he drove out of the county parking lot.

Somehow Jeff rationalized that the company should post the bond for his indiscretions. The afternoon following the hearing he took out the company checkbook and wrote a check for the ten thousand dollars. On the ledger he wrote "Performance bond as per zoning ordinance." He went to the bank first for a cashier's check, and then to Ortega's office, where he left it with the secretary.

The same evening, "Nacho" Ortega drove to the Sandoval house where he sat in the kitchen over coffee, explaining everything to Luis, Maria, and Lucinda. Ortega had grown up in much the same kind of house where a candle to Guadalupe burned day and night. He felt good to be able to give the family some sort of comfort against the domination of a different culture.

The first "Constellation" after the flood arrived from Los Angeles the day after Joe Bushnell's flight landed from Florida. Joe and Jeff spent the afternoon going over Joe's plan for a new sales strategy with the salesmen.

"I think I fired them up," Joe said as they sat down to dinner at the hotel.

"I damn sure hope so, Joe," Jeff said. "This entire project needs firing up with the flood and all."

"You should be sitting in Orlando waiting for Disney to make a decision."

"I guess I can't envy y'all on that score," Jeff remarked.

"I think we need another receptionist, Jeff," Bushnell continued. "Esther just doesn't cut it, know what I mean?"

"Yeah, I know. I just haven't got around to it."

"Who is that big-busted blonde waiting tables at the far end of the dining room?" Bushnell asked.

"That's Susie. Good waitress, and friendly."

"What we need at that desk is a good-looking broad with a smile and a nice set of boobs," Bushnell said. "I could care less if she can type or all that. Just so she smiles and gets these jokers excited about Río Oro."

"That sounds good to me," Jeff said.

"Get her over here, and we can see what she's like."

Jeff caught Susie Pardo's attention, and she came to the table. Joe Bushnell dominated the interview, and after twenty minutes, Susie Pardo became the new receptionist in the BIENVENIDO Building.

During the night a storm front eased into the valley, and by morning Sierra Diablo disappeared in a shroud of clouds. The buses arrived in a slow drizzle that showed no signs of clearing. Jeff gave the "kick-off" talk. Susie mingled with her cleavage and smile serving coffee and doughnuts. In spite of the weather sales met the average. The storm passed two days later, but the stream flow in the river had risen to a point where the construction foreman recommended against using the temporary crossing.

"That goddam river is goin' to break our backs," Jeff said to Bushnell as they sat in the office.

"Take it easy, ole buddy," Joe replied. "We ain't dead yet."

"Helluva year to start a development," Jeff replied.

Joe Bushnell had been back at Río Oro for a week when as he and Jeff dined at the hotel at their usual table, Joe fell silent for a few moments as he contemplated how to approach Jeff Stack about a question that had plagued him all afternoon. "I remember I paid all the performance bonds when I was here before," he said casually. "The planning director told me there wouldn't be any more that he could see."

"Oh, yeah, I forgot to tell you. They needed one for the bridge," Jeff lied.

"Damn, those bastards bleed a guy," Bushnell said.

"For sure, Joe."

"Incidentally, Jeff," Bushnell continued. "I think you forgot to take Lucinda Sandoval off the payroll. Orlando will keep sending her checks if you don't notify them."

"I guess I did forget. I'll take care of that first thing in the morning."

Jeff Stack felt trapped. He wondered if Bushnell had come out to help with sales, or to check up on him.

Lucinda Sandoval would have gladly traded the signed agreement and cash bond from Jeff Stack for the return of her parents' respect. A wall of coldness loomed between her, and especially her father. Her brother, Paco, sensed something different, but didn't understand it. He surmised that it came about because his sister had quit her job...nobody in the family had told him. He decided to follow Lucinda outside when she went to close up the chickens for the night.

"Hey, little sister, what's goin' on?" he asked.

"I'm just shutting up the hens from the coyotes," she answered.

"No, Lucinda, I'm talking about what's going on between you and the folks?"

"What do you mean, Paco?" She asked, trying to evade his questioning.

"They hardly talk to you, or you to them...It's been this way for a couple weeks."

Lucinda could tell that Paco would not give up until he found out. "Come on down to the river where we can talk," she said.

"Paco, if I tell you, I want you to promise me that you will not interfere," she said when they stood under a stand of cottonwood trees by the river. "I know your temper too well."

"OK, Lucinda, just tell me what in hell is going on."

"I'm pregnant."

"Mother of God!" he exclaimed as Lucinda went to her brother's arms.

"It's such a mess, Paco. He's married. He didn't tell me."

"Is it that bastard gringo at Río Oro?"

"Paco, you promised not to interfere," she said, after drying her tears. "He has signed an agreement to support the baby."

Paco Sandoval had always been close to his sister. He immediately became defensive on her behalf, and hatred for the mod-tailored Jeff Stack engulfed his emotions. They walked back to the house in silence. "You promised not to interfere," she reminded him as they approached the house.

Paco grunted an unintelligible reply.

The family ate supper in silence until the dishes were cleared away. Paco announced that he had a date with Yolanda, his current girlfriend. "Don't wait up for me, Mama," he said, and went outside to his car.

Paco's anger increased as he raced the souped-up Ford toward Río Oro. Once at the hotel he calmed as he walked to the registration desk in the lobby. "Mr. Stack, please," he said to the clerk on duty.

"Just a moment, sir," the girl replied. "I think he's in the dining room. I'll page him for you." She picked up the phone, and called the dining room hostess. "There's someone here at the desk for Mr. Stack, Helen."

Jeff and Joe Bushnell were lingering over after dinner drinks. Helen's message gave Stack a welcomed opportunity to leave, because he held a constant, uneasy feeling that the subject of the performance bond might return to their conversation.

Jeff had never met Paco, and was surprised when he introduced himself. "I'm Paco Sandoval, Lucinda's brother, Mr. Stack. Lucinda would like to talk to you. She's outside in the car."

"That's good. I've wanted to talk to her. Thanks," Jeff said, wondering what Lucinda wanted.

When they were well away from the hotel entrance, Paco, who had walked ahead, stopped, and turned toward Jeff. "Hey, what's going on?" Jeff asked, seeing the hatred leaping at him from Paco Sandoval's eyes. "Where's Lucinda?"

Paco's first punch caught Jeff on the corner of his mouth, splitting his lower lip and loosening some teeth. "Conniving gringo hijo de la chingada!"

The second blow cracked his nose. Without hesitating, Paco drove his fist into the stunned man's solar plexus, and as Jeff doubled over with the pain, Paco slammed his fist to the back of his neck. Stack hit the paved surface of the parking lot, peeling the skin off the right side of his face. Still enraged, Paco sent a swift kick into the unconscious man's rib cage. He reached down, and dragged him off the pavement onto the bluish-green graveled landscaping. "Dirty gringo son-of-a-bitch, I ought to cut off your balls!" he said, and strutted with completed vengeance back to the Ford.

Consciousness returned to Jeff as he lay on the hospital bed. Bushnell stood at his beside. "Thank God y'all's back, old buddy," Joe said when Stack's eyes seemed to stay open through the swelling. "I almost gave y'all up for dead by the time the ambulance got there."

Jeff's memory brought him back to the fierce look on Paco Sandoval's face a moment before the first tooth-shattering blow hit him. He tried to say something to Bushnell, but couldn't.

Bushnell looked at Jeff, and grimaced. His head looked like a huge bruise where the bandage didn't cover. "Who did it?" he asked.

Jeff again tried to speak, but the effort brought on a stabbing pain to his jaw.

"There's some busted ribs, y'all lost two teeth, and have a slight concussion. The doctor said you'll be OK in a couple weeks. Just stay here, and heal up. I wish y'all could tell me who the hell did this. I'll have the sheriff slap his ass in jail in a heartbeat. I'll be by tomorrow to see how y'all are doin'."

Bushnell saw that the swelling had somewhat subsided when he came by for a visit the next afternoon. "Y'all look like you might live, old buddy," Joe said in greeting.

Jeff had difficulty talking, and many of his words came out garbled. "I feel like I've been in a gator pit," he managed to say.

"Y'all looked like it last night when I found y'all lyin' on the gravel. Tell me who did this number on y'all, and I'll have the bastard locked up."

"No," Jeff said. "Let it go by."

"You must have made somebody madder'n hell."

Jeff Stack had decided that to cause the Sandoval family any more trouble would not be worth it in spite of his current dilemma. He also felt that he probably had it coming. "There's nothing quite as humbling as getting the shit kicked out of you," he thought to himself after Bushnell left the room.

Paco Sandoval revealed nothing to Lucinda or the rest of the family. After leaving the hotel parking lot, he had driven to Robles de Plata. He returned home early in the morning.

Lucinda spent the first part of her mornings helping her mother with household chores, trying to break through the barrier, but Maria Sandoval, as much as she may have wanted to, could not bring herself to a position contrary to her husband.

After she finished the household chores, Lucinda began her daily walks along the river over the landscape she loved. She looked at the changes the flood had caused, and marveled at the force of raging water. During these solitary walks she began to recapture the feelings of independence, which had been strong when she was younger. She thought about the baby, and what it might be like raising it without a father. There was the question about what she would do with her life, and where she would go. Thoughts of all that had happened, and the contemplation of them often left her confused. She began thinking about returning to the sketching and painting she had enjoyed while in school. One day she asked Paco to take her to town to look for art supplies, and returned with plenty to work with.

The following morning she hurried with the housework, and took her equipment to the river near Adams Crossing. She plodded through the sand until she came to a large mesquite log that had become driftwood during the flood. The river had left it stranded on the east bank, opposite a lone cottonwood tree that had escaped the fury of the flood. She sat on the log looking around at her surroundings. Everything in her view begged her to draw. She didn't know where to start: the Sierra Diablo, the cottonwood tree, the bend in the river, the rocks and boulders strewn with flood debris: it all deserved to be drawn.

The first subject she chose, the Sierra Diablo, gave her practice sketching. She looked at her progress, and was pleased that she hadn't forgotten what she had once accomplished with ease. At various locations she would stop to sketch a tree, a boulder, or just the way the river looked to her.

By April there was no mistaking her condition. She continued her walks and drawing on a daily basis except when the few rainy spells came into the valley from the west. In spite of the barrier at home she gained soothing contentment from her days along the river.

The cottonwoods were first to explode in yellow-green spring finery. The new leaves gave Lucinda inspiration to begin to use her watercolors. Her first attempt became the huge tree she had previously sketched when its skeleton of branches gave the winter winds an instrument to play. She played with the colors until she liked the mixtures. "Wow!" she said aloud. "It looks almost real." She looked at the painting critically, and decided that the tree needed a different background for contrast. Her concentration on her work made her oblivious to everything including the baby's movements inside of her. She didn't hear the man's footsteps in the sand as he approached.

The pair of faded denim pants and the equally faded chambray shirt, covered by a somewhat tattered buckskin jacket fit his thin build. His angular face wore a pleasant smile as he watched Lucinda's brushstrokes. An old, but respectable felt cowboy hat tilted slightly over his right eye. He stopped his approach at a distance not to disturb her concentration, and continued to watch her work on the painting.

At length Lucinda put her brush down, and held the painting in front of her with outstretched arms. The man saw the entire painting for the first time. "Hello," he said. "That's very nice."

"Oh!" Lucinda gasped. "You surprised me. I didn't hear you."

"I'm sorry to startle you," he said, walking closer. "I've been watching you work for quite a while. I tried not to break your concentration."

Lucinda's first reaction was a touch of fear, but that vanished with the man's gentle voice and friendly smile. "I must admit, I get very involved with this," she said.

"That's really a beautiful painting you're doing," he said. "You are very good."

"Thank you, uh..."

"Mike Moore. I live over in The Barn. I'm a writer. Do you live in La Flor with the artists?"

"Oh no," she replied. "I am Lucinda Sandoval. I live over near the mission."

"I thought you must be one of the artists in La Flor."

"I'm really not an artist," she continued. "I've only been doing this for three months. The people in La Flor are real artists."

"Huh," Mike grunted. "Your work is better than anything I've seen in La Flor."

"Well, thank you, Mike, that's a very nice compliment. What do you write about?"

"I'm really just starting too," he said. "So far all I've published is nonfiction, environmental stuff, but I'm working on a novel now."

Lucinda remembered her Aunt Ana, who worked in the post office, telling Maria about "The Writer" who never said much, and whose mail was mostly brown envelopes and occasional packages.

Lucinda found herself looking intently at Mike Moore, and looked away quickly, somewhat embarrassed. Mike sensed her uneasiness. "How about an apple?" he asked, withdrawing a shiny red Delicious from his jacket pocket.

"No...No thanks, Mike...I'm sorry I was staring at you, but you must be the one everyone calls 'The Writer.'"

"Who is everyone?" he asked.

"I was just remembering my aunt and my mother talking in the kitchen about a month ago. My Tía Ana gossips a lot. She works in the post office; the fat one."

"Ah yes, the fat one," Mike said. "Very pleasant, but she asks a lot of questions."

"That's for sure," Lucinda replied. "Lots of people around here call her a newspaper, and refer to her as 'The La Flor Daily Mistake.'"

Mike laughed with Lucinda. "Is her gossip always wrong?" he asked.

"Most of the time, because she hears one thing, and when she repeats it, there is a different meaning."

"There seems to be an oversupply of gossip in small towns," Mike observed. "La Flor probably isn't any different that way."

"But here you have the gringo gossip on one hand, and the Mexican gossip on the other," Lucinda said. "We call it 'cluck, cluck, cluck.'"

Mike laughed at the expression. "I'll have to remember that one," he said. He broke the apple in half with his hands. "Come on, Lucinda, share this with me."

"All right, as long as you have half," she said, as they both sat on the dead mesquite log.

"It's a wonder I haven't seen you before," he said. "I walk around here most every day. I must admit that my mind is generally on the novel. It's difficult to escape it, even when I walk to get away from it."

"I know what you mean. I seem to focus on my drawing. Of course the baby is always on my mind."

"When are you due?"

"The doctor says the last of August, but doctors are not always right."

"What does your husband do for a living?"

"I'm...I'm not married, Mike," she replied, looking away toward the river.

"Those things happen, Lucinda. I am the child of an unwed mother."

Lucinda looked at Mike as he sat next to her on the log. "He seems so open and warm," she thought to herself.

Mike stood up and stretched. "I guess it's time for me to leave you to your painting. It was really nice to talk with you, and I hope I see you tomorrow," he said, and smiled.

"I enjoyed meeting you too, Mike. Good luck with the writing."

Lucinda watched as Mike walked away from the river toward The Barn. He stopped, and turned around when he had gone about a hundred yards. He smiled and waved. Lucinda smiled and waved also, and then both turned to continue their separate pursuits.

She spent a good part of the evening making empanadas, the triangular pastry with fruit filling like "turnovers." There were enough for the house, and six to put in her case the following morning.

The leaves on her cottonwood tree had darkened as they unfolded further, and she decided to start another watercolor to depict the advance of spring. She spotted Mike walking toward her as the sun told her that noon had arrived. "Hello, Artist," he called when she looked up.

"Hello, Writer," she said returning his greeting.

"How's the painting coming along?" he asked. "I had to come by to see it."

Lucinda felt happy to see him. "When he smiles, his entire face shows something nice," she thought. "It's finished," she replied. "At least for now. I have started another to show the changes in the leaf color."

"May I see the finished one?" he asked.

Lucinda took out the painting, and held it up for him to see. Mike's bluish-green eyes sparkled. "That is really beautiful, Lucinda," he said. "I really like the way everything blends, just like nature."

"I'm glad you like it," she said. "Do you think it needs anything else?"

"I know nothing about art," he replied. "If I like a picture, I like it, and I like this one. It is harmonious... relaxing."

Lucinda put the painting back in the large brown portfolio, reached into her case, and brought out the empanadas. "Try one of these," she said.

Mike bit into the pastry. "Tasty," he said. "You make these?"

"Last night," she replied.

Lucinda had finished with the cottonwood tree with its darker leaves by noon the following day, and had started an ink sketch of a group of boulders around a hackberry bush when she saw Mike approaching at a distance carrying some lumber on his shoulder. "Hi, Artist," he called.

"Hi, Writer," she answered.

He lifted the boards from his shoulder, reached into his pocket for several carriage bolts, and began assembling the pieces together. "An easel!" she exclaimed. "How nice!" She stepped up to it and pretended to paint. "Did you make it?"

"Yeah. I hope it's the right height. If it isn't, I made some extra holes to adjust it."

Lucinda smiled. She felt like hugging him. "This is very sweet of you, Writer," she said. "I want you to know that it's special." She slipped one arm around his waist, and gave him an affectionate squeeze. Mike started to put an arm around her shoulders when she broke away, and looked up at him with tears in her eyes.

"Hey, why the tears, Artist?" he asked softly, and took her face in his hands.

"Half happy, half sad, I suppose," she answered, and walked to the log to sit down. "Ever since I told my parents

I was pregnant they have treated me like an unwanted stray dog. They feed me but they don't want to get attached to me. And here you are, three days ago a complete stranger, doing something just for me ... and me pregnant and unmarried doesn't seem to make any difference to you."

"I feel sorry for your parents, Lucinda. The prospect of a grandchild should bring them joy. They must be very straight."

"They are old-fashioned. And there's nobody straighter than an old-fashioned Mexican who thinks virginity is a must for marriage; for a daughter anyway."

"As for the easel," he said. "I made it for a beautiful woman who paints beautiful pictures."

"Thanks, Mike. I will treasure using it."

"Oh," he said as he reached into his pocket, and took out a steel tape for measuring. "I'd like to make a frame for the cottonwood picture, and I need the size."

Lucinda handed him the pad of drawing paper, and he wrote the dimensions on a slip of paper. "I thought you were a writer?" she said. "Are you a carpenter too?"

"I've been a lot of things, because it takes a long time to become established as a writer, and I need to eat. I started writing seriously five years ago, and I'm not what you would call established yet."

"Don't you ever get discouraged?"

"There are times when I wonder, but I love to write. I get frustrated when I have to work at some idiotic job in order to pay rent and buy groceries. I have learned to live very frugally, and someday I hope to be able to live entirely on my writing."

"You sound very determined," she said. "I guess I haven't been drawing long enough to wonder if I could ever earn my living doing it. I've never sold any, so I guess I'd better wait until that happens before I contemplate making a living by painting. I can always make a living with my typing skills. That's what I was doing at Río Oro."

"Hey, I might hire you to do the final copy of my novel when it's ready. I'll get a job as a carpenter to pay you."

"Mike, I'd type your novel for nothing, just to read it."

"Don't make any brash statements until you've seen it."

"You made the easel for me, I'll type your book."

"By the way," he said. "Let me know when you're ready to move the easel to another location, and I'll carry it for you."

"Will it be safe here?"

"Sure, just hide it behind the log. Anyway, if someone rips it off, I'll build you another."

Mike stopped writing early the next morning, and went outside to make the frame for Lucinda's painting. He chose an old, weathered, gray plank from a pile of assorted lumber he had gathered around the area. He measured, and cut the four sides of the frame, and assembled it with corner braces. Then he drove his battered Ford pickup truck to La Flor to buy the matting. After a cup of coffee with Brian McTavish he went to see if the artist Brian had recommended would sell him a sheet of white matting paper. The man was friendly, and not only sold Mike the paper at his cost, but also cut it to size. Mike returned to Brian's house across from Saint Lucia's, and the two friends walked over to El Sombrero for a pitcher of beer and sandwiches.

There were a few tourists having lunch when they walked in and sat down at a small table near the front window. A plain-looking, thin woman with long hair, and a star tattooed on each thumb came to the table for their order. "Hi, Gretchen," Brian said. "Bring us a large pitcher, two glasses, and a couple of tacos for me, please."

"How about you, Mike?" Gretchen asked.

"That all sounds good to me, Gretchen," he said, and turned to Brian. "How's everything in the *Peyton Place* of Arizona?"

"About the same, Mike. There are rumblings about forming a town council. I haven't paid too much attention to it though."

"How's the book coming?" Mike inquired.

"Tough...Goddam tough. I still need to do some more research into the history, and there's very little here in the historical library. I need to get up to the university special collections. How are you progressing with the novel?"

"It's going great. I get up at three or four in the morning, and after coffee I get right into it."

Their conversation continued through their lunch and another large pitcher. They enjoyed sharing their writing experiences with each other, especially since they were the only writers around La Flor at the time. Mike glanced at his watch as Brian poured out the last of the pitcher into the two glasses. "Damn, I better get going after this one," he said.

"Since when have you been in a hurry?" Brian asked. "You'd think you had a girlfriend."

"She's a friend so far, but I have to tell you, I really like her."

Brian dropped the subject, not wishing to intrude. They finished the beer, and returned to Mike's pickup. "Stop by when you can, Brian," Mike said as he put the truck into gear.

"You too. I enjoyed the lunch."

Mike drove back to the Adams crossing, and was happy that Lucinda had not left. He parked at the side of the dirt road, and walked over to where she stood in front of the easel. "I was almost ready to give up on you," she said.

"I'm sure glad you didn't. I'm ready for your painting. I just came back from La Flor with the matting. Can you bring it over tomorrow so I can put it all together?"

"What time?"

"Come over for one of Mike Moore's special lunches."

"Can I bring anything?"

"Just you and your picture."

"The picture and me it will be then," she said, tilting her head slightly to one side as she smiled. She put her hands on her expanding belly. "And, of course, the baby. I'm beginning to feel like I'm two people everywhere I go."

"You are very beautiful, Lucinda Sandoval," he said.

"So are you, Writer," she said, feeling a tingling sensation surge through her, leaving her almost breathless.

The big, black Labrador bitch, the hair on her back bristling as she barked at Lucinda's approach, looked quickly at Mike as he came outside. "OK, Noche. She's OK." The dog began wagging her tail, and walked over to sniff Lucinda's shoes.

"I would have been earlier, but I stopped to sketch an old, dead mesquite tree over by Diablo Canyon," she said.

"I think I know the one you mean," Mike replied. "There's a family of buzzards that roosts in it."

"Hmm," Lucinda pondered. "That would make a nice picture...sketching in the buzzards. I haven't tried birds or animals yet."

"You will have to be there before sunrise to find them."

"That will take some explanation at home," she said.

"Show them your work," Mike suggested. "They should understand why you need to be there early."

They went into the kitchen. "I will have to find another way, Mike. The gap between us seems to widen with every day. I don't even want to share my pictures with them."

Lucinda had never been inside The Barn. She had seen it many times from the outside. Now, inside, she looked around fascinated, not only by the construction of two-foot thick plastered adobe walls, and the mesquite pole rafters, but the way Mike had arranged his things of work and living. She could see that he spent most of his time writing. His housekeeping showed minimum effort, but she enjoyed observing the total essence of his environment.

Mike set the old knife-marked plank table, and brought stuffed bell peppers out of the oven. They sat down to lunch. "Don't you get lonely living here by yourself?" Lucinda asked.

"I keep too busy to think about it, and besides old Noche keeps me company. She used to follow me on my walks, but she's taken to staying home lately. She's sixteen. I do enjoy solitude, and as a writer I must have time by myself to be able to think out what I want to say, along with the actual writing."

"I can relate to that. I have always enjoyed being alone during my walks by the river. I never tire of seeing the river, even when it's dry."

"I have actually given quite a lot of thought to living alone in the past five years," Mike said, wrinkling his brow. "I lived with a woman for a while, and had to leave. She couldn't bear to be by herself, and couldn't respect my need for hours of solitude in order to accomplish my writing. I think a person has to learn to live with himself or herself in contentment before living with someone else."

"I agree with that, Mike. Jeff, the baby's father, had to be with someone all the time. When he finds himself away from people, he becomes nervous and upset. I don't know why I was ever attracted to him."

"Hindsight is always twenty/twenty."

Mike raised his coffee cup. "To the baby. May he or she be as beautiful as the mother."

"Mike, you have said I am beautiful twice today, and once yesterday...Why?

"No other reason besides the way I feel. I find you a totally beautiful woman."

"Please don't take me the wrong way," she said looking into his eyes. "I feel warm, and even tingling good each time you say that. Ever since my mistake, I have questioned myself. When I told Jeff that I was pregnant, he demanded that I get an abortion. That made me feel ugly and dirty. Then my parents' attitude has made me feel uglier and like an outcast. I feel much better now after the days along the river drawing and painting and giving me a chance to see myself better. Knowing you has brought me much peace."

"That's one of the reasons I see you as so beautiful," Mike said. "I sense what you have accomplished within yourself. I had to do that myself. But when you refer to your pregnancy as a mistake, I must disagree."

"Why? You may not feel that way, but everyone else seems to."

"Mistake is not a word I enjoy, because it is strictly a value judgment on the part of whoever uses it," he continued. "I have done things in my life that society would hasten to call mistakes. I could, like many, sit around and kick myself in the ass the rest of my life, but to what good? What would be the accomplishment? So, I have eliminated the entire concept from my vocabulary and my thinking. I only have experiences. It is difficult to regret experiences."

"Wow," she said. "You make things clear, so understandable. I have never known anyone like you. I now understand why you are so together, so collected, so mellow. You really help, Mike Moore."

"I'm glad," he said. "Hey, we have been sitting here half the afternoon, and I haven't framed your painting yet."

"Need any help?" she asked.

"No. Just sit and relax."

Mike left the kitchen, and walked to the half-barn, half-carport building where he had set up a crude workshop. He brought the frame, matting, and a few tools back to the kitchen. "It's time for your painting, Artist."

Lucinda took the painting of the old cottonwood tree sprouting its first spring leaves from her portfolio, and handed it to Mike. A few minutes later he had the painting matted and framed in the old barn wood. "I like it," he said. "How about you, Artist?"

"It is super-good looking."

The softness of the weathered wood blended with her subtle composition to enhance the landscape. Mike reached over to Lucinda, and rubbed his curled index finger on her cheek. "It's ready to hang," he said.

"I would like you to have it, Mike," she said.

"Really?"

"You have given me a part of yourself. The painting is part of me."

Mike put his arms around her shoulders, and she slipped her arms around his waist. Without hesitation he held her in a full embrace, kissing her tenderly as the passion that had been building between them all afternoon took over.

Mike drove Lucinda to the mission, and continued alone to the post office. The only letter in the box was from his literary agent in New York. He opened the envelope, and saw the check for nine hundred dollars. The agent had sold a short story he had submitted six months before. He wished he could drive to Lucinda's house to tell her his good news.

The following day next to the river, Lucinda received Mike's good news about his sale with jubilance. "Hey, Writer, I'm really proud of you," she said hugging him.

The valley simmered in the heat of June. Everything looked parched from the intensity of the sun radiating through the cloudless sky. Lucinda worked under the shade of cottonwood trees where Mike had moved her easel. She anxiously waited for middays to hear Mike's old truck coming to take her to The Barn for lunch and their siestas lying naked next to each other on the bed beneath the fan. She marveled that, in spite of her pregnant body, he wanted her.

San Juan's Day, the 24th of June, brought little hint of rain, but there were highflying thunderheads, cotton white against the clear blue sky. The thermometer on the porch of The Barn registered one hundred degrees. Tourist traffic on the streets of La Flor was noticeably absent.

July 4 came and went. Still no rain to cool the earth and bring life to dormant grass. The leaves of trees and brush on the foothills looked wilted. People in the valley who had planted gardens watered them twice daily. Mike and Lucinda spent more time in siesta.

Early in the morning of July 6 Mike saw that the thunderheads had lowered their flight pattern, and had slowed considerably. He began his day at the typewriter, and didn't give the sky another thought until eight o'clock, when he left The Barn to pick up Lucinda. In this the last seven weeks of her pregnancy she gave up the walks along the river, and Mike picked her up at the mission to drive her to

The Barn. She painted under the shade of the mesquite grove in the yard as he wrote until lunchtime came around.

By the time they returned from the mission the sky had blackened, and the clouds billowed and boiled as the intense heat from the earth lifted the warm masses of moist air quickly skyward, cooling them to condensation. Mike and Lucinda watched the storm build. He decided that watching the first storm of summer demanded his attention more than the typewriter.

Lucinda felt drawn toward Mike. Her parental situation gave her strong desires to be with him and his complete acceptance of her. "Perhaps once the baby is born your parents will change their attitude," Mike suggested, as the first thunder rolled by the cloud-covered Sierra Diablo.

"I doubt that, Mike," she said. "They may accept the baby, but their wall against me will never change. I don't really care about them anymore. My absolute certain feeling is that I love you."

"I love you too, Lucinda. I constantly wonder what it would be like to live together. I must admit it scares me a bit."

"I have thought about that too. I know I would be happier with you than with my parents, but we haven't known each other for very long, even though it seems longer."

"It does seem longer. I find myself wishing I had met you years ago."

All of a sudden a lightning bolt streaked earthward, followed by an earsplitting clap of thunder. They watched the rain travel quickly toward them across the abandoned field to the east.

"We had better head inside, or we'll get drenched," Mike said.

"Good, I like this storm. It is putting us to bed early, and I suddenly have a great desire to be next to you, Writer."

The July storms formed a spotty mosaic over the Río de la Concepción watershed. Most areas had received some rains, but other parts were more favored. The soil moisture gave the perennial grasses a good start, and the leaves on the brush no longer had their previous wilted look.

During the first week in August the frequency of storms increased so that the soil could hold no more moisture, and runoff became ubiquitous. Lucinda and Mike had taken shelter again in The Barn at noon as a huge squadron of black thunderheads rolled in with thunder, lightning, and a deluge of rain. Where most of the previous storms had come in and left after twenty minutes to a half hour, this one continued to unload its moisture steadily throughout the afternoon and evening. There was one storm cell after another, and the loud claps of thunder made it difficult for Mike and Lucinda to fall asleep. As they lay in bed in each other's arms Diablo Canyon sent a wall of water down its channel. Ochoa, though gentler, flooded its major fords. The river's ribbon of water left over from previous runoff began to flow in earnest, especially after its major tributaries donated their runoff to the cause. The *cienega* south of The Barn became a quagmire. Finally asleep, the couple didn't hear the roar of the river, but suddenly Lucinda awakened, and sat up with her left hand on the headboard to brace herself. Mike opened his eyes and saw the puzzled look on her face. "What's the matter? Are you all right, Lucinda?"

"I don't know. I just woke up and feel weird."

"Maybe you had a dream. I do that myself sometimes," he suggested.

She moved so that she was lying on her side facing him. "Hold me, Mike. Hold me," she pleaded. "For some reason I feel scared."

Mike put his arms around her, and ran his fingers through her long black hair, and rubbed her back to calm her. She closed her eyes and put her head on his chest.

"Oooh," she said suddenly. "Oh my God!"

She leaned away, and Mike saw the startled grimace on her face, and the sudden fear in her eyes. "I must be in labor!"

Mike leaned to look at the clock on the bookshelf. "Three twenty-five" he said.

"What?"

"It's three twenty-five," he repeated. "We need to time your pain intervals. At least that's what I read once."

"For God's sake," she said. "I'm not due for three weeks!"

"Nature is not always as precise as doctors are," he said.

Mike put his arms around her, talked softly, and tried to reassure her that there was plenty of time. "If need be, I can deliver the baby myself. I've delivered a lot of foals and calves. So don't worry, I am here with you, and I'll take good care of you. I love you, Lucinda precious."

"I know, Mike. I feel better already. Just being with you I feel safer than I would at home. Maybe we should drive to the hospital right now."

"It won't hurt to get ready. I'll help you get your clothes on." He went to the couch, and brought her blouse and maternity skirt.

"Oooh, there's another."

Mike looked at the clock again. "Three forty-five," he announced. "Did you feel any twinges before we went to sleep?"

"No."

"Well, there is nothing to worry about. We'll just keep timing the intervals. Remember, I'm with you."

"I'm fine, now. The fear is gone. I just don't know what this is going to be like."

"That's something I can't possibly tell you about," he said, and they both laughed.

Mike helped her onto the seat of the Ford, slammed the door shut, and walked around to the driver's side. He slid under the steering wheel, put the key into the ignition switch. "Old Ford," he said to himself. "Don't even think of failing me now."

The truck started, and Mike drove out of the yard toward Adams crossing. He had thought he had heard the river roaring, but decided to try the crossing anyway. "Damn," he said as the flooded channel came into view. "We aren't going to cross there," he said as nonchalantly as possible. "Let's see what Diablo's up to."

He drove carefully over the rutted dirt road until he saw that Diablo Canyon was as flooded as the river. "No chance through that one either," he said. "If Ochoa is full, we might as well stay home and get ready for the blessed event in The Barn."

They never made it to Ochoa crossing; the cienega presented such a quagmire of water and mud that Mike didn't think it was wise to try, and risk getting stuck in the middle. "Having the baby in our bed is better than in the cab of this truck," he said, and drove back to The Barn. During the search for a way across the river Lucinda had experienced two more contractions. He helped her undress, and put clean sheets on the bed. Then he brought all the clean towels he had, and spread two of them on the bed where she would be lying. He bent over and kissed her. "You've got to be the bravest woman in creation," he said.

"You are brave to do this," she said. "I think most men would be in a state of panic."

"I know everything will be fine. I know exactly what needs to be done."

"Oooh," she groaned. "That one was stronger."

"Eight minutes," he said. "I doubt that we would have made the hospital if the river had been dry."

"I was just thinking, Mike," she said. "I'm glad that I am having the baby here. At the hospital they do all sorts of things like shave all the hair, and enemas."

"A lot of babies have been born through wombs covered with hair."

The contractions increased in frequency and intensity until Lucinda's groans were close to screams. Mike went to the kitchen, washed his arms and hands thoroughly, and returned to Lucinda. He washed between her legs, and dried her. "Breathe deeply when you feel the contractions, sweetheart, then relax between them."

Mike began to realize that in spite of his experience with mares foaling and cows calving, this was Lucinda, a woman, and a woman he loved deeply. "Don't be breached," he thought. His thoughts flitted back to one cold January morning. A sorrel mare was having her first foal, and he had checked her every so often as the night progressed. Finally, at three o'clock in the morning the mare went down in labor. She stood up and went down several times as he watched with his flashlight. He saw the foal's tongue and one yellow hoof. "There should be two!" he had said to himself. He went to the mare, and kneeled down to grope for the other hoof. It was not far behind the first one, but it was obvious that the mare was having a problem forcing the shoulders out of her birth canal. Mike reached in, grabbed the hoof that was still inside, and pushed it back as far as he could. Then he pulled out and down in a synchronized force when the mare had her next contraction. The foal came quickly out sending Mike onto his back. He ended up looking at the foal's mouth just in front of his eyes. The rest of the foal lay on top of him. He was soaked with amniotic fluid. After crawling out from under the newborn foal, he cleared the mucous from its nose and mouth. Then he rushed to the house for a shower and dry clothes. When he returned to the corral the little filly with the slightly crooked stripe on its face was nursing the leathery bag of the sorrel mare. The placenta lay on the floor of the corral.

The fluid gushed out as Lucinda screamed. Mike looked down between her legs, and saw the baby's head begin to come out. He reached to keep it coming smoothly, guided it into the world. "Keep pushing, sweetheart, it's almost here...not much more...push...push." Lucinda bore down, groaned as she tried to push as hard as she could, and the baby came through and out into Mike's waiting hands. "You did it, it's here...everything is fine, my love. You have a son."

Mike's hands moved quickly and surely. He put the wrinkled baby boy on the blanket between Lucinda's legs after clearing a small amount of mucous from his mouth. Then he took a foot-long strand of dental floss he had previously boiled. He tied a clove hitch around the umbilical cord close to the baby's navel. After tightening another hitch, he repeated the operation further away. With the floss tightened, he took the knife he had also boiled, and severed the chord between the knots. Then he wrapped the boy in the blanket, and placed him on Lucinda's chest. She looked at her baby, and smiled. "He's beautiful," she said. Lucinda was exhausted, but fought sleep to be with the boy. "His name will be Miguel," she said. "I want to name him after his father."

Mike stood smiling at them. "Thank you, Lucinda. I am proud to be his father."

Two days later the stream flow in the river had receded enough for Ward Tuttle to drive the four-wheel drive service truck over the crossing at Río Oro. He radioed the dispatcher that he was going across the river to check on the transformer located near The Barn, a routine chore that had to be done after storms. When Mike heard the vehicle, he went outside, and was able to hail Tuttle as he passed by.

"Would you do me a big favor?" Mike asked.

"I'll sure try," Tuttle said.

"I need to get a message to Luis Sandoval over by the mission. He might be worried about his daughter, Lucinda. The message is that Lucinda gave birth to a baby boy, and that they are both fine. The telephone's out again."

"I'll see what I can do," Tuttle replied. "Where did all this happen?"

"Right here," Mike replied. "She was painting, and the storm came in quickly. She started into labor, but we couldn't get out. I delivered the baby here. Thank God there were no complications."

"My God, that's really something," Tuttle said. "I wouldn't have the slightest idea what to do. I'll get the message to old Luis if I have to drive over there."

"Sure do appreciate your trouble," Mike replied, and walked back to the kitchen.

Joe Bushnell and Jeff Stack listened on their extensions as Ernie Monahan spoke dejectedly. "That goddam Disney outfit changed locations on us, and all the options we exercised are worthless as tits on a boar-hog. We are in a world of shit, boys, and for the life of me I can't figure a way out. Y'all have any ideas?"

"Sales out here are pretty good, Ernie," Bushnell said. "There's a bunch of houses already finished, and a bunch more started."

"Y'all don't seem to understand what I'm sayin'," Monahan continued. "If we don't find some way to pull this Seminole stuff out of the barrel, the sales in Río Oro could triple and it wouldn't be enough to cover our ass."

"Why don't we fly back, and talk all this out together," Jeff suggested. "There's gotta be some way to pull this all out."

"That sounds good to me," Monahan replied. "Better make it fast, cause the bankers are already shittin' their pants."

"We'll be there day after tomorrow unless we can't get a flight," Bushnell said, ending the telephone conference.

Bushnell and Stack stared scowling at each other across the desk. Each wondered what the other was thinking. "This is about the worst thing that could happen, havin' Disney change their location," Bushnell said.

"I can't disagree there," Jeff answered. "I think I'll pack all my gear."

"You may be right, Jeff. At least out here it was the river that busted us, not some outfit changin' their mind. All we've had are bad breaks, but I'm glad I salted a little away, I think I'm goin' to need it."

"You're lucky, Joe," Stack said, leaning back in his chair. "I'm broke. I don't know what to do, or where to go. Peggy's old man will have a lot to gloat about."

"Hell's fire, y'all can snap back. Everybody needs a good salesman. The 'gray stud' will gallop again."

"Joe, the 'gray stud' is done gallopin'. The 'gray stud' is goin' to walk."

Two weeks later, the word of L.D.I.'s failures flew through the valley. For the residents of La Flor it didn't mean much except for something to talk about.

As soon as the Adams crossing became passable Mike drove Lucinda and Miguel to the Sandoval house. "I really dread going home, Mike," Lucinda said as the pickup truck pulled up in front of the house.

"If it's too bad you can always come back to The Barn," he said. "I'll be here tomorrow morning."

"Come in and meet my mother, will you Mike? It will be easier if you were there with me."

Maria Sandoval met them at the front door. "Mama, this is Mike Moore. He delivered the baby. Look at little Miguel, Mama."

Maria nodded to Mike, and peered into the blanket viewing her grandson. She smiled at the baby, and looked back at Lucinda. "Your father is very upset with you, Lucinda," she scolded. "Why were you across the river having the baby?"

"I didn't know the baby would decide to be born this soon."

"Your father is at work today. I hope you can explain all this better to him."

Mike felt embarrassed in front of Maria's scolding. "Lucinda, may I talk to you a minute alone?"

Lucinda walked back to the pickup with him. "Listen to me, sweetheart. I can't stand to listen to your mother's scolding. I think you should hand me Miguel, go into the house, get as many of your things as you can, and come back with me now instead of in the morning. This will spare you another night listening to your father. In time they may come around, and if not, that becomes their loss."

"I was thinking the same thing, Mike. I wasn't even thinking about getting my things, but maybe I should."

She left Miguel snuggling in Mike's arms, and returned to the house. Ten minutes later she appeared at the door with a suitcase and a large box. Before leaving she turned to

Maria. "Mama, I must go with Mike. We love each other, and I belong with him. I'm no longer a little girl, and Papa needs to understand that...so do you. Please tell Paco to come and see me at The Barn."

She left her mother speechless, and carried her things to the truck.

"There are some things that have to be done, even though it's difficult to do them," Mike said as they drove off to check the mail, and go home.

A week later Paco drove up to The Barn with the rest of Lucinda's belongings, and a letter from Florida addressed to her. She opened the envelope, and read the letter:

Dear Lucinda,
By this time your baby must be reality. I hope
all is well with both of you. I am sorry for all the
trouble I caused you, and tell your brother, Paco that
I hold no grudge. He actually taught me a good lesson. I am also sorry to tell you that L.D.I. has folded,
and I am out of a job. I will not be sending another
check, so go to Judge Ortega with this letter, and you
will receive the ten thousand dollars cash I put up as
a performance bond. Peggy, my wife is divorcing me.
Again, I'm sorry for all the trouble I caused.
Jeff Stack

Lucinda put her hand over her mouth in shock at Jeff's letter. "Mike, look at this letter from Jeff Stack," she said.

While Mike read the letter Lucinda turned to Paco. "What lesson did you teach Jeff Stack, brother?"

"I couldn't help it, Lucinda," Paco answered. "I lost my temper when you told me about being pregnant, so I went up to Río Oro, and beat the hell out of that gringo."

"I guess all that doesn't make much difference any-more," Lucinda said. "Mike, that ten thousand dollars will come in handy with three mouths to feed.

"I think we should put it away in a sound investment so that when and if Miguel wants to go to college, he'll have the money to do it," Mike said. "I'm not worried about the mouths to feed, my writing is starting to sell. I can always find a day job. We'll make it."

# The Miner

**J**ack Magruder counted the blasts from the shaft of the Little Josie. He had set eight sticks of dynamite to explode and crumble the hard rock to penetrate the shaft in the direction where he figured his lost vein of silver might be. When the eighth explosion went off he was glad. He walked slowly to the shack, opened the rough planked door, and made for the stove where an old blue-enameled coffee-pot sat waiting on the still hot cast-iron round plate above the fire-box, keeping the strong, bitter brew hot.

Magruder grabbed the yellowed, chipped mug from the old, gray, battered table, and walked to the stove. He took a hold of the coffeepot handle with his bare, heavily calloused hand, and filled the mug. After spooning two measures of sugar into the brew and stirring it haphazardly, the miner sat down on the old kitchen chair that had been missing four doweled back stays for as long as he had owned it.

The brew tasted good, but the restfulness of the chair felt better than anything Jack Magruder could imagine. If the blast had uncovered the vein he would be ecstatic. If there was only the rubble of worthless rocks, he would drill more holes in the rock, pack them with dynamite, caps, and fuse wires to try again. It would take a while before the acrid smoke from the blasting would dissipate allowing him to grope his way through the shaft and to the end of the drift to discover the results of his weeklong labor. The mongrel dog, thumping his tail slowly at Magruder's feet, seemed to know his master's hopes. The long-eared, shaggy-haired burro outside looked toward the shack with her ears forward. The miner sat, sipping his coffee, hoping he had found the vein he was certain had to be there. He didn't know exactly where, but he had been following it before it disappeared.

Jack Magruder had been working the Little Josie claim for twenty years, eking out a living. It had been a solitary life, suiting Magruder's nature. It wasn't that he didn't like people; he just didn't feel comfortable around more than one person at a time. That inner attitude had been a part of him all his life as far as he knew, but the twenty years of long days and nights working alone at the Little Josie seemed to have intensified it.

As he had done often, Jack thought back over his life, not only after he became a miner, but also when he was growing up in New Rochelle, New York. He remembered loathing school, because it meant being taunted and teased by his peers because of his painful shyness. He had no idea why he was shy, he just felt at ease when he was alone, walking in the woods, along the shore of Long Island Sound, or over the country roads outside this suburb of New York City. As he grew older and entered junior high school he spent most of his winter afternoons in his room reading books about the

West, especially about the mining towns and miners. During his senior year in high school he had found a book about Arizona from which he developed a strong desire. Jack Magruder wanted to go to Arizona to live.

Jack's father, Dennis, was a successful lawyer in Manhattan, and had always assumed that his only son would go to college and Columbia Law School. The farthest thing from Jack's mind was to go to any college, much less law school. After the 1926 holidays the pressure began when Dennis Magruder discovered that his son, Jack, wanted to go to Arizona and become a miner. Jack's mother, Josephine Magruder, sided with her son, but not in front of her domineering husband. It was she who convinced Dennis to give Jack enough money to travel to Rinconada after his high school graduation, and live for a year while he looked around for a place to settle.

He had grown to five feet, ten inches, and Jack was strong. The taunting stopped because none of his peers had any desire to tangle with him. His ruddy face, blue eyes with bushy, black eyebrows, was topped by black hair that had a natural wave to it. Isabel Ives found him ruggedly handsome and his shyness charming. Jack Magruder thought Isabel was the prettiest girl in high school, but without her encouragement he would never have considered asking her for a date.

From that time he didn't walk alone. Isabel went with him practically everywhere. It was while they were walking in the woods one evening two weeks before graduation that she pulled him to the ground on a grassy glade surrounded by oak and larch trees, hidden from the world. Jack Magruder wanted Isabel forever after that experience.

The day before they graduated Jack told her about his plans to go to Arizona, and asked her to go with him as his wife. "How in the world will you be able to support us?" she asked. "You should go to college and on to law school like you told me your father wanted."

"Isabel, I love you, but you are asking the impossible. I'll get established with a mine in Arizona, and then I'll send for you."

"Suppose I don't like Arizona, Jack. I love you, too, but I don't want to live with rattlesnakes and scorpions. They say those creatures are all over the place there."

"I'll write and let you know what it's like."

Jack Magruder took his shyness with him to Rinconada by rail. He found a room near the university, and spent a month reading not only about the mines around southern Arizona, but also the geology. The Arivaca area attracted him.

While buying a geologist's pick in a hardware store Jack met Roland Clayton, who was buying paint for his office building. Clayton was a successful real estate dealer, and was looking for someone to apply the paint he was purchasing. It was Clayton who struck up a conversation with Jack Magruder, and Jack took Roland's offer to paint the stuccoed adobe building, a block north of the courthouse.

During the week it took to do the work, the two men became friends. Jack impressed Clayton by his diligence, not only in the painting, but also with his self-study of geology and mining.

After packing his few belongings that included the geologist's pick Jack took a bus from Rinconada to the junction of the Arivaca Road and the Tucson-Nogales Road. From there he walked west for twenty odd miles until he arrived in the tiny mining and ranching hamlet that had been called La Aribac during the Spanish colonial period of southern Arizona history.

He wrote a long letter to Isabel Ives describing the country he felt was an absolute paradise. A month later he read her reply that told him she was engaged to one of their classmates who was studying to become an engineer. Jack read the letter over and over with tears rolling down his cheeks.

Magruder spent three months poking around the hills looking at the geology, and picking at rocks he found around the Cerro Colorado Mountains. He bought a jennet burro from a man in Arivaca and named her Isabel. A .22 caliber rifle kept him in rabbits, venison, and an occasional javelina. He had brought maps showing the locations of mines so he limited his searching to areas where few if any mining claims had been filed. The nearest mine to the Little Josie was north of a hill that separated two arroyos. It was called Lucky Angel. The basis for his filing on the Little Josie was a ledge of igneous rock that he had found hidden behind a thick stand of catclaw. He had camped a short ways from the brush, and was gathering dead wood for his fire when he spied the ledge behind the prickly tree. The brush with its sharp curved thorns was difficult to clear away, and required a great effort on Jack's part seeing as he had only a small hatchet to work with. Once cleared of its wall of thorns the ledge looked promising. Magruder spent two days picking away at the formation and examining the observable minerals. One particular sample revealed a trace of silver. Jack Magruder built his monuments, and went to Rinconada. The Little Josie was born, and became his hope.

After filing his claim, Magruder went to Roland Clayton's office, and told his friend what he had accomplished. Clayton offered to stake Magruder while he worked on sinking a shaft, hoping to strike a vein of silver. Jack was grateful, and accepted because the money he had brought with him from New York had diminished considerably.

# THE MINER

Roland Clayton drove Magruder back to Arivaca. While there the two went into La Gitana Bar at Clayton's insistence. Jack had his first taste of mescal. It would not be his last.

Clayton drove Magruder back to the Little Josie, arriving just as the sun began to bathe the mountains in spectacular crimson. Jack started a fire, made a pot of coffee, and the two had a supper of venison jerky as the darkness of night invaded the rough, rocky terrain. As the two men sat by the fire their conversation centered on Jack Magruder's plan to begin his shaft by the outcropping, and explore from there. Clayton had little knowledge of mining, and was interested in the way Magruder explained his theory that the slight show of silver at the surface might indicate richer mineral deposits deeper below.

The first project in developing the claim was to build a shack to live in. Magruder made it from used lumber he found in Arivaca, and hauled out to the Little Josie on Isabel's packsaddle. When that task was finished, he built a rock masonry cistern in which to store runoff water from the shack's guttered roof. A week later Magruder went to the village to purchase a "double-jack" sledgehammer, some drills, a pick, shovel, and an old wheelbarrow. Two weeks later he returned for a box of dynamite, caps, and fuse.

Magruder worked at a steady pace from before daylight to dusk. It took six months of drilling, blasting, and mucking out the crumbled rocks before he saw "color," and took the rocks into the assay office. The report was promising, and he found he could sell his ore locally in Arivaca. It wasn't long before he struck a thin vein of rich silver ore in the shaft, and when he sold what he had high graded, after mining the ore, Magruder went joyfully to Rinconada to give Roland Clayton half the proceeds.

Clayton was happy with Jack's progress, and again drove him back to the Little Josie. The benefactor found it astounding that Magruder had made such progress on the shaft. He was also impressed with Jack's diligence, and when he returned to Rinconada he bought a Model A Ford coupe that the previous owner had converted into a pick-up truck. Clayton drove it out to the Little Josie to surprise Magruder.

Jack was grateful, but wondered if the fuel to run the vehicle would prove to be an unnecessary expense. Isabel did her job of hauling supplies from town and ore to the assay office. Magruder did see that the Ford would make his trips into Rinconada much easier.

One day, in spite of having the pickup, Jack had gone to the general store with Isabel. The man who ran the store and sorted the mail handed Magruder a letter from a member of his father's Manhattan law firm. Jack went out on the street in front of the store to read the correspondence, and found that his mother had died after a long and costly illness, and that his father had jumped in front of the Boston–New York express train after leaving all his assets to a scholarship fund under his name at Columbia Law School.

"I'll be damned," he said aloud, and walked to La Gitana leading Isabel. "You stay here," he said to the burro, as he wrapped the lead rope around the old, worn hitch rack. "I'll be back in a little."

Magruder went into the bar. He was the only customer, and Kenny Jameson, the owner/bartender, had poured a shot glass full of mescal before Jack sat on the worn, cracked, leather-covered bar stool supported by four square oak legs blackened by age and neglect. The legs were braced by four rectangular pieces of oak, fastened to the legs by mortises and tenons. All the braces showed the years of wear by thousands of cowboy, miner, and hunter boots, shoes worn by travelers from the city, or the occasional hob-nailed boots the geologists used when searching the area for minerals the Spaniards, Mexicans, and gringo prospectors might have overlooked.

He drank the fiery liquid straight down without a pause, placed the glass down on the bar in front of him, and watched as Jameson filled it again.

"I just got a letter telling me that my mother died and my father jumped in front of a train," he said. "How do you like that shit?"

"That's a shame, Jack. I'm sorry to hear that."

"The funny part is, the old man left everything he had to his goddam law school. I know him well enough to know that he did that to try and teach me a lesson."

"What the hell kind of a lesson?"

"Since I didn't want to go to law school he'd give his money to someone who would. One of the reasons I left home was to escape going to law school. Hell, I didn't even want to go to college."

Magruder drank the second shot, and Kenny refilled the glass again. Magruder had come to know Jameson, and felt more comfortable talking to him than to anyone in town except his burro, Isabel.

"That seems like a helluva way to try and teach you a lesson, Jack," Jameson said.

"He just didn't realize that I didn't give a good damn about his money. He always thought he could hold his money over my head and he could get me to do anything. When I came west it was my mother who made him give me enough to get located with. If it had been up to the old man, I could have walked out the door with the clothes on my back. I named the Little Josie after my mother."

Magruder finished the third shot. "Want a refill, Jack?" Jameson asked. "You generally stop at three."

"Yeah, Kenny," Magruder said. "Give me one more. It isn't every day a man finds out that both his parents are dead."

"Well," Kenny said. "At least you knew your parents. I had to grow up in an orphanage."

"I reckon we all have our separate stories," Jack said, left the bar, and untied the lead rope from the hitch rack. As usual he rode Isabel overland using a trail, rather than the road, that cut several miles off the way back to the Little Josie. Sam, Magruder's mongrel dog, with his tail wagging as he barked, trotted out from the shack to meet them.

The following day Magruder went back to work early in the morning. Pounding away steadily with his double-jack he drilled holes in the rock face of the shaft to fill with powder. It took a week for him to get the holes ready for blasting, and when the smoke cleared he went in as usual to inspect the results. Magruder was disappointed when he saw that the thin vein of silver he had been surviving on had disappeared. Nothing but worthless rock confronted him.

Tenaciously he began a drift to the north as soon as he had cleared out the crumbled rock and dumped it on the pile of tailings outside the shaft. He drilled, blasted, and mucked the drift for two weeks without any sign of the vein he had lost. After two months of strenuous effort he had almost decided to start a drift in a different direction. One more blasting was ready. As usual he counted the explosions to make sure there would be no live charges left that could explode while he was in the shaft.

Drinking coffee in his shack as he waited for the acrid smoke to clear, he thought about where he would begin another drift to try and pick up the vein again. He thought about the times he had had with Isabel Ives. He thought about his parents, dead and buried. He thought about Roland Clayton, and how the man seemed more like a father to him than Dennis Magruder ever did. He wondered about the shyness that followed him everywhere.

When enough time had passed for the air to clear in the shaft Magruder lit his carbide miner's lamp, and pushed the wheelbarrow with his pick and shovel into the opening. The smell of exploded dynamite still lingered in the air as he went slowly inward toward the end, almost a hundred feet from the entrance.

As he first glanced around judging the effectiveness of his blasting he was satisfied. Looking at the rubble of crumbled rocks on the floor of the shaft he knew that everything had gone as he had planned. Upon closer inspection of the newly exposed walls he spotted the new, much wider vein of silver halfway up the wall of the drift. His eyes dropped to the ore piled on the floor, and he began quickly shoveling the rocks into the wheelbarrow. He wanted to get them out of the shaft and into the sunlight to see them better. With a full load he began the trip back to the entrance of the mine.

Once his eyes became accustomed to the bright sunlight Jack Magruder couldn't believe the richness of the ore he had in the wheelbarrow. He took his small geologist's pick, and broke the rocks into smaller pieces to inspect the ore further. "Well, my friends," he said to the dog and burro. "I think we have found our vein of silver."

After working the first wheelbarrow load, he returned to the drift for another. The process went on until nearly dusk, and the pile of ore looked large enough to fill the back of the Ford several times. But he would high-grade the ore further. His excitement over the new vein continued through the evening, after he had broiled some venison and had drunk several mugs of coffee. He decided to transport the ore to Rinconada rather than sell it through the assay office in Arivaca where word of the strike would speed through the village.

Dominating his thoughts was the promise of being able to pay back Roland Clayton's stake, as well as a profit to the man who was his benefactor. Jack Magruder was a happy man. He worked steadily as usual, drilling, blasting, and mucking ore, loading the high grade into the back of the Ford.

Roland Clayton was very happy to hear about Magruder's strike at the Little Josie. It was not only happiness for Jack, but also pride in himself that he had had faith in Magruder. When Jack brought enough money to Clayton's real estate office to pay off the stake with a substantial profit Clayton thought about the twenty years of hard rock mining that had been Magruder's sole occupation.

"Jack," he said. "You have paid me half of every one of your pay days on the stake. This money here not only pays the stake in full, but also more than enough interest."

"A deal is a deal, Roland," Magruder said. "If it wasn't for your stake, I would probably have had to find something else to do."

"Let me have enough to pay off the stake, and you take the rest to buy some drilling machinery. All that hand work will make an old man out of you."

"I might lose an arm on one of those drills."

"Whatever," Clayton said. "You take this bundle, I'll take this other bundle, and we'll call it square. But if you ever need another stake, let me know. You'll have it."

"You are a good friend, Roland. If you should need anything, anytime, just get word to me."

# THE MINER

Magruder didn't buy any drilling machine. He was happy as he continued to work the mine with a double-jack sledge and star-drills. The vein provided him with a good living, and enough to build an addition to the shack. He couldn't remember how many drills he had worn out or how many sticks of dynamite he had packed into the holes over the years. His fourth burro named Isabel provided him with transportation back and forth to La Gitana, his one respite from the long hours he spent in the shaft. He never drank enough mescal to get drunk because he never stayed long enough to drink that much.

The sight of Magruder astride the floppy-eared burro going to the one general store and La Gitana was familiar to the few permanent residents of Arivaca. The June heat had set in. As the burro plodded slowly down the dirt main street of the town a small gust of wind whipped up the dust and blew toward them. Jack closed his eyes against the dust and the Mexican straw hat shifted on his head. He reached up to keep it from blowing away. The burro closed her eyes too, but kept her slow pace toward the bar in the middle of the small village of adobe buildings.

Magruder leaned to the left as the burro stopped at the hitch rack. His left foot easily touched the ground, and he let his right leg slide over the burro's curved, sloping rump to the ground. "You stay here, Isabel," he muttered. "I'll be back in a little."

He gave the burro a brief scratch between her hairy, floppy ears, and walked toward the open doorway at one end of the eroded adobe building.

Kenny Jameson, tall, thin, and now balding, bartender at La Gitana for many years, had already poured a shot glass full of mescal, and placed it on the old, scarred, pine bar in front of Magruder's favorite stool. "Afternoon, Jack," Kenny said, as the miner walked in the doorway.

"Hello, Kenny," Magruder said.

"Comin' on hot out there, eh, Jack?"

"Just like every June," Magruder said. "Dry as flour, too."

Magruder emptied the shot glass with one gulp. "That sure helps wash the dust out," Kenny said, as he filled the glass again. "There was a feller in here yesterday askin' for you, Jack. Didn't give his name, just asked where he could find you."

"What did you tell him?" Jack asked, and sipped half the mescal from the shot glass.

"I told him I had no idea," Jameson said. "As long as I've known you, Jack Magruder, I don't know where you live."

"I'm glad you don't, Kenny. I don't need company more than Isabel, that old burro out there."

"The man said he'd be back again today," the bartender said. "You might want to know that, Jack."

"What did this jasper look like?" Jack asked.

"Oh, kinda tall, about my height. Forty years old, or so, and he has a full head of sandy colored hair and a short red beard. He was wearin' Levis and a shirt with initials on the left sleeve. He seemed all right, but not someone I'd think would be lookin' for you."

"Doesn't sound familiar," Jack said. "Probably some crazy insurance salesman."

"He didn't have a briefcase with him, so I doubt if he was an insurance salesman. The initials on his shirtsleeve were HSC; I remember that."

Magruder finished his drink, and looked up at the ceiling trying to put the initials to a name as Jameson refilled the shot glass.

"I sure don't know anyone with those initials or by your description, Kenny," Magruder said.

The bartender, hearing a vehicle pull up and stop, glanced out the window toward the street. "Well, Jack, you'll find out in a minute. Whoever it was just drove up in the same green pickup he had yesterday."

Jack Magruder didn't turn around, and sipped his mescal. He listened to the footsteps approach the bar across the old wooden floor. He wished he hadn't come to town.

"Howdy," the stranger said. "Remember I was here yesterday?"

"Yeah, I remember," Jameson said. "What'll it be today, another bourbon?"

"That will be fine," he said, and sat down four stools from Magruder.

Jameson took a glass from a shelf behind the bar, free-poured it full of whiskey, and placed it in front of the stranger. Magruder wanted to get up and leave, but his curiosity prevailed. He glanced casually at the man. To his knowledge he had never seen him before. The stranger sipped his whiskey and lit a cigarette.

"You haven't seen Jack Magruder today, have you?" he asked Jameson.

"Matter of fact, he's sittin' right there," Jameson said, motioning with a nod of his head toward Magruder.

"Mr. Magruder, I'm Harrison Clayton. You remember my father, Roland?"

Magruder turned to the man who claimed to be the son of his benefactor. "I know Roland Clayton very well," he said. "He never mentioned having a son, though. How is Roland?"

"I'm afraid I have sad news for you, Mr. Magruder. Dad passed away a month ago. He had a massive coronary."

Magruder dropped his lower jaw, completely taken aback by the news. He sat staring at the man for a few moments. "I'll be damned," he said finally. "That's a damned shame."

"That's the reason I have been looking for you, Mr. Magruder," Harrison Clayton said. "We have some business to take care of since I am the executor of my father's estate."

"I haven't seen Roland in almost a year," Magruder said, still shocked at the news of his friend's death. He looked intently at the man who claimed to be Roland Clayton's son, but he didn't resemble his former benefactor in any respect. Magruder wished Roland were there to identify the man.

"Mr. Magruder, now that I have found you, I would like to see the Little Josie Mining Claim."

"I'm afraid that is something you will keep wishing for," Jack said. "I don't invite anyone to the Little Josie."

"As I said, Mr. Magruder, I am the executor of my father's estate. Since the Little Josie shows up on his ledgers, I must see it."

"Roland and I settled our business several years ago. There's no reason for you to be looking for me or the Little Josie."

"According to my father's ledgers, Mr. Magruder, there is a ten-thousand-dollar debt outstanding. That's why I must see the mine."

Kenny Jameson busied himself polishing glasses as he listened intently to the conversation between Jack Magruder and the man with HSC stitched on the left sleeve of his blue, Oxford cloth shirt.

"Mr. Clayton, or whoever you are," Magruder said. "You claim to be Roland Clayton's son, but in all the years I knew Roland he never mentioned having a son, or any children, for that matter. You are telling me that Roland is dead and some ledgers say that the Little Josie owes ten thousand dollars. I have a good memory, and I remember the day Roland and I settled our accounts. Therefore I suggest you go back to wherever you came from, because I am damned sure not taking you out to the Little Josie. What's more, I'd just as soon not see you again."

"I hoped you would be a reasonable man, Mr. Magruder. You will be hearing from my lawyers."

"I don't talk to lawyers, Mr. Clayton, or whoever the hell you are," Magruder said, turning back to Kenny Jameson, and motioning for another mescal.

The man with the initials on the sleeve of his shirt left the bar, climbed into the dark green, half-ton Chevrolet pickup truck, consulted a map briefly, and drove away in the direction of Rinconada.

"Looks like you got rid of that jasper all right, Jack," Jameson said.

"Somehow, I don't think I've seen the last of Harrison Clayton, or whoever he is," Jack said.

Magruder finished his drink, went to the general store for a few provisions, and rode the burro back to the Little Josie over the familiar trail. The trail ended at the Little Josie west of the two-track mine road, so Magruder didn't see the fresh tire tracks heading toward the Lucky Angel shaft on the far side of the long, rounded hill that hid the Lucky Angel from view.

In the past Magruder had seen limited weekend activity at the Lucky Angel shortly after he had begun working the Little Josie, but he never went over to meet those he assumed owned the claim. Jack Magruder minded his own business, and kept to himself. The only visitors at the Little Josie in twenty years were occasional hunters.

Magruder was not aware of the dark green pickup truck parked at the Lucky Angel until four days later when Deputy Joe Stoddard drove up to his shack as Jack was getting ready to blast.

Magruder looked up as the patrol car stopped, and a short, uniformed deputy got out and began walking toward him. Sam, the old mongrel dog, barked at the deputy. "All right, Sam," Magruder said to the dog.

"Is your name Jack Magruder?" the deputy asked, squinting through his bi-focaled eyeglasses.

"I'm Magruder," Jack said, as he stood up to face the man.

"The bartender at La Gitana told me you know a man named Harrison Clayton," the deputy said.

"I met a man at La Gitana four days ago who claimed to be Harrison Clayton," Magruder said.

"The bartender also said you were not having a pleasant conversation with Clayton."

"That's about right," Magruder said. "I have reason to believe the man is up to something no good pertaining to me."

"What was it all about, Magruder?"

"He is claiming that I owe Roland Clayton ten thousand dollars, and I know I settled everything with Roland. Besides, I don't think he is who he claims to be."

"Why not?"

"During the years I knew Roland Clayton, he never mentioned having any children."

"Does that mean he didn't have any?"

"The man who claims to be Harrison Clayton doesn't resemble Roland Clayton in any respect."

"Mr. Magruder, your story seems to check with the bartender at La Gitana, but I have a missing person bulletin on Clayton. He was last seen leaving La Gitana going this way in a dark green, Chevrolet pickup. That coincides with the bulletin."

"I haven't seen the man nor his pickup since he drove away four days ago."

"What did you do after you left La Gitana?"

"I went to the store, bought some beans and coffee, and rode back here like I always do."

"How is that?"

"On the back of the burro," Jack said, annoyed with the questioning. "How else would a man ride a burro?"

"What I meant is, which way did you ride home?"

"The usual way," Jack said. "We follow a trail that goes across country. It saves several miles."

"Where does the trail end?"

"Right there," Jack said, pointing to the shack.

"Does your trail pass on the other side of that hill?" the deputy asked, pointing to the hill that kept the Lucky Angel out of view.

"No," Jack said. "What are you getting at anyway?"

"I followed the road to that other mine. There were some recent tire tracks on it. I found the dark green pickup truck over there, but there's no sign of Clayton."

"Did you look in the shaft?"

"No," the deputy said, waving his arms to indicate he did not like the idea of going into a mineshaft. "I sent for assistance. The range deputies should arrive in an hour or so. In fact, I'd better get back to the Arivaca Road so they will know where to turn. We may need you for further questioning," the deputy said, opening the door to the patrol car. "Where can we find you?"

"Right here, unless I take a notion to ride to town."

Magruder watched the patrol car leave, hoping it was the last he would see of it. An hour later, as he was assembling the dynamite, caps, and fuse wire to take into the shaft, he heard the sound of vehicles on the road leading to the Lucky Angel. He began to wonder what the officers would find in the shaft on the other side of the hill, and decided to postpone blasting until the following day.

Three hours later the deputy who had questioned Magruder, and two range deputies wearing broad-brimmed hats drove into the yard by Magruder's shack. They got out of their vehicles, and approached Magruder, who had come out of the shack to meet them.

"Magruder," Deputy Stoddard said. "We found Clayton's body at the bottom of the shaft."

"What's that got to do with me?" Magruder asked.

"You were the last person to see Clayton alive, and we found his corpse at the bottom of your next door neighbor's mine shaft. We want you to come with us to Rinconada for further questioning in this matter."

"Well," Magruder said. "I think I'll just stay here, and take care of my burro."

"I'm afraid I have to take you into custody."

"Do you have a warrant?" Magruder asked.

"He's right, Joe," one of the range deputies said. "Besides, there's no sign of any violence on the body."

"Probably bad air," Magruder said. "I went down that shaft to check if my vein went under the hill. It didn't, but my carbide lamp went weak, and I scrambled out of there as quick as I could."

"All right," Stoddard said. "I'll let you stay here, but you are not to leave the premises until I either bring a warrant for your arrest, or an autopsy report clearing you of suspicion."

The sun was almost beyond the rugged western horizon when the deputies left with the wrapped up swollen corpse of Harrison Clayton in the bed of the dark green pickup truck.

Magruder felt uneasy about the situation he found himself in. He knew he was completely innocent in the death of the man who had claimed to be Roland Clayton's son. Yet, the fear of unjust accusation persisted, causing him a fitful night with little sleep.

Early the following morning he made his pot of coffee, contemplating packing Isabel with provisions, and going into the Cerro Colorado where the chances of discovery would be next to impossible. But the thought of constant worry and hiding chased away the idea. "If I could depend on justice, I wouldn't have to think such thoughts," he said to the burro.

As the rising sun bathed the mesquite-dotted landscape in reds and pinks Magruder opened the powder house door, took out his blasting paraphernalia, and went down the shaft to the end of the drift. He packed the holes with the explosives. An hour later he counted the muffled explosions as he stood outside the entrance to the mine. The count was right, eight dull sounding booms. No worry from unexploded charges, but a knotted feeling in his stomach persisted. He went into the shack, hoping that something to eat would alleviate the feeling. After every blasting in the past he would be anxious to enter the shaft as soon as the bitter-smelling smoke dissipated, but today he could think only about his precarious situation with the law. He finished a bowl of beans, and sat for a while in contemplation before going outside.

"Let's go to town, old girl," he said to the burro as he slipped the old, cracked leather halter over her head. "I need to talk to Kenny Jameson. Sam, old man, stay here and watch things."

As he rode Isabel toward La Gitana he felt the eyes of several onlookers, but he didn't turn toward them. At the hitch rack he slid off the burro and wrapped the halter rope around the well-worn pole. "You stay here, Isabel," he said. "I'll be back in a little."

"Howdy, Jack," Jameson said as Magruder walked through the doorway.

"Hello, Kenny," Magruder said, and again sat on his favorite bar stool in front of the full shot glass the bartender had poured.

"The deputies findin' the body of that Clayton jasper has sure caused excitement in town," Jameson said.

"Yeah," Magruder said. "I wish I'd never seen the son-of-a-bitch. I knew he'd mean trouble when he was in here claiming to be Roland Clayton's son."

"The deputy was in here askin' me all kinds of questions."

"I know," Magruder said. "He told me. How did he know where to find me?"

"The jasper mentioned the Little Josie Mine. I told that to the deputy."

"What else did you tell the deputy?"

"Just what I heard you two talkin' about. I also told him you were pretty much a loner."

"I am," Magruder said. "All I want is to live and work in private without deputies coming to my place and accusing me of killing some bastard I don't even know."

"As long as you didn't kill the bastard, you have nothin' to worry about, Jack."

"If you believe in justice, I suppose you're right, Kenny. But that deputy was ready to take me in for 'further questioning.' If it wasn't for one of the range deputies I would probably be in Rinconada."

Jameson poured another shot into Magruder's glass. "I wouldn't worry about it, Jack," he said.

"You would worry if someone came to town, found you, and told you that you owed ten thousand dollars, and you knew you didn't. Then you have an unpleasant conversation with the bastard, and he goes out and dies in your neighbor's mine shaft."

Magruder drank two more shots of mescal than usual. He was contemplating another just as two men parked their new Jeep in front of La Gitana, and walked in the doorway.

"What'll it be for you?" Jameson asked, when the two had seated themselves.

"Couple of beers," the stockier of the two said. "Make it A-1."

"You fellers look familiar, somehow," Kenny Jameson said.

"We own the Lucky Angel," the stocky man said. "The sheriff told us that someone was killed in our shaft, and suggested that we take measures to see that no one trespasses. Seems we are liable even if a trespasser comes snooping around and falls in."

"Ya hafta wonder whose side the law is on these days," Jameson said. "Right, Jack?"

"That's for sure," Magruder said, and walked out of the bar, unwrapped the halter rope, and mounted Isabel for the ride back to the Little Josie.

"That was Jack Magruder," Jameson said. "He works the Little Josie. The deputy wanted to take him in for questioning about the dead guy."

"The sheriff told us that he was still investigating the incident," the taller man said. "This is the first time we have ever seen Magruder. We used to work the Lucky Angel on weekends just for the hell of it, but it got to be more work than fun, especially when all we were hauling out of the shaft was worthless rocks."

"That would discourage me, too," Jameson said. "How come you never ran into Magruder before?"

"We went over to the Little Josie one time, but he wasn't around. There was just an old dog that didn't seem very friendly."

"Magruder doesn't take to visitors very well," Jameson said.

Magruder didn't feel any better about his dilemma. He was also hot from the ride home in the intense heat of the June afternoon. The way the two owners of the Lucky Angel talked bothered him, and increased his wondering about justice. Again he found himself thinking about riding into the Cerro Colorado. Any other time he would have gone into the shaft to see what the blasting had uncovered, but he sat on the doorstep of the shack with a lukewarm mug of coffee in his hand as the sun dipped behind the Baboquivari Mountains to the west.

"Sam, why am I content with just you and Isabel around? I've been out here so long, I can barely talk to anyone but you and Kenny Jameson. Now I wonder if I would be better off not talking to him."

When Deputy Joe Stoddard stood at Laura Clayton's open door, and informed her that they had found her husband's dead body at the bottom of the Lucky Angel shaft, she looked at him in shocked silence for a few moments.

"Come in, officer," she said.

"I told Harrison he was foolish to try his scheme," she said, finally.

"What scheme are you referring to, Mrs. Clayton?"

"It's a long story," she said, and raised her arms to run her fingers through her long, dark brown hair. "Harrison is, or I guess I should say, was such a greedy bastard. That's one reason I think that caused his stepfather to send him packing when he was twenty years old. Harrison hated Roland Clayton, even though the man adopted him, then supported him after Harrison's mother died. Harrison was jealous over his stepfather's friendship with some miner. Roland had compared his miner friend with Harrison, trying to soften Harrison's greed and laziness."

"You mentioned some scheme, Mrs. Clayton," the deputy interjected.

"I thought it was a stupid idea," Laura Clayton continued. "Roland Clayton died broke. The real estate holdings he had accumulated over the years withered. He sold out to join a land syndicate up north, and as those deals often go, one of the partners embezzled the money, and ended up in Brazil. Roland Clayton wound up with only his small social security check. The entire episode probably caused his heart attack."

"What about the scheme, Mrs. Clayton?"

"I'm getting to that," she said impatiently. "When Roland died without a will, Harrison became his sole heir. Harrison was disgusted that the estate included only this small house. He got himself appointed executor of Roland's estate to have the house put in his name. Then he found Roland's ledgers. While looking through the ledgers Harrison saw a note slipped in with the Little Josie Mine account. The note said that Jack Magruder had settled the account with Roland. But Roland never entered that in the ledger."

Laura Clayton paused long enough to get her thoughts together. "Harrison, that greedy bastard, was going to try and get the court to force Magruder to pay ten thousand dollars or transfer the mine to him. He went out to Arivaca in my pickup to find Magruder and have a look at the Little Josie Mine. He doesn't, or rather didn't know a damn thing about mines."

"You don't sound sad that your husband is dead, Mrs. Clayton," Joe Stoddard said.

"I had already decided to leave Harrison, deputy. His latest scheme was just another dishonest act on his part. I was sick to death of him, to tell you the truth. He was also physically and emotionally abusive. I was planning to leave as soon as he came back with my pickup. That's why I called your office to report him missing. I want to go to my family's ranch in Colorado."

"We noticed that the pickup is registered in your name," Stoddard said. "I wonder if you could show me the Roland Clayton ledgers."

"Yes, I'll get them for you," she said, and went to the desk in the adjoining room. She brought two light-green ledgers, and handed them to Stoddard. "You'll find the Little Josie account in this one," she said, pointing to the ledger on top.

"Would you mind showing me the Little Josie account, Mrs. Clayton? The rest is really none of my business."

Laura Clayton opened the ledger to the Little Josie account, and handed it back to Stoddard.

"Looks like your husband could have made a good case in court with this," he said.

Laura went back to the adjoining room, and returned with an envelope. She opened it and withdrew a sheet of paper. "Not with this," she said, handing it to Stoddard. "Harrison threw this away, but I found it and saved it. It's the note stating that Magruder settled his account, which Roland never entered in the ledger."

"What did you plan to do with this?"

# THE MINER

"I was going to find Magruder before I headed for Colorado, and give it to him. I would appreciate your giving me directions to the Little Josie so I can apologize to him for my greedy husband getting him into all this mess."

"The autopsy report isn't in yet, Mrs. Clayton. I wouldn't advise you to try and find Magruder until he is cleared of causing your husband's death. He doesn't appear to enjoy visitors under any circumstances."

"Just give me the directions. I'll wait until you tell me it's all right to go see him."

The autopsy report on the body of Harrison Clayton reached the sheriff's office the following day at 3:00 P.M. The coroner determined that the cause of death was by accidental suffocation, due, as Magruder had assumed, to bad air at the bottom of the shaft. Deputy Sheriff Joe Stoddard, followed by Laura Clayton in her green pickup truck, drove to the Little Josie to inform Jack Magruder that he was no longer under investigation.

Magruder had finally gone into the Little Josie mineshaft to look at the results of his blasting. The heavy, burdensome, thoughts plaguing him disappeared when he saw what looked to be a small part of the wide vein of silver he had lost a second time. He was coming out of the shaft pushing his rock-loaded wheelbarrow when Stoddard and Laura Clayton drove up to the shack. Sam, the mongrel dog, who had been waiting for Magruder at the entrance to the shaft, ran out to meet them, barking, until Magruder called him back. Magruder stood waiting for the two people to approach. He was curious about the woman who had driven up in the same green pickup that Harrison Clayton had left at the Lucky Angel. As she walked toward him, Magruder stared at her. She carried herself in a statuesque manner

100

that reminded him of Isabel Ives, except she was darker complected, and her face had a slightly weathered look about it. Her nose was straight and thin. The closer she came the more uneasy Magruder became.

"I've brought you some good news," Stoddard said.

Magruder shifted his eyes toward the deputy.

"You're off the hook. The coroner's report says that Clayton died from accidental suffocation."

"I told you it was bad air," Magruder replied.

"I don't know a mine shaft from a hand-dug well," Stoddard said. "Sorry this caused you any trouble."

Magruder wanted to say, "no trouble, just sleepless nights and constant worry because I don't trust any of you," but he kept silent.

"Magruder, this is Mrs. Laura Clayton, Harrison Clayton's widow. She wanted to meet you so I had her follow me out here."

"Pleased to meet you, Mrs. Clayton," Magruder said, wondering why she wanted to meet him. "I'm sorry about your husband."

"Mr. Magruder, it's a pleasure to meet the man my husband was so jealous of," Laura said. "And you don't need to feel sorry for me about my husband. I was already through trying to deal with him."

Magruder was puzzled by Laura Clayton's words, but he didn't ask any of the questions that were swimming through his mind.

"Well, Magruder, Mrs. Clayton," Stoddard said. "I have to get back to Rinconada. Again, I hope this didn't cause you any trouble. I had to do what I had to do."

Jack Magruder gave Stoddard a slight wave without any enthusiasm, and returned his attention to Laura Clayton. He was surprised at himself to wonder what she might look like in a dress instead of the tight-fitting Levis and white peasant blouse. He looked at her brown eyes that looked directly at him, and he had to look away, feeling awkward in her presence. Magruder had not been around women for so many years that he didn't know what to say even though he wanted her to stay.

"May I call you, Jack?" Laura asked.

"Jack's fine," Magruder said.

"I'm Laura, and I came out here to tell you about what that bastard Harrison had planned. I also wanted to meet you. Do you mind me being here?"

"No, not at all," Magruder said. "I'm just not used to people here at the Little Josie. You'll have to excuse me for being awkward."

"You're not awkward at all, Jack," she said. "Do you have any coffee made, or would you let me drive you into town for a drink?"

Magruder stood speechless. He didn't want Laura Clayton inside his shack to see how he lived in spite of the half pot of coffee there.

"I guess we could go to La Gitana for a drink, Mrs. Clayton," he said.

"Laura, OK?"

"OK, Laura," Magruder said.

As she drove the pickup over the rutted, bumpy road Laura Clayton told him about her dead husband's scheme to try and get ten thousand dollars or the Little Josie from Jack Magruder. She also told Jack about Harrison Clayton being adopted, and the bad relationship he had had with Jack's friend, Roland. It was the first time Jack had heard about Roland Clayton's financial difficulties, and he wished he had known in time to offer his help.

# THE MINER

By the time they reached Arivaca Jack Magruder had learned more about his benefactor, Roland Clayton, than he had ever known. He had also become more comfortable in the presence of Laura Clayton.

Kenny Jameson walked out from behind the bar as Jack and Laura took seats at a small table. "Hello, Jack. What'll it be for you folks?"

"I'll have a bourbon-on-the-rocks, please," Laura said.

"Your usual, Jack?"

"Fine, Kenny," Magruder said, and turned his attention back to Laura Clayton.

"There is something else I want you to know, Jack," Laura said, after Kenny had brought their drinks, and returned to talk to the two men drinking beer at the bar. "Roland Clayton's house is about all he had left. Harrison was in the process of having it transferred into his name. With Harrison dead, I'm next in line since I'm his widow. I think that Roland Clayton would have wanted you to have the house, and as soon as it is in my name I plan to deed it over to you."

Magruder couldn't believe the complete contrast between Harrison Clayton and his widow. "I appreciate your offer, Laura, but what would I do with a house in Rinconada?"

"Hell, I don't know, Jack," she said. "You can always sell it."

"How about you? Where will you live?"

"I was going back up to Colorado. My family has a small ranch near Pagosa Springs. I just wanted a place to go to get away from that bastard, Harrison."

Magruder and Laura Clayton talked through several drinks, before and after eating a supper of Kenny Jameson's "Baboquivari Barbecue." It was close to midnight when they left La Gitana for the Little Josie and Jack's shack. The closer they came to the mine the more nervous Magruder became. He wanted to be hospitable to Laura Clayton. He even found himself enjoying being with her, but the thought of her spending the night in the shack was something he couldn't imagine.

Laura sensed Jack's increasing uneasiness. When they reached the mine Laura turned off the lights and the ignition.

"I know this is awkward for you, Jack, but I would like to spend the night here. I have had too many drinks to be driving down that winding road to Rinconada. It was bad enough getting here from Arivaca. We don't have to sleep together. I'll keep my clothes on if you want."

Magruder was silent for a few moments. He felt himself calming away from his nervousness.

"I would like you to stay, Laura," he said. "My house is not much to offer someone like you."

"Nonsense, Jack Magruder," she said, and patted his shoulder. "If it's good enough for you, it's perfect for me."

# Soul of the Hob-Nailed Boot

**H**arry Kennedy rummaged around his old, dilapidated mining shack where he had lived for nearly twenty-two years. He was looking for the box containing his fuses and caps. He hadn't blasted in three years, but he remembered putting the box inside to keep it out of the weather and separate from the wooden keg of dynamite sticks he kept in the small powder house fifty yards from the entrance to the main shaft of the Lonesome Buzzard Mine.

He took off his old, dilapidated felt hat and scratched the balding scalp that was once covered by thick, brown hair. "I wonder where I put that box," he muttered to himself, and plopped the hat back on his head, and rubbed the three days' stubble of gray whiskers on his narrow chin.

Three years before, the narrow sliver of yellow color had played out, but Harry set four more charges, hoping there would be more of the vein of gold he had lived from for nineteen years. But, as he mucked out the rubble there was nothing but rocks, just a few more wheelbarrow loads to add to the tailing pile. It was then that Harry decided to take life easy for once, and live on his small Social Security check.

As a "powder monkey" for twenty-three years with the big mining companies in Butte, Montana, and over at Silverbell, Arizona, he had put in enough quarters to easily qualify for "guvment money," as he called it. The check bought his food and other essentials, but Harry didn't need many essentials except for an occasional bottle of Black Velvet and Louis L'Amour paperback books to read. He drove his old pickup into Bandino, Arizona, once a month for his meager supplies including a couple of books, stopped at the post office to check "general delivery," and drove back to the Lonesome Buzzard. His yearly trip to Tucson was for a new pair of Levis, some chambray work shirts, drills, and blasting supplies.

A life of leisure was a drastic change for Harry, who had worked since he was twelve years old. First it was milking his father's cows and putting up hay in the summer. Harry called the place a "pitchfork ranch" because they put up hay all summer to pitch out to the cattle all winter. That was in Sheridan County, Wyoming.

Just before his eighteenth birthday, Harry's father got himself kicked in the head by one of the mules as he was hitching the team to the old McCormick-Deering hay mower. He was dead before Harry's older brother, Dave, got their father into Sheridan. Dave married soon after that, and then the following winter the boys' mother died from some new flu virus that was going around.

Dave, being the oldest, and having a strong tendency to be bossy around Harry, told "Little Brother" he had better look around for a job because the ranch wasn't big enough to support both of them. Harry figured it was Dave's wife who had influenced his brother. A disgruntled Harry left the ranch the next day.

A feeling of relief from having to work on the "pitch-fork ranch" made Harry decide to look for work other than on ranches. After reading an advertisement for miners in the local newspaper, Harry bought a bus ticket to Butte, Montana. He arrived in the bustling mining town in the late afternoon, too late to apply for work.

He was eating a supper of chicken-fried steak in a small cafe when he overheard a conversation at the adjacent table. "If you're a powder monkey, they'll hire you right off, but who in hell wants to be a goddam powder monkey?"

Harry had watched his father set charges of dynamite to blow tree stumps out of the new hay field. That was just enough to make him answer the personnel interviewer, "Powder Monkey," when the man asked what kind of a job Harry wanted to apply for.

The job proved to be rewarding in several ways. Harry earned a larger paycheck than if he had been a plain miner. He was able to work on his own because nobody wanted to be around dynamite. And, the rest of the miners had respect for a man who had a cool attitude toward dangerous work. After fifteen years at the Butte Mine, Harry wanted a change, not only from that mining operation, but also to live in a warmer climate. That is when he moved to Silverbell. After eight years there, he had saved enough money to strike out on his own, prospecting for gold and silver, hoping to hit pay dirt.

Bandino is a small village nestled in the foothills of a high mountain range. Bandino's past was a combination of cattle raising and mining. Harry quit his powder monkey job at Silverbell, and headed for the hills around Bandino. Six months later, he filed a claim and called it Lonesome

Buzzard. For nineteen years he blasted, mucked ore, and had it assayed. The Lonesome Buzzard provided a living, and that was all that interested Harry. He had never married. Watching his brother's demanding wife impressed Harry that he didn't want the same to happen to him. He had his girlfriends along the way, but he never proposed marriage to any of them.

A year after the vein of gold ore played out Harry had just driven his old pickup back from Bandino when a green carryall drove up and parked behind Harry's old, paintless Ford. The district forest ranger got out of the U.S. Government vehicle, and walked toward the shack where Harry was putting away the things he had brought from Bandino.

"Mr. Kennedy," the ranger called out.

Harry came to the door. "I'm Kennedy, what can I do for you?"

"Mr. Kennedy, I'm James Hawthorne, district ranger. I need to talk to you about a new forest service policy."

All forest rangers looked the same to Harry, but this one, with his neatly trimmed blond mustache and narrow, jutting chin made Harry feel that he couldn't trust the man. It was not unusual for Harry not to trust men in uniforms no matter what they looked like.

"Let me get some coffee started, and I'll be right with you."

Harry went back inside the shack to put the pot of morning coffee on the hot part of the old cast-iron wood-burning stove. He finished putting away his groceries, and opened the official looking envelope that he had picked up at the post office. After reading the letter, he knew what the ranger was referring to as "new policy." Harry tossed the letter onto the scarred wooden table in the middle of the room, poured out two chipped mugs full of coffee from the blue enameled pot, and carried them outside.

"Here's some coffee. What's all this new policy business?"

"Well, Mr. Kennedy, the forest service has adopted a new policy toward old mining claims that are no longer productive. The Lonesome Buzzard is one which the forest service intends to condemn, and return the area to its natural state."

"You mean to say you're goin' to fill up my shaft?"

"We will seal the shaft. Otherwise it would constitute a hazard to the public. The Lonesome Buzzard claim is in the middle of a proposed campground and trailhead."

"Well, Mr. Hawthorne, you'd best be makin' your campground somewhere else because Lonesome Buzzard's a patented claim. I own this chunk of ground."

"I'm sorry, Mr. Kennedy, but the forest service has the authority to condemn any parcel within a national forest for purposes of enjoyment by the public."

"I am part of the public, and I've enjoyed livin' here for twenty years. Go find somewhere else for your damn fool campground."

"Have you received our letter of intent in the mail?"

"I picked it up today. I haven't had a chance to study it yet."

"When you read that letter you will better understand our policy. There is nothing to get panicky about. You will have two years to vacate the property."

Harry's face became crimson as anger flooded his brain and body. "Mr. ranger, you can tell you're goddam forest service they'll have to carry my dead body off Lonesome Buzzard. I've been here twenty years, and I intend to stay the rest of my life."

"Mr. Kennedy, when you read the letter of intent, you will see that the government will compensate you for the appraised value of the property."

"Compensate my ass. There's no price on Lonesome Buzzard and never will be. Now, get your goddam guvment ass off my ground."

"Mr. Kennedy," Hawthorne started to say.

But, Harry had turned around and headed for the door of the shack. The district ranger tossed the untasted coffee on the ground, and left the chipped coffee mug in the bed of the old Ford.

When Harry heard the carryall start up and back down the narrow two-tracked road, he poured himself a half tumbler of Black Velvet. He took a large swallow, set the drink back on the table and waved his clenched fist in the air.

"The sonsabitches," he muttered, several times.

Harry Kennedy drank several half-full tumblers of the Black Velvet that afternoon. He didn't remember seeing the sun set when he awakened later than usual the next morning. The hangover that he suffered was brutal. Never in his sixty-three years had Harry felt so sick. As he pushed himself up from his bed to start the fire in the stove, his head throbbed and his stomach felt raw. He recalled how the Mexican miners would complain about *la cruda*, meaning "raw." "I've damn sure got a cruda this morning," he mumbled as he started the fire, and a fresh pot of coffee. His eyes caught the nearly empty bottle of Black Velvet where he had left it on the table next to the tumbler. Glancing in the old mirror with one corner broken off, Harry looked at his bloodshot, green eyes that looked more sunken than usual, and shuddered. Even the tiny red capillaries on his almost bulbous nose looked more prominent.

A year later Harry was nailing some new sheets of corrugated roofing on the shack, replacing the rusted roof before it started to leak. He looked up from his work, and spotted two men in green forest service uniforms. One carried a surveyor's transit, the other the rod and a long steel measuring tape rolled into its bracket. For six months Harry hadn't thought much about the ranger's prior visit or the letter of intent he had received in the mail. He felt a surge of anger and his stomach muscles tightened.

"You men have no business trespassin' on my ground," he yelled.

The surveyors stopped, and turned toward the shack.

"We're surveying the Lonesome Buzzard claim as part of the appraisal," the man with the transit called.

"I don't give a damn what you're doin', get the hell off my ground," Harry yelled back. "See those rock cairns," he continued, and pointed to the piles of rocks marking his claim. "Stay the hell outside them. You might as well go back where you came from because Lonesome Buzzard ain't for sale."

"The Lonesome Buzzard claim is being condemned, sir," the transit man replied.

"Condemned, hell," Harry growled. "I'll condemn you two if you continue to set foot on my ground. Now, get!"

The two surveyors turned around, and walked back to their green carryall, stowed their surveying equipment, and drove back down the road from the Lonesome Buzzard.

When he had finished nailing on the new roof, Harry walked down the road to the northern boundary. He took a well-used tape measure from his pocket, and measured the width of the rutted dirt road he had used for many years. That afternoon, he drove the old Ford into Bandino, and bought two old railroad ties, some two-by-six planks, some carriage bolts, two heavy hinges, a four-foot length of bright galvanized chain and a padlock.

Three days later, after working slowly and methodically, Harry struggled with the heavy wooden gate as he lifted it onto its hinges. He wrapped the chain around the gate and the railroad tie post on which the gate swung shut, and locked the padlock through two links on the end of the chain. With his tools in the back of the old Ford, he drove the hundred yards back to the shack. That evening, as he sat on the aged, gray, weathered bench in front of the shack puffing on his pipe and sipping Black Velvet from the tumbler Harry felt good at having finished the gate.

The next morning he drove into Bandino, and bought a small can of black enamel paint and a half-inch-wide brush. When he returned, he meticulously painted the words, PRIVATE PROPERTY KEEP OUT, on the top two-by-six plank of the gate.

Harry settled back to his life of a retired miner, reading western novels or, when the weather was good, sitting on the bench thinking about the years he had spent on the ranch, working for the mines, and blasting out the shaft of the Lonesome Buzzard. Ultimately his thoughts would turn to the girls he had known, and on occasion he would drive into Bandino to sit in Emma Dalton's kitchen sipping coffee and talking with her.

Ten months to the day, after he had told the surveyors to leave, the district ranger drove up to the gate and got out of the new green carryall with a short-wave antenna sprouting from the roof. Harry was sitting on the bench.

"Mr. Kennedy, I'm James Hawthorne, district ranger. Remember me?" the man in the green uniform called out.

"Just stay where you are, outside my gate," Harry yelled back.

"Mr. Kennedy, I'm hear to talk to you about vacating the premises."

"Then you might as well leave. I ain't vacating these premises."

"Try to be reasonable, Mr. Kennedy. Your property has been condemned and the government will send you a compensation check as soon as you vacate."

"I told you once that Lonesome Buzzard ain't for sale. Go back to where you came from and leave me in peace."

The ranger reached in and took a brown envelope from the dashboard of the carryall. He waved it in the air over the gate.

"This is an eviction notice, Mr. Kennedy. I am leaving it here for you," Hawthorne called, and slipped the envelope behind the padlocked chain. "You have sixty days to vacate, Mr. Kennedy."

"In sixty days, I'll still be sittin' right here."

Hawthorne shook his head in disbelief at Harry Kennedy's stubbornness, returned to the carryall, and backed it down the road.

"Sonsabitches," Harry muttered as the vehicle went out of sight.

He walked down to the gate, and pulled the brown envelope out from behind the chain. As he sat down at the table inside the shack, Harry opened the envelope, and read the "Notice Of Eviction From Condemned Property."

"Sonsabitches," he muttered. "Sonsabitches."

One morning, a month later, Harry drove his old Ford into Bandino to have coffee with Emma Dalton. When she heard the old Ford pickup drive up and stop in front of her house, Emma quickly ran a brush over her long, straight white hair and dabbed a little light pink rouge on her slightly sagging cheeks. Smoothing her blue gingham dress, she went to the door, and invited Harry in for coffee. After fifteen minutes of chatting and sipping coffee, Harry handed the brown envelope to Emma. She took the eviction notice out of the envelope and read it.

"Where are you going to go, Harry?"

"Not goin' anywhere. The Lonesome Buzzard's been my ground for twenty-two years. It ain't for sale."

"But, the government is running you out, Harry. You've got to leave in thirty days according to this notice."

"How can the guvment run me out of my own home, Emma?"

"The government can do just about anything they choose to."

"I always thought the guvment was us, the people."

"I reckon it's supposed to be, Harry. But one person hasn't much chance against them when they decide to do something like running you off your claim. I think you'd best pack up your stuff and move in here until you figure out where you want to live."

"I can tell you one thing, Emma, I ain't leavin' my ground."

It was on a Wednesday, the last day of the month. Sitting on the bench, Harry watched the gray carryall, carrying white U.S. Government license plates, stop at his gate. Three men got out. The district ranger in his green uniform led the others, wearing cowboy hats, white shirts, and Levis, to the gate. Harry cradled his thirty-thirty carbine in his arms.

"Mr. Kennedy," Hawthorne called out. "These two men with me are federal marshals. We are here to carry out the eviction notice. You need to put your rifle away."

Harry pulled the lever down, and up again to slide a .30 caliber shell into the chamber of the carbine.

"Leave me be," Harry yelled. "I ain't movin' from my ground."

Hawthorne turned to the two marshals. "There's no telling what that old coot might do if we were to try and take him."

"I don't hanker to take a chance with that carbine pointed our way," the taller of the two marshals commented. "Tell him we'll be back in the morning at 10:00. We might need more people. There's no sense in taking chances with the old devil."

"Mr. Kennedy," Hawthorne called. "We will be back tomorrow morning at 10:00. It will be your last chance to be reasonable about all this."

"Just don't come past my gate onto my ground, you sonsabitches."

The three government men returned to the gray carryall with bars on the back windows. Harry eased the hammer on the carbine to its safety position as the carryall backed down the road from the gate.

He remained on the bench deep in thought for an hour. Entering the shack, he went to the cupboard next to the stove, opened the rickety door, took out an old tobacco can, and shook the cash out on the table. After stuffing the money into the brown envelope the eviction notice had been in, Harry ambled out to the old Ford to drive into Bandino.

His first stop was the small grocery store where he bought a package of Muriel Cigars and a top sirloin steak. At the liquor store he took a bottle of Black Velvet from the shelf, and paid for it. At Emma Dalton's they talked over coffee. As he was leaving, he handed Emma the brown envelope.

"Keep this for me until I come for it, Emma."

"All right, but when will you be back?"

"Don't know," Harry mumbled. "You take care, Emma."

Back at the Lonesome Buzzard late in the afternoon, Harry started a fire with mesquite wood in the middle of the fire circle that was off to one side of the shack. When the wood had almost burned down to coals, he put the old, greasy, refrigerator rack he used for a grill onto the fire. Sitting at the table waiting for the flames of the fire to abate, he poured a tumbler full of Black Velvet and lit one of the cigars.

Before placing the steak on the grill, Harry sprinkled it with ground red chile, salt, and black pepper. He sat down on the bench to watch the steak cook as he sipped his drink and puffed on the cigar. When the fat around the outside of the steak began browning, he flipped the steak over with a fork, and went inside to get an old chipped plate he had used for many years. He stabbed the steak, and put it on the plate.

"Nothin' like a good steak cooked on mesquite coals," he mumbled to himself as he walked back inside the shack.

Before sitting down at the table, Harry removed the glass chimney from the coal-oil lamp, lit the wick, and replaced the chimney. The yellow flame from the lamp gave the inside of the shack a pleasant glow. He ate the rare meat slowly, relishing each mouthful, taking occasional sips from the tumbler.

As usual, Harry finished every morsel on his plate. Then he filled the tumbler again, lit another cigar, and began to read his copy of Louis L'Amour's *The Strong Shall Live*. He had read half of the story, "Duffy's Man" and had almost finished the tumbler of Black Velvet, when he put the paperback book on the table, spread out to keep his place. After sipping down another tumbler of Black Velvet, Harry ground out what was left of his cigar into the tin ashtray that had once had "Golden West Saloon" printed on its rim. He staggered over to his bed, and was soon asleep.

The sun colored the cloudy sky crimson with streaks of brilliant orange before it rose over the far ridge the next morning. Harry watched the sky as it constantly changed color, and marveled at the beauty.

After a second mug of coffee he began rummaging around inside the shack to find the box of fuse and caps. Then he remembered he had left it under the bed. He took the box outside, and put it on the bench. The three-foot by two-foot door to the powder house had swollen, but he managed to open it after several tugs. After dragging a full keg of dynamite sticks out of the powder house, Harry brushed the dust off the keg and carried it over to the bench. The lid came loose easily when he had removed all the screws that held it shut.

Reaching into the keg, he took out a half-dozen sticks, and put them on the bench. With black electrician's tape, he joined the sticks together, along with the cap and fuse. Leaving the end of the fuse hanging out, he put the wrapped-up dynamite sticks back in the keg. He put the wooden top back on the keg. By the sun, Harry judged the time to be around nine o'clock.

The bottle of Black Velvet was still a third full after he poured out half a tumbler, and put it and the bottle on the bench next to the dynamite keg. After bringing the book out and lighting a cigar, he sat on top of the keg, and began reading "Duffy's Man." He had leaned his carbine against the front of the bench.

The sound of several vehicles laboring up the road to the Lonesome Buzzard came to Harry just as he was finishing the story. He reached over, grabbed the bottle, and filled the tumbler again. Then he grabbed the thirty-thirty, and laid it across his lap.

There were four government vehicles in a line, stopped at the gate. Altogether Harry counted twelve men as they walked up to look over the top two-by-six plank. Six other men in green uniforms accompanied the district ranger. The two federal marshals from the day before had one additional man dressed similarly. Harry recognized the remaining two men as deputy sheriffs.

"Mr. Kennedy," Hawthorne yelled. "We are here to remove you from the premises. We have a court order from the federal judge in Tucson. I would advise you to come peacefully so nobody gets hurt."

"Ranger, you don't seem to get it through your thick skull that I'm not leavin' my ground."

Hawthorne pulled back the left sleeve of his green Eisenhower jacket, and glanced at his wristwatch. "It is 9:45, Mr. Kennedy. You have fifteen minutes to vacate."

Harry pulled his last cigar out of his shirt pocket and lit it. After a swallow of Black Velvet he yelled, "You sonsabitches have fifteen minutes to get the hell out of my sight or we'll all blow sky high."

"What's that crazy old man talking about, Hawthorne?" one of the federal marshals asked.

"I have no idea. He has his carbine on his lap. We need to take every precaution that he doesn't shoot anyone."

"I think it would be prudent if we surrounded him, and took him from behind," the new marshal advised.

Hawthorne looked at his wristwatch again. "Ten more minutes."

"If we stand here at this gate, we're going to end up with a Mexican standoff," the other marshal said.

The shorter of the two deputy sheriffs held a pair of binoculars to his eyes. Lowering them, he announced, "That old man is sitting on a dynamite keg with a fuse stickin' out from under the lid."

"I don't think Kennedy is crazy enough to do anything like that," Hawthorne said. "That keg is probably empty, and the fuse sticking out is most likely his bluff."

"I wouldn't count on him bluffing, Hawthorne," The taller marshal warned. "I've seen too many crazy bastards go nutty when they're cornered."

Hawthorne looked at his wristwatch again. "It's 10:00, gentlemen," he said, and turned to the federal marshals. "It's up to you now. You're carrying the authority with your badges."

"All right," the tallest marshal said. "We need to spread out and keep close to the oaks and manzanita. If the old coot starts shooting that carbine, hit the dirt until he runs out of ammo."

The lawmen began walking in two directions as they began spreading themselves away from each other. When they began crossing onto the Lonesome Buzzard claim, Harry took a swallow from the tumbler, puffed deeply on his cigar, and flicked the ash from the end with his little finger.

"I told you sonsabitches to keep off my ground. I reckon you don't believe a citizen has any right to a home anymore. All you sonsabitches better hit the dirt, or I'll blow you all sky high."

The lawmen continued their slow approach. Harry grabbed the fuse, and touched the lighted cigar to the end. It sizzled as it snaked its way toward the keg.

"Adios, you sonsa......"

The explosion took them all by surprise. The twelve men fell to the ground and crouched with their hands over their heads. Pieces of rock and debris from the exploded shack began falling all around.

When the dust had cleared, the men got up slowly, close to being in shock from the horrible experience. All they could find of Harry Kennedy was the hob-nailed sole from one of his boots.

# Antonio Sings His Song

**E**very time his father returned from working in the United States, Antonio listened to the stories. Each year, for as long as Antonio could remember, Ignacio Beltrán left his family at the *milpita*, the small farm, and traveled north to work for dollars in the fields. A few months later Ignacio would step off the rattling old bus that stopped in the village of Tinaja Verde, and walk home. Antonio and his brothers and sisters always ran to greet their father on the dusty path long before he reached the small adobe house where their mother waited for her husband. Antonio remembered his father hugging and kissing his mother with the small ones grabbing at his legs. Those were happy times.

After *la cena*, the evening meal, Ignacio would sit in the old chair with his family gathered around, and tell what had happened to him during the months away. He always began with the trip to the border, and crossing through the fence without getting caught by the *migra*, the Border Patrol.

Antonio liked the part of the story where his father walked along the river that flows north, hiding during the days, and walking nights by the moonlight.

Ignacio told about friendly ranchers or farmers who gave him food for work, or sometimes just food. There were some who slammed the doors, and he would hurry back to the river and hide from the migra. It was always the migra in their green uniforms and green trucks that Ignacio had to watch for. One year they caught him, put him in their green car, and drove him back to the border. The next day he was walking along the river that flows north again. It was a long walk to the big farms where he could earn dollars working in the fields.

Antonio liked the stories. The stories made up for the months his father had been away. He would listen until he fell asleep. He was the last of the children to fall asleep because he was the oldest.

Now it was his turn to travel north to work in the fields. It was his turn to send dollars back home. His father needed to plant *maiz*, *frijoles*, and *calabazas*, corn, beans, and squash, in the milpita. Ignacio was tired of the long walk, the long hours, the hard work. He wanted to stay home with his family. Antonio was the oldest. It was his turn to go. Antonio bent down, and looked in the small mirror over the washtub in the yard. He was taller than both his mother and father. He felt the black, silky hairs of his mustache, which had been growing for two years without trimming. With the comb he had carried in his pocket since he had met Noemi he ran the teeth through his bushy, black hair. It was his turn to go.

Ignacio gave him directions, drawing his map in the dirt with a stick, telling where to go and where not to go. Where the friendly ranches were and where the people slammed their doors. He told Antonio about the farm where he had worked two weeks and the farmer did not pay. Instead the farmer called the migra. That was two weeks' work with no dollars to send back to the family.

Antonio learned about Mendosa, his father's friend in Tucson. Mendosa lived *seis cuadros*, six blocks, from the river. Mendosa might find him work to earn the bus fare to Phoenix where the fields were. The farmers needed workers.

Ignacio made him practice English: food, for *comida*; please, for *por favor*; thank you, for *gracias*; work, for *trabajo*; water, for *agua*; where, for *donde*. "When they ask your name, tell them Tony."

He would miss playing his guitar. He would miss singing to Noemi.

Neighbors came over the evening before he left. They said, "*Buena suerte*, good luck," and tossed coins in his hat. The next morning there were hugs from his brothers and sisters, and a teary good-bye from his mother. "May it go well for you," his father said as they gave each other *abrazos*, hugs.

Antonio walked away from the adobe house toward the village and the old rickety bus. He turned around to wave one last time. The frijoles wrapped in corn tortillas felt heavy in the old flour sack his mother had packed for him. He hoped the food would last until he got to Tucson. Then he realized he had no idea how far he would have to go to reach Tucson. Everything would be new.

The rickety, old bus chugged along the rough, rutted road into the village, and came to a lurching stop in front of Tienda Ochoa, the only store in Tinaja Verde that sold groceries. It was also the official bus stop. Nobody knew what the bus had looked like when it was new because it was old long before it first made the daily trip from Esquinapa through the small farming villages. It might have been green, blue, or yellow. When the dust cloud it had churned up with its wheels passed by, Antonio walked to the always open front door and stepped aboard. He was the only passenger from Tinaja Verde that morning.

After handing the driver three pesos, he walked toward the rear. The bus lurched again before he had reached the empty seat next to a dirty, fly-specked window. He grabbed the back of the seats as he half stumbled along the aisle. Only an old woman dressed in *luto*, mourning black, holding a red laying hen on her lap looked up as he passed by. He looked into her clouded, gray eyes beneath the dusty, black shawl covering her head. One wisp of white hair had escaped, and hung lazily over her faded, brown, heavily wrinkled forehead. Antonio felt like telling all the road-weary passengers that he was Antonio Beltrán, and he was going to the United States to work and earn dollars for his family.

The young adventurer looked out the dirty window as the bus bounced and rocked back and forth over the road through the countryside sprinkled with small farms, some not large enough to support the families living in the small adobe houses. He smiled at the dirty-faced children dressed in old, tattered clothing waving at the once-a-day bus.

By the time the bus had stopped at four more villages there were people standing in the aisle, hanging to the well worn rails near the top, or the backs of the worn-through seats, polished shiny from the many years and many hands. Some carried bundles, some were empty-handed. All had looks of forced patience until the bus struck the pavement with a bounce at the edge of Esquinapa. Then a young man in a wrinkled Guayavera shirt, carrying a plastic briefcase, began edging his way toward the front of the bus as the wheels plunked through pot-holes in the street. The other standing passengers moved just enough for the man to pass. He was the first to leave when the driver braked the bus to its destination stop in front of Café Aguila.

The passengers shuffled toward the door. Antonio waited for the old lady with the hen to get slowly up from her seat, and limp hesitantly to the front of the bus. At the front he slid by her, jumped to the ground, and offered his hand. "Thank you, boy," she said, her old voice crackling slightly, and allowed him to hold her free arm as she stepped from the bus.

"You're welcome," Antonio said.

The old one, hunched over with the burden of a long life, stopped momentarily as Antonio returned her arm. She turned her head slightly, looked up at him and smiled. Antonio gave her a slight pat on her shoulder, and turned to walk the five blocks across town where the big highway bus stopped on its way from Tepic to Mazatlan.

The thought of eating crossed his mind as he stood waiting for the big bus. "I will wait until later so the food will last," he said to himself. He walked back into the building where he had bought his ticket to Mazatlan. The young girl smiled coyly at him from behind the lunch counter across from the ticket window. "Café, por favor," he said to the girl.

She took a chipped, thick, dingy-looking mug from a shelf, and went to the wood-burning stove by the window. Antonio took a fifty-centavo coin from his pocket, and put it on the countertop as she filled the mug with inky, black coffee. "Gracias," he said, and reached for the blue enameled sugar bowl.

"Por nada, Señor," the girl said, and stood watching him put two spoonfuls of brownish-colored sugar into the mug, and stir the coffee. Antonio took the mug from the counter without looking at the girl, and went to a bench near the door. He had promised Noemi that he would be hers.

The hot coffee tasted good enough, but it was not as *rico*, rich, as his mother's brew. She roasted the beans with sugar in the frying pan over the red-hot coals in the fireplace outside the adobe house. He had just finished the coffee when the big bus came to a stop on the street outside. He put the empty mug on the counter, noticing the girl was still watching. "Adios," he said.

"Que le vaya bien," she answered.

"Gracias," he said, over his shoulder as he walked out the door.

He sat down in an aisle seat next to an elderly man wearing a cowboy hat. His face was carved into creases from a life in the sun, and his hands showed that they had labored with rope and reins. The old cowboy looked up when Antonio sat down. "Where are you heading?" he asked.

"I am going to the United States to earn dollars," Antonio said, proudly.

"Good idea," the cowboy replied. "When I was your age I went there, too. I was a cowboy in the mountains for a while, and then I worked ten years in a feedlot where they fatten cattle."

The bus started, and pulled away from the curb, heading toward the highway to Mazatlan.

"I am going to work in the fields like my father did," Antonio said.

"You work at what you know," the cowboy said. "I was a cowboy so I worked as a cowboy. You should do

126

what I did. I got a green card and worked in the feedlot for ten years."

He leaned over, and took his wallet out of his hip pocket. Leafing through some cards he pulled out the immigration card, and handed it to Antonio. "I still carry my green card."

Antonio looked at the white card with the printing on it. "Why do they call it a green card when it's white?" he asked.

"¿Quién sabe? Who knows, but everybody calls it a green card. Maybe green means go, and you can go across the border with a green card."

"How do I get a green card?" Antonio asked.

"You have to find an Americano who will sponsor you, and that's not always easy. I worked for ten years in the feedlot, and went home and got married. When I reached sixty-two years old I started getting a check from the U.S. Social Security system every month."

"Why didn't you keep working in the feedlot?" Antonio asked.

"I had worked long enough to get Social Security, and I wanted to go and get married to my wife. We have a little rancho near Concordia where they make furniture."

"Is that where you are going?"

"Yes," the cowboy answered. "I went to Tepic to visit my sister. She is old. Now I am going back to the rancho this side of Concordia. I have to change buses at Reunión. That's where the highway starts that goes over the mountains to Durango."

"Have you seen Durango?" Antonio asked.

"I went there once when I worked with Rancho Santa Barbara. They say Durango is full of scorpions, but I didn't see any."

"How long did you work with Rancho Santa Barbara?" Antonio asked.

"Only two years while the Americano was the *mayordomo*, the foreman. The land reformers invaded the biggest rancho in México. Now it is all divided up into small ranchos, and the Americano left for Téjas, Texas. My wife and I went back to our rancho near Concordia."

The bus slowed as it entered the crossroads village of Reunión, and stopped at the terminal building. "Reunión," the driver called back.

Antonio got up from his seat to let the old cowboy out into the aisle. "Well, young man," the cowboy said. "You think about working ten years in the United States so you can get Social Security money some day."

"I will think about it," Antonio said, and watched as the bow-legged old cowboy walked down the aisle to the front of the bus. He slid over to the seat by the window.

The bus moved slower than before as it traveled toward Mazatlan. Antonio had never seen so many buildings as when the bus entered the city. The terminal was full of people. Some were rushing to board. Some were sleeping in seats or on the floor. Some were reading magazines or newspapers. Others were just standing around waiting. The voice over the loudspeaker announcing arrivals and departures was difficult for him to understand. He went directly to the glassed-in window, and asked the clerk for a ticket to Nogales, Sonora, as his father had instructed him to do.

The obese clerk looked like he would spill off the stool with the swivel seat. He wore a constant scowl on his pockmarked face. The flabby jowls jiggled as he moved his lips under the thin, carefully trimmed, black mustache. Antonio put a one-hundred-peso bill through the opening at the bottom of the window. The clerk snapped it up with his pudgy fingers, and swiveled around so that he faced the rack of tickets. Tilting his head back to look at the tickets through his smudged bifocals, he reached over, and thumbed a ticket from its place in the rack. From underneath the counter he counted out Antonio's change, and wordlessly slapped the ticket and the change on the counter, and slid both together through the opening at the bottom of the glass.

Antonio took the ticket and change. "Gracias," he said. But the clerk only replied with his scowl. Antonio concluded that the clerk did not enjoy his work in the slightest. He hoped he would enjoy working in the fields.

He found a seat in the waiting room and began trying to understand the voice over the loudspeaker. Every time there was a volley of names of cities there would be people getting up from their seats or off the floor, gathering their belongings, and heading for the gate to the loading area.

Antonio tried to listen over the din of the waiting room noise. He heard Guadalajara during one volley. He listened for Nogales, but didn't hear it mentioned. He thought he heard Culiacan, which was on the way to that northern city. He rose from his seat, and walked to the gate. A man in a disheveled uniform was standing just inside the loading area. "I am looking for the bus to Nogales, Sonora," he said, and showed the man his ticket.

"You had better hurry. Number eighteen is about ready to pull out for Culiacan," he said, pointing to the bus parked in slot number eighteen.

Antonio trotted over to the bus, and went up the steps to face the driver with his ticket in his hand. The driver punched it, and handed it back. Antonio put the ticket in his hip pocket, and walked toward the rear of the bus.

There were no vacant seats. He walked toward the rear, stopping in front of three other passengers standing in the aisle. A young woman with a sleeping baby in her arms sat looking out the window below where he stood. The older woman in the aisle seat next to the young mother looked straight ahead, with her hands folded on her lap, looking like a statue except when she blinked her eyes or slightly moved her nostrils. Four more passengers mounted the steps, handed their tickets to the driver, and walked back to stand in the aisle.

The door wooshed and thunked as it closed behind the last passenger to board. Antonio listened as the diesel engine whined its way through the gears. When the bus finally reached the north/south highway the engine stopped whining and went into a steady humming sound. He heard a mixture of voices as some of the passengers talked with one another. The view out the window was a blur of trees and rocks as the bus cruised over the highway. He crouched once, and saw the blue of the ocean in the distance. The young mother looked away from the window, and saw Antonio looking at the ocean. His eyes met hers for a fleeting moment, and he saw her smile. He returned the smile, and looked away at the passengers standing next to him. Thoughts of Noemi raced into his mind.

Every time the bus passed another vehicle on the highway the engine labored, moaning heavily. Only a handful of cars passed the bus on the narrow road. He wondered how long it would be before they reached Culiacan and the chance for a seat.

The baby finished its nap, and looked up into the young mother's adoring eyes. Antonio watched as the baby moved its tiny lips over empty gums. He had seen the same thing with his younger siblings.

The baby began to whimper. The young mother lifted it to her shoulder, and began patting the baby's back with her right hand as she bounced it gently with her other arm under its bottom. The baby seemed satisfied for the moment. The bus continued on its way, both standing and seated passengers swaying as the driver pulled out to pass a car or truck, and then darted back into the right-hand lane.

The baby's whimpering changed to crying. Hungry. Antonio watched intently as the young mother slipped her right hand between the baby and herself to undo the top two buttons of her blouse. She shifted the baby lower to nurse. The baby stopped crying as it felt a familiar position. With her hand under her round, firm breast the young mother guided her nipple into the baby's anticipating mouth. She looked up, saw Antonio watching, and smiled. He smiled back, and continued to enjoy looking at the baby nurse. He thought about Noemi, and hoped that someday she would nurse his baby. But, that would have to wait until he earned enough dollars in the United States. It might be quite a while.

He thought about what the old cowboy had said about working ten years to get a monthly check from the U.S. Social Security system when he reached sixty-two years old. No, he would not wait ten years to watch Noemi nurse his baby.

The bus rumbled through the streets of Culiacan until it pulled in to the terminal and parked. The young mother and baby left the seat, squeezing past the statue-like old lady. Antonio smiled at the young woman as she left, and took a seat vacated by a couple across the aisle. He was hungry, and opened the sack for some of the food his mother had packed.

He was almost asleep when the bus driver announced Los Mochis. The stops in Navojoa, Ciudad Obregon, and Guaymas barely made him stir. Somewhere between

Guaymas and Hermosillo the sun came through his window, and Antonio awakened to his second day on the road to the United States. He wanted to get up from the seat to stretch, but a woman had sat down next to him at Guaymas and was dozing. He didn't want to disturb her.

The Hermosillo terminal was full of travelers. Antonio had to change buses. He felt lucky to find a seat in the crowded Tres Estrellas bus heading for the border city of Nogales, Sonora. From there he knew he would have to walk. The walking wouldn't require money for tickets, but across the border he would constantly be sought by the American migra, the U.S. Border Patrol. His father had told him where to go and where not to go, but there was always the chance of getting caught. He wondered about being illegal. Wherever he would be it was the earth. How could he be illegally on a piece of the earth? Ignacio had told him about laws, but he didn't understand. But, he would be careful, and try not to be caught by what his father called "Los Chiles Verdes," the green chiles, because of the color of their uniforms and vehicles.

The bus pulled in to the Nogales, Sonora terminal. Antonio walked out to the sidewalk, and looked north. He saw the fence. Just beyond was the United States. First he had to get through to the other side to begin the long walk to Tucson. There was a man leaning against a building across the street smoking a cigarette. Antonio looked toward him when the man said, "Hello, muchacho, come here a moment."

Antonio walked across the buckling pavement toward the man. "Did you just come in on the bus?" the man asked.

The stranger was wearing a wide-brimmed straw hat, cowboy boots, pressed blue jeans, and a dark blue shirt. He had his thumbs hooked in the front pockets of his blue jeans, and the cigarette dangled from his lips.

"Yes," Antonio said.

"Where did you come in from?" the man continued.

"Near Esquinapa," Antonio said.

"You going through the fence?"

"Maybe," Antonio answered. He was beginning to feel uneasy with the stranger's questioning.

"Hey, man, I'm your friend. I'll tell you how you can make a lot of money. Much more than you will ever make in the fields."

Antonio remembered what his father had told him about the drug traffickers. The stranger had to be one of them. "I am a farmer," Antonio said. "I work at what I do."

"The fields are a long way to walk," the man said. "Work for me, and you will make more in a night than you will in a month in the fields. And, you will not have to walk so far."

"No, gracias," Antonio said, and turned away to walk to the main street called Obregon where his father had told him about a restaurant. He was hungry. He had finished the last of the food from his mother that morning. Now he carried the rolled-up flour sack.

Sitting at the small table in Leo's restaurant, waiting for his meal, gave him a chance to rest from the long bus ride. The stranger made him remember what his father had said about the drug traffickers. That they made getting north to the fields more difficult because the Americanos had put more migra near the border to stop the drugs. Ignacio had also told him about the easiest places to get through the fence.

The hunger left. The waitress brought him a plastic jug with water just as his father had said. Antonio paid the bill, and began walking. He stopped at a *changaro*, a small store on a side street to buy tortillas to put in the old flour sack.

The first obstacle was the high hill to the east. Small houses, all with different colors, perched on the hillside overlooking the downtown section of Nogales, Sonora, and Nogales, Arizona, on the north side of the border. At the top of the hill Antonio rested before making the descent toward the Río Santa Cruz. The half-moon's light outlined the other hills beyond that he would have to climb to reach the place his father had described.

The chain-link fence changed to four strands of barbed wire. One more hill to climb. The trail was well worn from thousands of feet from the south searching for a safe crossing from which they would begin the long walk north. He passed the monument that marked the International Border. Another kilometer.

The wires were loose from many others. Getting through was the easy part. Keeping hidden from the migra was the real challenge. There were still four hours of darkness left to reach the mesquite bosque, the large grove of mesquite that grew close together near the river, the river that flows north. He was tired from climbing up and down the hills, but he could not risk resting before he reached the bosque. His spirits rose when he came to the river. Another hour to the bosque. He would spend the day asleep under the thick growing trees. He thought about Noemi and wished she could be walking with him in the moonlight.

Antonio reached the bosque just as the moonlight faded. He remembered not to walk in the sandy river bottom where the migra could easily pick up his tracks. There were many things to think about. Too many. He was asleep before sunrise.

# ANTONIO SINGS HIS SONG

The rattling sound of an old pickup truck on the nearby road brought him out of his sleep. He could barely catch a glimpse of it through the dense thicket of catclaw and Jerusalem thorn beyond the bosque. It was dirty white, not green. Back to sleep until dusk.

Cold tortillas were better than no tortillas. He didn't want to start a fire to signal the migra where he was hiding. He ate three, and drank some water. He would reach the friendly ranch by morning. His father told him they were Mexicanos from Sinaloa who had become Americanos. Pochos, but they were good pochos. They worked for a rico, a rich man, but they remembered when they walked along the river. Their name was Chávez. Antonio started north again, away from the bosque. The sunset cast a beautiful array of reds, oranges, yellows, and purples through the clouds on the horizon.

The noise of the southbound train with its bright white headlight dancing in the dark made Antonio stop walking. He watched and listened as the railroad freight cars clicked along the steel tracks, and rumbled toward the border. There was an abandoned field between him and the tracks. A small white house was at the far end of the field. He hoped there was no dog to bark an alarm, and after crawling through the old wire fence, he walked as quietly as he could through the field.

Ignacio had warned him not to leave footprints near the railroad crossings because those were easy places for the migra to look and still remain in their comfortable, green cars. He crawled under the next fence by the tracks, and began walking over the wooden railroad ties. They made walking easier, and he could travel at a greater pace.

The white, crossed signs ahead shone in the moonlight. Antonio approached the crossing with caution. There might be a green car with its lights turned off waiting for him. He stopped walking to listen for voices. Silence. He stepped slowly on the ties until he reached the side of the narrow, dirt road. He stopped again, looking up and down the road. The moon was suddenly hidden behind a large cloud. Antonio walked on a rail to leave no tracks in the dirt. At the other side he returned to the ties. Safe.

The cloud passed, and the moonlight bounced off the dome of the old mission church his father had told him about. No food there, it was Americano government place. He kept walking steadily, trying to reach the Chávez place before sunrise.

The faint, early morning light had just begun invading the valley when he saw the light coming from the window of the small wood-frame house west of the railroad track. The Chávez casa, right where his father had said it would be. Antonio came to the crossing, and carefully walked on the rail, balancing himself, until he could walk through the grass along the two-rutted dirt road leading to the house.

Three mongrel dogs came barking and bounding from the yard toward him as he approached. He stopped as the dogs surrounded him, and he spoke to them. The dogs continued their unwelcome greeting until a man opened the door, and walked out on the porch to see what the commotion was all about. "Señor Chávez," Antonio called. "Soy Antonio Beltrán."

Chávez called the dogs to him. Antonio walked through the open gate in the wire fence that surrounded the yard littered with half-broken children's toys, a few pieces of scrap iron and four worn out automobile tires. "I am Antonio Beltrán," he repeated. "I am the son of Ignacio Beltrán, from Tinaja Verde."

"I remember your father, come in, come in," Chávez said. "Where is your father?"

"He stayed at Tinaja Verde. It is my turn to find work in the fields."

Chávez introduced Antonio to his wife Rosalia as she was stirring the contents of a blue enameled pot on the stove. Antonio sat with Chávez at the old wooden table, and Rosalia brought them each a mug of hot coffee. Antonio looked into the next room, and saw four young children watching him.

The hearty breakfast of sausage and eggs wrapped in a large flour tortilla, and the generous portion of frijoles satisfied the hunger Antonio had been feeling for several hours. He thanked Rosalia when he had finished, and Chávez took him outside to an old barn-like structure, and told him he was welcome to sleep there during the day, just as his father had.

Chávez went back to the house for a few minutes, and then left in a well-used Nissan pickup truck for his job in the village of Tubac. Chávez was good at building with adobe, and was working on an old house bought by a rich woman from Grand Rapids, Michigan. He had told Antonio he could get some work for him, but the house was too close to the road to keep hidden from the migra.

Sleep came quickly for Antonio. The old mattress felt good after his first night on the ground in the bosque. It was late afternoon when Chávez returned, and Antonio awakened at the sound of the Nissan coming into the yard. Chávez invited Antonio to stay for supper. As the sun was setting over the Tumacacori Mountains Antonio walked back to the railroad track with his flour sack full of food from Rosalia, and the plastic jug full of water.

# ANTONIO SINGS HIS SONG

Antonio wondered about the United States. So far, he had not found life much different than in Mexico. The Chávez family ate the same kind of food, and their house wasn't adobe, but inside it looked the same as most of the ones he had seen in Mexico, and they spoke Spanish. "Why is there a border and migra when the people are the same?" he asked himself as he walked along the railroad ties.

Another bunch of dogs came out of a yard to investigate him as he walked opposite Tubac. He ignored them, and continued walking. They stopped barking, turned around, and trotted back to their yard. Antonio saw a few lights from the village. His father had told him about several "safe houses" in Tubac, but he didn't need to stop since Rosalia Chávez had filled his flour sack.

The moon peeked over the Santa Rita Mountains as Antonio passed a golf course. His father had said that he should stay away from there because the people were afraid of Mexicanos. He continued following the railroad tracks. From Ignacio's description he recognized Green Valley's lights and the groves of *nueces*, the pecan trees that grew in straight lines. Then, as the first morning light eased into the valley again he found another bosque to spend the daylight hours in sleeping, hidden from the migra. He crawled under some dense underbrush, ate some beans wrapped in a tortilla, and stretched out to sleep. He could hear the sounds of cars and trucks traveling on the highway several kilometers to the west. Then the purring of an airplane's engine caught his attention. He looked up through the thick canopy of underbrush, and saw it flying along over the river.

He pulled the flour sack under him to hide its whiteness. His father had said he might see the airplane that looked for him. Antonio didn't move until the aircraft had flown south. He felt safe because his father had said that if the man in the airplane had seen him the airplane would begin circling around until the green cars came. Antonio was glad that the airplane had continued south without circling.

The staccato sound of a diesel engine slowing on the highway roused him from his sleep in the late afternoon. He felt the dank, humid heat in the bosque. The sun was still bright. He would eat, and wait for sunset. He had walked too far to take a chance on getting caught. He would have to follow the river from the bosque into Tucson because the railroad track was next to the highway and the green cars of the migra. The dangerous place was where the highway crossed the river over a bridge. Antonio waited patiently for darkness.

From the bosque he walked through a pecan grove to the bank of the dry, sandy-bottomed river. He followed the bank for a ways until he came to an arroyo tributary, using it to drop down into the main channel. The bridge was just ahead. He saw the headlights of the occasional cars and trucks passing over it as he plodded through the heavy sand. After the bridge the channel widened, and Antonio found the sand firmer and easier to walk on. The moon rose to give him a view of where he was heading. In the far distance he noticed the glow of city lights from Tucson, a sprawling city of over half a million people. He followed the river, keeping close to the east bank and in the shadows.

Just as the channel went into a long sweeping curve to the south of a hill studded with saguaro cactus, standing like sentinels in the moonlight, he stopped and finished the last of the food Rosalia Chávez had given him. The plastic water jug remained a third full. He came to another bridge, this one much larger and higher than the others. Antonio walked slowly in case the migra were watching from the highway. His father had told him that he would pass under several bridges. He must count them, and climb out of the river channel at the fourth bridge to find Mendosa's house before sunrise.

There were six young people sitting under the third bridge drinking beer and laughing. "Cerveza?" one of them called after he spotted Antonio walking.

"No, gracias," Antonio said. He must find Mendosa's before sunrise.

*Puente cuatro*, the fourth bridge. A narrow path led to the top of the riverbank. He stopped momentarily at the road, turned right, and walked to the next street going north and south. One block south and then turn left. Three more blocks, the tan house on the corner with the front porch. Mendosa's name was written on the mailbox in front. Antonio felt relieved that he had found his Tucson destination.

"Go around to the rear, and knock on the kitchen door," his father had instructed him.

Mendosa opened the door, and looked at Antonio, standing in front of him with his empty flour sack and partially filled, plastic water jug. "I am Antonio Beltrán from Tinaja Verde," Antonio said. "My father is Ignacio Beltrán."

"Well, yes," Mendosa said. "*Pásele, pásele*, come in."

Antonio entered the house. There were more furnishings than in the Chávez house, but it was still Mexican. He felt comfortable. Mendosa spoke with friendship.

After breakfast Mendosa told him about four days' work washing dishes in his restaurant nearby. The regular dishwasher had gone to Nogales for a visit. Antonio could start work with the evening meal. Mendosa gave Antonio a "Raiders" cap, and showed him the toolshed in back of the house where he could sleep. "Wear the Raiders hat, and you will look like you belong here," Mendosa said.

# ANTONIO SINGS HIS SONG

Antonio had never seen so many dirty dishes. The waitress kept bringing them in, and piling them next to the sink. He wondered if the work would last all night. Finally the waitress told him that the restaurant had closed, and there were only a few more dishes to wash. He walked back to Mendosa's house, and went to sleep in the toolshed again.

He went to the restaurant the following morning, washed breakfast dishes, lunch dishes, and supper dishes. After four days Mendosa paid him with dollars, and told him about a friend who would take him to Phoenix in a truck. The truck would stop in front of the house before sunrise.

Antonio was ready to leave when the truck stopped in front of Mendosa's house, and the driver came in for a cup of coffee. The man hauled produce from the fields outside Phoenix to small grocery stores in and around Tucson. He always tried to find something to haul back to Phoenix on the return trip. Sometimes his only load was illegal farm workers who had stopped at Mendosa's.

The driver told him that there were melons to pick in Phoenix. He would take Antonio right to the fields because he was hauling melons to Tucson. Antonio put the Raiders cap on and climbed into the cab of the truck. When they were stopped at a traffic light just before entering the interstate a green migra car pulled up alongside. Antonio looked straight ahead. The light turned green and the migra car sped away to enter the interstate going south. The Raiders cap must have fooled them.

Antonio went to work picking melons. It was three weeks of bending over all day, and sleeping in the old shacks along the irrigation canal. Evenings were spent in conversations. One man from Michoacan who had been picking melons for fifteen years explained that Americanos wouldn't do

141

the fieldwork, especially for the wages the farmers paid the Mexicanos, but the Americanos complained that the Mexicanos were taking jobs away from them.

After the first week Antonio and the man from Michoacan went to the post office and bought money orders to send home to their families. The man from Michoacan told Antonio that he always missed his wife and children when he came to the United States to work, but they needed the money to live on.

When the melons were picked the man from Michoacan and Antonio traveled to Idaho to pick fruit. They saw some of their other friends from the melon fields in Phoenix. Picking fruit didn't require bending over all day. At one orchard Antonio worked in the packing sheds. He wondered how his family was, and he thought about Noemi. It seemed to him that he always thought about Noemi. He wondered how many years he would have to come to the United States to work.

Antonio always went to the post offices with the man from Michoacan. He learned how to buy the money orders speaking English. He learned a lot from the man. When the fruit-picking season ended he learned that some of his fellow countrymen went out to the highway to be easily found by the migra in the green cars. The migra would stop, lock them in the cars, and take them to a detention center where there was food and shelter. Then a bus would take them all the way to the border. It was a free ride!

Antonio and the man from Michoacan went from Idaho to California to work in the vineyards. There was a lot of bending over again. Antonio learned his work quickly, and his hands performed almost like a machine. He thought about Noemi. He wanted to go out on the highway for a free ride to the border, but the wages were good. It would not be long.

## ANTONIO SINGS HIS SONG

The man from Michoacan approached Antonio one morning as they were getting ready for the day's work. He handed Antonio a wrinkled brown paper sack with something inside. Antonio opened the sack and found an Oakland Raiders jacket inside. He held it up admiring the black fabric with the silver-colored Raiders logo on the front. He turned it around and looked at the large silver-colored letters across the back that spelled "RAIDERS." Antonio thanked his friend, and put the jacket on.

One afternoon the boss man took Antonio and the man from Michoacan aside, and asked them if they would stay after the harvest was done. The boss liked the way the two worked, and he needed help planting a new vineyard. The man from Michoacan agreed to stay. Antonio thought about Noemi. He thanked the boss for his offer, but told him he had to go home. He would try to come back next year.

The next day he went to the post office to send most of his money home. That night he talked with the man from Michoacan. They planned to meet next year in Tinaja Verde to go to the border, and walk to Tucson together. The man from Michoacan understood why Antonio didn't want to stay in California. He had been in love once too. He was still in love with his wife, but the money was too good to turn down. His wife would understand. She always accepted his working in the United States. That had become their way of life.

Antonio said good-bye to his friend the next morning. He put his money in his shoes, took off the Raiders cap, stuffed it in his back pocket, and replaced it with a tattered straw hat to attract the migra. The Raiders jacket was rolled up and under his arm as he walked four miles to the highway to wait for the migra. The sun was hot. He wondered why the migra didn't drive by when he wanted them to.

ANTONIO SINGS HIS SONG

A policeman stopped, and asked Antonio for identification. The *policía* opened the rear door of the patrol car, and Antonio slid in on the seat. The policía talked on his radio. Ten minutes later the green migra car pulled up behind the policía. Antonio was led to the green car, and put into the backseat. The migra, who opened the door, tried to speak Spanish, but Antonio could not understand what he said. The migra driver did not say anything.

Antonio spent three days and nights in the detention center with others who had been picked up by the migra. All were waiting for the free bus ride to the border. Antonio slept with his shoes on. It was early on the fourth morning that they were herded almost like cattle aboard the green bus with bars on the windows. Antonio wondered why the migra put bars on the windows. None of them would try to escape. All of them wanted the free ride to the border.

After dark the bus arrived at the Calexico migra station. They were herded off the bus, and into the detention center. After stopping at the desk they went to a big dining area, and filled their metal trays with the food from the steam table. Free bus ride. Free food. The United States was a good place to work.

After breakfast in the morning they were herded into the green bus again, for the ride to the border gate. They stepped off the bus and walked into Mexico. The Mexicali bus depot was close to the border. Most of his companions walked there to buy their tickets home. They bought tickets to as far away as Colima, Guadalajara, and Mexico City. Antonio took his dollars from his shoe and bought his ticket to Esquinapa. He changed the rest of his dollars into pesos. This bus would go to Santa Ana in Sonora. The next bus would go south to Mazatlan. The bus for Tepic would stop for him to get off in Esquinapa. Antonio thought about

# ANTONIO SINGS HIS SONG

Noemi as he stood waiting in the crowded depot, listening for the loudspeaker to announce the loading of his bus to Santa Ana.

The trip across the desert seemed endless. He wondered how long his friend from Michoacan would stay. He looked out the window as they traveled through the Pinacate Mountains. In the distance he could see remnants of old volcanoes. The bus stopped in Sonoita, and he ate some lunch at a small café near the bus station. At Santa Ana he changed buses.

Antonio found a seat near the rear of the Mazatlan-bound bus. He was happy to be traveling south, away from the border, getting closer and closer to Tinaja Verde. The darkness of night obscured any view he might have had through the window so his thoughts focused on what his homecoming might be like.

He began thinking up the words to a *corrido*, the long story-telling ballads he had heard men sing about the travels of men and of horses. The words began to fall into place in his mind as the bus sped southward toward Hermosillo. He concentrated on every detail of his life since leaving Tinaja Verde eight months before. It was early spring then, and now it was getting along toward late fall.

He woke up when the bus parked in the Hermosillo terminal. He disembarked with the other passengers, and walked to the lunch counter for a cup of café. The sleepy-eyed girl drew a cup of hot water from an urn, and placed it in front of him along with a jar of Nescafé and a bowl of sugar. He spooned in the powdered coffee and two sugars. As he stirred the coffee he thought again, as he had so many times, about how good a cup of his mother's coffee would taste. He bought a small packet of Gancitos, the chocolate-covered sponge cake with a drop of jelly on the top.

The bus driver finished his coffee and *torta*, sandwich, and was laughing with the sleepy-eyed waitress. When he rose to leave, Antonio followed him through the gate and into the bus. He walked back to the seat he had occupied before. Words and music for his corrido began flowing in his mind again. At Guaymas another driver took over. When he opened his eyes again the sun was just poking its way over the top of the Sierra Madres.

The stop at Los Mochis was long enough for him to eat a breakfast of sausage with eggs with a large spoonful of frijoles on the side of the plate. Another cup of powdered Nescafé. He felt better after the meal.

The words and music kept going through his mind so that the remainder of the trip became a blur until the bus stopped at Mazatlan, where he made another change. This time he was able to understand the voice over the loudspeaker. He wondered about the young mother nursing her baby, and when he would see Noemi doing the same beautiful thing. He was the only passenger to leave the bus at Esquinapa.

He walked to Café Aguila, and discovered that the bus for Tinaja Verde would not leave until early morning for its daily trip around the villages. He had forgotten. The gnawing feeling in his stomach told him it was time to eat again. It was not the same young girl behind the counter he had bought the coffee from on his way north. An older woman took his order for a plate of *carne machaca*, the dried beef that was so delicious mixed with green chile and onions.

After his feast he ambled over to a park with a bandstand in the middle. The place stood vacant except for a man and woman sitting entwined on one of the benches. Antonio rolled up the Raiders jacket, and bunched it under his head as he stretched out on the bench. He remembered the man from Michoacan, and wondered if they would meet again in Tinaja Verde next year. He thought about the words and music for his corrido again. He fell asleep just after remembering the night in the Calexico detention center.

The rickety bus pulled away from Esquinapa at sunrise. Antonio looked out the dirty flyspecked window as the bus bounced and slithered over the narrow dirt road around the villages. Tinaja Verde was next, just ahead. The bus lurched to a stop in front of the Tienda Ochoa. Antonio jumped out of the always-open door, and walked quickly down the path to the milpita.

He heard a shout, and then his brothers and sisters came running to greet him. He hugged them, and reached down to take little Dorita into his arms to carry her to the adobe house. His mother was standing in the doorway. His father, Ignacio, rose from his chair in the yard. It was as tear-filled a welcome home, as it had been a good-bye eight months before.

They were all anxious to hear about his adventures, and what it was like in the United States. He looked bigger and taller. He had new shoes and Americano jeans. Yes, the giros, the money orders, had arrived. Yes, the corn crop was fine, and the frijoles were sweeter than the year before.

Antonio walked into the house, and took the guitar from its hook on the wall. "I will be back soon," he said. "I have something I want to do."

The siblings were suddenly quiet. His mother smiled. Ignacio sat back down in his chair. Antonio walked back over the path to the village. Noemi had seen him through her window, and now she waited in the doorway. Antonio hung the guitar on her gatepost as she ran to meet him. She held out her hands to him, knowing her mother would be peeking through the kitchen window. She kissed Antonio quickly, and turned toward the open door of the house. "Mama," she called. "It's Antonio. He is back from the United States. We are going for a walk."

When they reached the secluded grove of cottonwood trees by the arroyo Antonio laid his guitar on the ground and took Noemi into his arms. Then they walked over to an old deadfall, and sat down on its barkless trunk. Antonio plunked at the guitar, and tuned it. "This is a song I have written for you, Noemi. It is called, 'El Corrido de Antonio Beltrán.'"

# Padre Mirandi

**A**lberto Mirandi proved to be a rebellious child even before he was born to Julio and Carmelita. Carmelita spent the most difficult nine months of her entire life when she was pregnant for the first time. The fetus made her constantly nauseous and wondering if she would live to see the baby born.

After he arrived in the world on May 4, 1730, little Alberto became petulant, screaming, and sickly. It was one thing after another until puberty struck with an unseen force that made everything fine except that Alberto developed an extraordinary interest in the opposite sex. By age fourteen at least ten girls in the small community of Begosia, in northern Italy, had succumbed to Alberto Mirandi's insistence. All but one of the ten *signorinas* sheltered happy memories of Alberto. The other, the daughter of a wealthy merchant, became instantly with child, and her father threatened to have young Alberto thrown into jail for his philandering.

However, long before he took such a liking to girls, the parents of young Alberto had decided that he should become a priest. They used their promise to the Church, the pope, God, Jesus, and the Virgin Mary to get their son away from Begosia just ahead of the town police chief, a good friend of the merchant father of the pregnant girlfriend.

A few years later Alberto Mirandi became an ordained priest in the Society of Jesus, Father Alberto Mirandi, SJ. On the surface, a more fervent spreader of the Gospel and doctrine of the Society never walked the cloistered halls of Saint James. While waiting for assignment, Father Alberto visited his family in Begosia. It would be the last time he would see any of them because Father Alberto Mirandi's assignment placed him at the Mission San Pablo de Guroki, in the Pimería Alta of New Spain, a long way from his native Begosia.

From Italy Alberto traveled overland to Cadiz, Spain, and finally to Palos for embarkation in 1754. Christopher Columbus had left from the same obscure port on his famous journey to the New World. But in the case of Father Alberto Mirandi, SJ, he was only a passenger. He sailed aboard the *Esmeralda*, destination Veracruz, the major east coast port in New Spain, where Cortez had made landfall on his way to conquer the Aztec civilization.

Mirandi had never yearned to be a sailor, and the voyage to the New World proved his early feeling. He became seasick as soon as the *Esmeralda* left the harbor of Palos, and he remained in his cabin for most of the trip. His most fervent hope came to be that he would remain in New Spain for the remainder of his life rather than have to walk up the gangway of another seagoing vessel.

Freshly arrived Jesuits were required to go through an indoctrination period before heading for their assignments.

# PADRE MIRANDI

Alberto was to have spent three months studying the mission system and learning rudimentary O'odham, the language of the O'odham Indians who were to be his charges. However, Padre Alfonso at San Pablo de Guroki had fallen ill with malaria, and Father Alberto Mirandi, SJ, found himself traveling north as the stricken Jesuit's replacement after only a month in the New World. Mirandi traveled north with four Spanish soldiers as his military escort.

Once installed in the mission Mirandi dismissed the soldiers, and proceeded to acquaint himself with his new surroundings, including his charges. In Europe the charges would have been called parishioners, but the major task of the priests in Pimería Alta was "taming Indians." This responsibility included teaching the Gospel, Spanish, and baptizing. He was also burdened with the task of insuring that couples would marry under the auspices of the Church rather than live under the traditional conditions of their tribal culture. In addition to the social dicta, Father Alberto was charged with the farming and raising livestock for the mission.

Most of the mission Indians were reticent, and reluctant to approach the new padre until the soldiers made their departure. The first to walk slowly to the small adobe structure that served as the rectory was Diego, the foreman of the mission farming enterprise. Spanish soldiers had brought him and his wife Mumara to San Pablo de Guroki from Arispe. Diego was appointed overseer of the resident O'odham farm workers. In Arispe the Spanish officials had considered him a "tame" Indian. But unlike most Opata, Diego did not agree with the mixing of Opata with Spaniards, or any other group. He was proud of his Opata lineage and was determined to keep it Opata, not only for himself, but also for his children.

Diego stopped twenty yards from the only entrance to the house. He had served the former padre as foreman, and he assumed that he would continue in the same capacity with Padre Mirandi.

Diego stood just over five feet six inches, and his stocky build held strong muscles from a lifetime of laboring in fields. He stood with his straw hat held in front of him with both calloused hands. He had been chosen *mayordomo* by the Spaniards in Arispe because of his alacrity at accepting baptism. What the Spaniards didn't know was that Diego understood that accepting didn't necessarily mean believing. But he had heard from certain itinerant traders how to become a mayordomo instead of a field laborer.

Diego had asked the former padre to marry Mumara and him in the mission even though they had two sons, seventeen and nineteen, and Keewa, their beautiful fourteen-year-old daughter. The padre had changed Diego's name from Dawa. He changed Mumara's name to Mariana, and Keewa was Christianized to Katarina. The sons became Felipe and Antonio. They used their Christian names around the padre, but elsewhere they went by their Opata names, given at birth during a presentation ceremony. Their Christian names sounded awkward to the Indians, and were a source of joking between them.

After waiting for half an hour Diego almost left for the fields, just as Padre Alberto opened the door of the rectory, and emerged into the sun. The priest stood looking at Diego momentarily as if waiting for the Indian to speak. Mirandi didn't know what to say. "Hello," the priest said finally.

"Hello," Diego answered.

It took ten minutes before Alberto Mirandi figured out that Diego wanted to report in as the mayordomo of the mission farms. Diego then took the padre on a tour of the fields to show what was planted and where, and to show his new boss the livestock owned by the mission. The latter consisted of fifty head of cattle, a few sheep, goats, and a small pen of hogs. There were four horses in a small pasture. Diego informed Mirandi that the mission owned several mares that were turned in with a stallion belonging to a neighbor. There was an orchard of fruit trees, peaches, and apricots that stood leafless as skeletons in the cold winter air.

The padre enjoyed seeing the fields, the orchard, and the livestock, but he didn't understand much of what Diego had told him. It wasn't because of the explanations; it was because Alberto Mirandi SJ didn't know much about farming. He realized that he must rely on Diego's knowledge.

They walked back toward the rectory where Katarina, now sixteen and blossoming into a beauty, waited demurely by the building. "This is Katarina, my daughter," Diego informed the priest. "She will cook for you and wash your clothes as she did for the other padre."

Mirandi's face lit up with a smile. "I am happy to meet you, Katarina," he said. "It is nice to know I will not go hungry or have to wear dirty clothes."

Looking at Katarina made Mirandi tingle. He could see an exotic beauty in her that seemed out of place in such an isolated spot as Mission San Pablo. He saw a certain refinement in her features not present in most of the Indian women. He had not looked over the papers left by the previous rector so he didn't know that Diego and his family were Opata rather than O'odham. Their facial structure was sharper than the O'odham, and they tended toward a taller stature. The Opata originated in the area of Río Sonora and had been "tamed" before the O'odham. The Spanish policy, when it came to the O'odham missions, was to bring already "tame" Indians to new missions to oversee the work of farming and livestock raising. This policy had backfired at one mission to the south in 1695.

The O'odham of San Pedro y San Pablo de Tubutama had rebelled against their overbearing Opata mayordomo, who didn't speak the same language. They killed him, and went on to murder the padre of the mission in Carborca to the south.

Father Mirandi had heard of the rebellion that had occurred during the time of Eusebio Kino, the Jesuit missionary and explorer who founded many missions in northwestern Mexico and the southwestern United States, but the thought of the Indians of Guroki rebelling didn't cross his mind. He was correct in his assumptions because Diego had learned the O'odham language, and he didn't oppress his charges. His benevolent attitude stemmed from his desire to get along with both his workers and the padre who resided at the mission. Had he been without a family he might have thought differently, but Diego was happy with his woman, his sons, and especially with Keewa, the daughter who had become very beautiful.

Katarina smiled. Mirandi stared at the girl for a moment, then turned back to Diego. "Thank you for showing me around the fields, Diego."

Upon his arrival at San Pablo de Guroki, Alberto Mirandi, SJ, had wondered if he had been shipped to the end of the earth in spite of the indoctrination sessions he had attended. The rectory was small, the mission was no more than a bower, and the surrounding country, except for the Río Concepción, looked wild and desolate in winter. He had wondered about the Indians and how the work would be accomplished. After meeting Diego and Katarina he felt better about the situation. He wondered about

Katarina's status and went to the rectory to read the mission census made by the former priest. He learned that Diego and his family were Opata, from Arispe.

As he looked at the census records Mirandi noticed that the former priest had included the Opata names of Diego and his family. He questioned the virtue of Christianizing Indian names. "Keewa," he said aloud to hear how Katarina's Opata name sounded.

He wondered if he was giving the name the correct pronunciation. Then he spoke the Opata names for the rest of the family. He remembered the Indian beauty of Keewa, and how different she looked compared to the O'odham women he had seen on his arrival. He felt good that Keewa would be doing his household chores rather than one of the others.

Diego hoped that he might be able to return to the Río Sonora with his family to find women for his sons and a man for Keewa. With the new padre's arrival at San Pablo de Guroki his hopes had risen. His plan involved working diligently for a while before asking for permission to travel to his homeland. Should the new padre refuse his request Diego planned to steal the mission horses and escape under the cover of darkness. He knew that he could go a long way off before discovery and without horses the padre would have great difficulty in pursuing him and his family. Diego had never discussed his thoughts with his family. He had only admonished Keewa to stay away from O'odham men and his sons not to think of taking a wife from among the O'odham women. When the sons asked what they should do for their desires, Diego told them to do whatever they had to do except that they would eventually settle with Opata women. They did not question him further.

Alberto Mirandi began his routine of offering mass to his charges, baptizing babies, and performing Christian marriage ceremonies. He enjoyed watching Katarina go about the rectory chores, and thoughts about what she would look like naked prevailed much of the time his eyes followed her. After two months in residence at San Pablo de Guroki Alberto Mirandi, SJ, began thinking that perhaps his vow of celibacy should not apply to Indian women. He began teaching Katarina Spanish.

Once a month Mirandi looked forward to visiting the resident priest at San José de Tawaki, a four-hour ride downstream, the nearest mission to Guroki. Padre Fritz Krampetz, originally from Bavaria, had been at San José for six years. He was fifteen years older than Mirandi, and often expressed a desire to return to his native land. Krampetz looked forward to the monthly visits from the new man at Guroki. The previous Jesuit rarely came downstream even before the malaria struck, and Krampetz, with his crippled left hip from a fall off a mule, stayed close to his mission.

Keewa liked the Spanish lessons. She also found the priest attractive, and could sense his attraction to her. But she kept those feelings to herself mostly because she didn't fully understand them.

The mass to celebrate his six months at San Pablo de Guroki caused Mirandi concern because many of the Indians did not attend. He wondered if it might be sullen resentment on their part, and decided to ask Diego what he thought might be the cause.

"These people may come to your masses most of the time," Diego said, haltingly. "But they still have their own beliefs, and their own gods."

"I understand that, Diego," Mirandi replied. "But why were so many missing from mass today? The women were here, but the men seemed to have disappeared."

Diego did not wish to continue the conversation. He knew what had happened, and he feared that the priest would punish everyone if he discovered the reason so many men had not attended the mass.

"I do not know," he said.

"Where are they?" Mirandi questioned. "You must know where they are. After all, you are the mayordomo!"

Diego felt trapped. He knew where the men were and what they were doing, but he didn't want to say anything. What the O'odham men did belonged to them, and it was not part of the Opata tradition. Opata might drink the fermented drink from the agave, but they didn't experiment with datura.

"If you want to speak to the men," Diego said. "Go to the far end of the fields, take the trail down by the river, and you will come to a grove of large mesquite trees. You will find the men of Guroki there."

"Lead me to them, Diego."

"I cannot do that. I am Opata, they are O'odham. Their beliefs are different from mine."

"You are all Christians! What kind of heathen practices are going on at a Christian mission?"

"You must find that out for yourself, Father."

Diego knew that if he was to interfere with the O'odham ritual of datura his life might be in danger. However, he did not think that they would harm the padre should he happen to find them. Besides he knew that most would be in a helpless state of mind from the hallucinogenic datura.

Father Mirandi decided that to pursue the matter any further with his foreman would be a waste of time and energy. He walked through the fields until he found the trail leading to the grove of mesquite. The sight of the

O'odham men under the influence of datura left him stunned with confusion.

The men sat entranced in a circle surrounding the prostrate bodies of three of their companions. They moaned in a sad cacophony as they waved their arms wildly about their heads. Mirandi stopped and stared at the three who appeared to be dead, or at least unconscious. For a moment he thought about storming into the circle to confront the men for missing his mass, but after watching their erratic behavior the priest turned around and returned to the rectory with a feeling of complete frustration.

Keewa was sweeping the dirt floor when he arrived.

"Katarina," Mirandi said. "What is going on in the mesquite grove? Why are the men acting crazy?"

"I do not know, Father. I have never seen them when they take the datura."

"What is this datura?"

"It is the plant with the big leaves and big white flowers."

"What do the men do with this plant?" Mirandi asked.

"I only know from my father," she replied. "He told us that they cut the plant at a certain time below the flower, and the plant bleeds. They eat the plant's blood and do strange things in the mesquite grove. Sometimes they die."

"Thank you for telling me this, Katarina," he said, and fell into silence as he thought about what all this meant. He wondered if the three prostrate bodies were, in fact, dead. *What can I do to stop this heathen practice!* he wondered to himself.

The following morning Diego came to the rectory before going to the fields. Keewa had told her father about the priest's questions, and the answers she had given. Diego needed to give the priest further explanation or risk falling from the father's trust.

"Padre," he began when the priest came to the door of the rectory. "Three men died from the datura yesterday. They will be buried by the others before night."

"Why do they not tell me about this?"

"They do things their own way, Father. They have their own ceremony after datura."

"How often does this happen?"

"It does not always happen with the datura. I think it happens when the datura speaks too strongly to them. I do not know because Opata do not talk to datura."

"The dead need a Christian burial, and I must know their names for the records," Mirandi said.

"Padre," Diego said. "They will bury their dead themselves. I will get the names for you, for the records."

Mirandi went back to the rectory disturbed at what he had learned about the datura and its potential to take life. He also felt that Diego was not in control of his workers. He didn't realize that Diego wanted no part of telling O'odham what they should or should not believe. As far as he was concerned his duty was to oversee the work in the fields and with the livestock.

Through the doorway he saw Katarina preparing strips of beef over the mesquite coals. As she bent over to turn the meat her loose-fitting blouse fell to reveal her firm, brown, round breasts. Mirandi felt himself surge with desire.

When the meal was ready Katarina brought in a plateful for the padre. "Which name do you like better," he asked, "Katarina or Keewa?"

The question startled the girl because she didn't realize that the padre knew her real name. "I don't know," she said.

"Did I pronounce Keewa the correct way?"

"Yes."

"I like the sound of Keewa better than Katarina," he said.

"I like it better too, but the padre before you told us that to be Christians we had to have Christian names."

"Do you know what a Christian is, Keewa?"

"The padre told my family we were Christians."

Alberto Mirandi paused to ponder Keewa's answer. He wondered if all Indian converts would answer in the same manner.

"Your food, Padre," Keewa said, observing that he had not touched the meat she had cooked.

"Oh yes," Mirandi said. "I was thinking you are very beautiful, Keewa."

Keewa smiled at the compliment. "I must return to our house now."

"We will have a Spanish lesson tomorrow after mass, and after breakfast," he said, and closed the door behind the girl.

"Tell your father I will need a horse to ride to San José de Tawaki," Mirandi said to Keewa after the lesson. "I will spend the night there, so you don't have to cook supper or breakfast in the morning."

Keewa left to tell Diego to saddle a horse for the padre. As she walked out to where he was watching his men working on an irrigation ditch she wondered why Mirandi wanted to go to Tawaki so soon after his visit only a week before.

Diego caught the big, gentle, buckskin gelding for the father. After he had him saddled he left the horse inside the corral, and went back to the ditch. Mirandi walked to the corral, and led the buckskin back to the rectory where he lifted a bundle of bedding and tied it behind the cantle with the saddle strings. He didn't bother with food because he would arrive at Tawaki in time for dinner, prepared by the old, wizened, O'odham woman named Ruth, who served Krampetz as his housekeeper.

# PADRE MIRANDI

Mirandi couldn't understand why Krampetz kept Ruth as his housekeeper when there were plenty of young and more attractive O'odham women in the Tawaki parish. *Perhaps if he had a housekeeper as pretty as Keewa he wouldn't want to return to Bavaria,* Mirandi thought as he urged the buckskin along the trail to Tawaki.

Krampetz sat on the bench outside the rectory when Mirandi rode up. "Hola, Alberto," the older man said without rising. "What brings you back here so soon? Have you done something you need to confess?" Krampetz chuckled at his own humor.

"There is nothing to do in this entire valley to confess for," Mirandi said, at the same time thinking about the thoughts he continued to have about Keewa.

"Put your horse up in the corral, and I'll have Ruth fix you a plate."

Mirandi, still mounted, rode the buckskin to the corral, unsaddled, and tossed in some hay he found under a ramada. Then he walked back to sit next to his fellow Jesuit. "A strange thing happened at the mission," Mirandi began. "The O'odham men went crazy from datura. Three of them died as a result. What kind of heathen behavior is this?"

"I have seen the same thing here many times, but I recall only one poor soul who died."

"Is there nothing we could do to put a stop to this heathen ritual?" Mirandi asked.

"Alberto, you have been among these people for only six months. You will come to know that whatever you may do or say to them they will not stop their barbaric ceremonies."

"But they are Christians, and Christians don't behave like barbarians."

"Father Alberto, you are so young. I hate to disillusion you. I have been in this godforsaken place for six years.

Before that I lived five years in another godforsaken place far to the south. I have grown cynical through these years. These people come to live at these missions because the living is easier than elsewhere. They are fed and cared for. They come to mass and mimic. They don't understand or believe in Christianity. Look into their round, pumpkin-like faces and you see nothing. At first I tried holding confession, but they said nothing. They have no guilt. They have nothing to confess. The Spaniards would come for them, and put them to work in their mines if it had not been for Eusebio Kino insisting on the *cédula*, the rule, that prevents that exploitation."

"Then why are we here?" Mirandi asked.

"We are supposed to teach the Gospel to these heathens. We are supposed to tame them, and integrate them into the Spanish way of life. But there is no Spanish way of life here. These Indians only put up with us priests because they are afraid of the Spanish soldiers. When you have been here as long as I have you will have learned to while away your time as best you can. If you don't learn that, your life will be filled with daily frustration."

Mirandi sat in silence contemplating the words of the older man. What he had spoken seemed to be true. He, too, had held confession. Three Indians showed up, but they didn't speak a word. They didn't even answer his questions. And the datura.

"I suppose you are right, Father Krampetz. I should not concern myself so much, but this datura ritual they do is beyond my comprehension."

"It is beyond your comprehension because you are not an Indian."

Ruth had warmed a bowl of beans mixed with small chunks of meat, and handed it to Mirandi. He looked up to her expressionless face, and thanked her. He savored the first spoonful despite it being almost too hot for his tongue. "This is really delicious," he said.

"Yes," Krampetz agreed. "Ruth is an excellent cook. I taught her how I like my food cooked. How is the food at San Pablo? Do you have a good cook?"

"Katarina, Diego's daughter, is my housekeeper," Mirandi said. "She is an adequate cook, but doesn't compare to Ruth."

"Ah yes, I remember the girl when I went to see Father Alfonso. She is very pretty. You might have to ride over here for confession if you don't teach her how to cook." Krampetz laughed, and noticed the color flush into Mirandi's face. "That's why I keep Ruth. She is a good cook, and you can see she is no source of temptation."

Alberto Mirandi felt foolish. He turned his face away from Krampetz but the hot feeling persisted. He suddenly wished that when the Father Visitor arrived Krampetz's wish to return to Bavaria would be granted.

Mirandi spent most of the night sleepless, thinking about the hopelessness of being a missionary to the O'odham. He also thought about Keewa and how he should resist the pull he felt to take her into his arms. The more he thought about her the more his passion rose. *Perhaps I should trade Keewa for her mother. There would be no temptation from Mariana.*

He didn't wake up until he heard the door slam behind Krampetz as he hobbled out to the ramada for mass. He dressed quickly, left the rectory, and took a seat on a log that had been placed behind the crude altar. Mirandi watched as the Indians genuflected whenever Krampetz genuflected. Mimicry. Krampetz knew what he was saying.

When mass ended the two priests returned to the rectory where Ruth served them a breakfast of eggs cooked with chile and onions. "We have done much to improve the lives of these Indians," Krampetz said, attempting to start a conversation.

"I suppose you are correct, Father, but livestock and crops are one thing, saving souls is another."

"One cannot save a soul that does not want saving, Alberto. Remember what I said yesterday about frustration."

Alberto Mirandi rode the buckskin slowly south along the trail that followed the Río Concepción, stopping once to watch a family of beavers work on their dam. He was fascinated to see them slapping mud against the willow and cottonwood saplings they had cut with their teeth, dragged to the dam, and placed with some sort of engineering knowledge they possessed. He admired their patience and industriousness, and wondered if he could somehow acquire the same patience in ministering to his charges.

He unsaddled the buckskin, and left him in the corral. Keewa rose from the bench at his approach. "Hola," he said.

"Hola, Padre Mirandi. I have the names of the dead men for the records."

"Let me get the book," Mirandi said, and went into the rectory. Keewa followed.

"They were Daniel, Pedro, and Pablo. Pedro and Pablo were brothers."

Mirandi wrote the names in the registry under the heading, "Death by datura," and closed the book after making sure the ink had dried. He looked at Keewa, a downcast look on his face. "You must not worry so, Padre," she said with concern.

"Keewa, I cannot help worrying about something that baffles me."

"It baffles me too, but I don't worry about something I don't understand."

Mirandi reached for her hand, sat down on his bed, and pulled her next to him. Keewa was surprised, but not afraid. "You are wise for a girl of your age, Keewa. I wish I could share your attitude toward this thing that datura has done."

"My father says that the O'odham do what they do, and we Opata do not have to do the same."

Mirandi put his right arm around the girl's shoulders, and drew her closer to him. Keewa offered no resistance. The closeness was something she had wondered about. Mirandi began shaking, slightly, yet uncontrollably. He brushed his left hand across her breasts, and felt her nipples stiffen beneath the cotton blouse. Keewa sighed as she felt herself becoming aroused. She put her right hand to his neck as she turned to him.

Mirandi slipped his hand and arm beneath the blouse and ran his smooth fingers across the hardened nipples. His passion quickened beneath the black robe until he desperately wanted this girl who seemed to have no inhibitions. He reached for her face and kissed her. She joined him with her mouth, and sighed again as she gave in to her feelings.

Mirandi pulled away. "I must latch the door," he said as he rose from the embrace and walked to the entrance. *My God, I should not be doing this. What about the vows?*

Keewa lay on her back with her eyes closed as he returned to the bedside. "What are you thinking, Keewa?"

She opened her eyes and turned her face toward him. "I am remembering watching my father and mother, and I am wanting to feel what it is like. My body is wanting to know."

"A priest is not supposed to do this," he said.

"Is not a priest a man as well?"

Mirandi reached for her hands and pulled her up into a sitting position. He then took the cotton blouse and lifted it over her head exposing the beautiful, brown, young body. He put his hands behind her shoulders and guided her back on the pillow. He no longer contemplated his vows. Nothing went through his mind except his fervent desire to make love to his beautiful Keewa.

The black robe fell in a heap after he tossed it on the floor. He slipped next to her. For a moment Mirandi remembered the last girl he had been with back in Italy, but Keewa again took over, obliterating all his thoughts except the ecstasy he experienced. Her mind went blank to everything except the strange new yearning she felt inside her that gradually strengthened. She felt herself slipping quickly out of control and cried out in complete, newfound joy. She felt herself falling dreamily into slumber.

Mirandi sat up on the side of the bed, and looked down at her. He smiled, and then when he saw the small spot of blood, he gasped. From what she had said he knew that he would be her first man, but the sight of the proof gave him a sudden surge of guilt.

Keewa slept for two hours. She opened her eyes to see Mirandi dressed again in his black robe, seated at the small table reading. He looked around when he heard her stir. Seeing that she had awakened, he left the table, walked to the bed, and took her into his arms. "I was your first man, Keewa?" he whispered.

"Oh yes."

"It is supper time and you will have to leave soon. You must not tell anyone what we did, not your parents, and not your brothers. It must remain our secret."

"It will be our secret, my first man."

Keewa rose quickly, put on her clothes, and went outside to heat a bowl of beans on the coals from the dying fire. When the beans were warm she brought the bowl to Mirandi. Then she went to the woodpile for enough logs to last through the night. "I must go home now," she said.

Mirandi sat outside on the bench watching the fresh mesquite logs smoke, flicker, and finally burst into flame. His thoughts rushed from guilt to happiness, from wonder to fear that Diego would somehow find out what his daughter was doing with a priest. He thought back to the wealthy merchant's daughter in Begosia, and how his parents had whisked him away just in time to avoid the chief of police. He had taken the vows, and until this day had been true to them. Now that he had broken the promise, what should he do? Certainly he could not confess this carnal sin to another priest, least of all to Krampetz, who would have a big laugh over it.

The heat from the fire felt comforting during all his contemplations. He watched the moon rise over the Sierra de Piedras, and flood the valley with its light. Thoughts about the afternoon with Keewa came often to chase away any others. He marveled at her exotic beauty and her freedom to act without any guilt whatsoever. When the moon had risen to a third of its way across the sky he went into the rectory.

Keewa was asleep before the moon rose. She had eaten the supper of venison that Mumara had prepared, but went to her bed early to have her thoughts in privacy. At least, as private as she could in the one-room dwelling. She didn't hear her parents or her brothers go to their beds. Her thoughts about the afternoon soothed her into sleep.

The sound of loud snoring awakened her. This had happened before, coming from her brother Antonio, who snored every time he slept on his back. Sometimes she would shake him to make him stop snoring, but this night she sat up from her deerhide bed to listen. Soft sounds of night breathing came from all except the snoring Antonio.

She quietly slipped on her moccasins, got to her feet, and walked slowly toward the hide-covered entrance to the wattle-and-daub hut. She paused before leaving to make sure again that everyone slept, and then carefully pushed the hide doorway far enough so that she could slip silently beneath it. Once outside she paused again, listened for any movement inside, and then tiptoed away in the direction of the rectory.

Alberto Mirandi snapped awake to the knock on the rectory door. "Who is it?" he said.

"Keewa."

He scrambled out of his covers and went to unlatch the door. "What are you doing here, Keewa?" he asked when he had opened the door to find her standing in the moonlight smiling up at him.

"I woke up thinking about this afternoon. I wanted to be with you again."

"What about your parents? What if they should wake and find you gone?"

"I have already decided to tell them I could not sleep and was walking by the river. They will believe me because I have done that before."

He stood aside to let her pass. She went directly to the bed and removed her blouse. Mirandi had turned to light a candle. Then he turned to see the naked Keewa in the candlelight waiting for him. Alberto Mirandi walked to the bed and took her into his arms.

He saw her walking toward him from her dwelling as he prepared to serve mass. She took her usual seat in the front row of log pews. Mirandi looked around his small congregation of O'odham. The rest of Keewa's family sat in their usual places toward the rear. He felt his nervousness subside as he began with the opening words.

Diego approached him after the service ended. Mirandi's nervousness enveloped him again until Diego started telling him that with planting time coming soon he might need more seed corn to plant in the new field that they had cleared over the winter.

Mirandi tried to seem nonchalant. "Perhaps, Padre Krampetz at Tawaki has enough to lend us some. The next time I go there for a visit I will ask him."

"The mesquite trees will soon be showing their leaves to tell us it is time to plant," Diego said, trying to impress the new padre that his request was important if the new field was to have a crop.

"I will be riding there soon, Diego. And, I won't forget the seed corn."

The nights were still very cool, and Mirandi didn't think there was any rush to get seed corn from Krampetz.

"Perhaps I should ride to Tawaki today and ask the padre," Diego said. "If he does not have enough for us, we will have to find it somewhere else. That is unless you don't care if there is corn in the new field."

Mirandi understood after Diego's patient explanation. "All right, Diego, ride to Tawaki today, and tell Padre Krampetz that I am requesting the seed corn. Wait one moment and I will write a note to him."

Mirandi went into the rectory, scribbled a short letter to Krampetz, and returned to hand it to his mayordomo.

Keewa listened to the conversation as she prepared Mirandi's breakfast. She was glad to hear that her father would be away until dark with his errand to Tawaki.

Diego saddled a bay gelding for himself, and put an empty packsaddle on the mule to haul the seed corn back if there was any in Tawaki. Before leaving he outlined to the farm hands the work he expected to be accomplished in his absence.

Mirandi and Keewa were in bed long before Diego reached Tawaki. By the time he reached the mission and handed the letter to Padre Krampetz the two lovers had returned to the bed in spite of Mirandi's pleading that he had work to do on the reports to the bishop.

Krampetz read the letter requesting seed corn, and sent Diego to find his mayordomo, Anselmo. Krampetz waited seated on his bench. "Do we have any spare seed corn, Anselmo?" Krampetz asked when the two Indian men approached.

"I think we can spare some, Padre," Anselmo replied.

"How much do you need, Diego? The letter doesn't state the amount you want to borrow."

"Two sacks will be enough. It is not a large field, and we have enough to plant half. The two sacks will plant the rest."

"Give Diego two sacks of seed corn, Anselmo. I will write it in the records."

Krampetz envied Mirandi having Diego as a mayordomo. The yields from the Guroki fields surpassed Tawaki every year in spite of Tawaki's lower elevation. He wondered what Diego did to achieve such yields. What Krampetz failed to understand was the difference in the soil. The fields of Tawaki were laced with former river channels even though it was not noticeable when one walked through the farmland. Guroki's fields held deeper soils, and were more easily irrigated from the river.

Mirandi had exhausted himself by midafternoon. Keewa, on the other hand, wanted to make love again. "Wait until tomorrow, Keewa," he pleaded. "It is time for you to cook supper anyway. I'll have to eat more than a bowl of beans to get back my strength."

Keewa relented with an impish smile. "I will feed you so much, my first man, that you will be ready when I sneak away tonight."

"I don't want you to sneak away tonight, Keewa. I must sleep. I must sleep all night."

She went outside to stir the coals from the fire. Then she trotted to her dwelling to get a good-sized strip of venison from the carcass her brothers had brought back from their hunt three days before. "What are you doing?" Mumara asked.

"I am taking some venison to the padre. He is tired of the beans."

"Tell him to hunt his own deer," Mumara said.

"Priests do not hunt deer," Keewa countered. "Besides, he is too busy with the reports to hunt deer."

Mumara waved a hand in disgust, and went back inside the hut. Keewa walked back to the rectory, and put the strip of venison on the coals.

Diego returned as the sun began splashing the Sierra de Piedras with scarlet as it set beyond the western Sierra Cimarron. He rode directly to the rectory with the pack mule laden with the two sacks of seed corn. "We have enough, now," he said. "The new field will have a crop."

"That is good, Diego," Mirandi said, and smiled. "You have done well today."

171

# PADRE MIRANDI

Keewa woke up in the middle of the night, but she didn't leave the hut. She thought about her recent experiences with the padre, and wondered what it would be like to live in the rectory with him. She felt herself, and then moved her hands to fondle her own breasts, imagining it was Alberto Mirandi.

Mirandi went to bed shortly after finishing his supper. He had no thoughts about anything. He was in a deep sleep within minutes.

Two weeks later Diego rode up to the rectory as Mirandi was finishing breakfast. Keewa was busy sweeping the dirt floor beneath the ramada. She had heard her father early that morning tell Mumara that the mesquite trees had sprouted their new leaves, and it was time to announce the planting time to the padre. She made sure to be busy outside when her father arrived.

"Hola, Diego," Mirandi said as the foreman rode up on the buckskin.

"The mesquite tells us to plant, padre. We should start today."

"Very well, Diego," Mirandi said. "Do you need extra help with the planting?"

"I have announced the planting to all the O'odham. They will send their young women."

"Thank you, Diego," Mirandi said.

Diego had no idea why Mirandi was thanking him for doing his job as mayordomo. "I must go to pack the mule with seed sacks," Diego said, and reined the buckskin around to head toward the corral.

Both Keewa and Mirandi laughed when Diego rode away. "They will be too busy to bother us for the next two weeks," Keewa said.

"We have the same thoughts, my dear," Mirandi answered.

Alberto Mirandi had given up thinking about his vow of celibacy. In fact, he had given up thinking about much of anything except Keewa, and how much he had come to love the beautifully exotic Indian girl. Keewa, too, adored the padre, and referred to him as Alberto unless others were in the vicinity.

The morning after planting began she arrived as usual to attend mass and fix his breakfast afterward. However, she seemed downcast as he watched her prepare the food. "What is the matter, Keewa?" Mirandi asked. "You look sad this morning."

"It is my time," she answered. "The blood started this morning."

For Mirandi the news of Keewa's period was welcome. It meant that there was no baby on the way. "We cannot make our love during my time," she continued. "Opata do not make their love during the blood."

"It will pass soon, and we will be free again," Mirandi commented.

Alberto Mirandi needed the rest. The activity had worn him down to almost lethargy. He walked over to Keewa and took her into his arms.

The first white clouds came in high from the south. The heat of early June became more intense with every day's passing. The crops in the Guroki fields showed vigorous growth from the almost constant irrigation. The squash put out its first blooms, the corn reached for the sky, and the beans sent their tendrils to wrap around the stalks of corn. The trees in the orchard had shed their blossoms to display the young fruit that would be harvested and dried before fall.

Keewa had missed her second time. For a month she had kept her morning nausea a secret within herself. She had mixed feelings about being with child from a priest. Now she was sure that there was another life growing inside her. She had heard descriptions from her mother, and she had seen O'odham women retch in the mornings as they worked around their huts. It was time to tell Alberto.

Mirandi had finished his breakfast and sat at his desk inside the rectory working on his report to the Father Visitor who was due within a week. Keewa finished banking the fire and cleaning up the utensils. It was time. She walked into the rectory. "I must talk to you," she said.

"I cannot talk now," Mirandi said without lifting his eyes from the ledger. "I must finish these reports for the Father Visitor."

"When can we talk?"

"Perhaps in the afternoon."

Keewa left the rectory disappointed that she was not able to speak with Alberto to tell him about her condition. She walked away from the rectory toward the river. She sat on a dead cottonwood log looking and listening to the water gurgle as it made its way in the channel. She felt happy about having Mirandi's baby inside her, but she was also afraid. She remembered how insistent Alberto had been that she should not speak about his or her lovemaking to anyone. Now, when she wanted to share what she knew with him he had refused to talk because of the records. *The records. The new life inside me is more important than the records!*

Keewa left her seat on the log, and walked with determination toward the rectory. Without knocking she opened the door and walked in. "There is new life inside me," she announced. "I think you should know this and be happy."

Mirandi had looked up momentarily when she entered, but returned to the ledger immediately. After hearing Keewa's announcement he remained staring at the ledger after dropping the quill pen from his fingers. "There is WHAT?"

"New life, Alberto, a baby!" She smiled.

Mirandi whipped around and stared at her. "How do you know?"

"I just know. Two moons have passed without my times. I am not well in the early mornings, and my breasts feel tight. I have heard other women tell about this, and I am the same."

Mirandi sat speechless staring at her for a few moments. His mind had been dashed into total confusion. "We must do something," he said finally after dropping his eyes to the floor.

"Do something? Are you not happy that we will have a child?"

Again he was speechless. *Happy? My God, how could I be happy? I have broken my vow of celibacy, and now I have fathered a child from an Indian girl who is sixteen years old,* he thought to himself. "Keewa, this is an awkward situation. Perhaps you don't fully understand that as a priest I am not supposed to do with a woman what I have done with you. I am not allowed to be your husband, least of all the father of your child."

"I do not understand all of this," she said sadly. She dropped her eyes to the floor, no longer smiling, feeling tears begin to well up in her eyes.

"The Father Visitor will be here soon, Keewa. I will ask him what is the best for both of us...and the baby."

Keewa turned and fled through the door. "Keewa, come back here. Please come back here!"

Mirandi rose quickly from his desk and followed her. She was running toward the river. He walked at his usual pace so that it wouldn't arouse suspicion in anyone who might be watching. She was sitting on the cottonwood log sobbing. Mirandi sat down next to her and put his arm around her. "Keewa, don't cry, of course I am happy. It just came as a surprise."

He reached out and took her face in his hands, and brought it up to wipe her tears away. He kissed her tenderly. "It is all right, my Keewa. It is all right."

She stopped sobbing and put her arms around his neck. They stayed that way for a few minutes without speaking. "Let us go back to the rectory," he said finally. "I will walk back, and you follow behind a ways."

She didn't answer, but he knew she would do as he asked. He rose from the log, and began walking back over the trail from the river. The initial shock accompanied by fear surged through him as he traveled. *I must hide my feelings from her. What will the Father Visitor do when I tell him what I have done? How will Diego react when he finally knows?*

He waited for her inside the door of the rectory, and took her into his arms again when she arrived minutes behind him. "Do you feel better?" Mirandi asked.

"I feel better now. I thought you were angry with me when I first told you. I would feel even better next to you in the bed."

Ignacio Quiroz, SJ, the Father Visitor, arrived a day ahead of the schedule he had sent in his letter. Mirandi went over the San Pablo de Guroki reports with him, and turned them over for the Father Visitor to hand-carry to the bishop. Mirandi spent two nervous days going over the reports and showing the church official around the fields. The evening before Quiroz was due to depart, Mirandi knew it was time to discuss the matter of Keewa's pregnancy with him.

"Father, I have something to confess to you," Mirandi said.

"Do you want me to hear your confession?"

"Perhaps later, but I would prefer to seek your advice first."

"Certainly. Tell me what is on your mind, my son."

"Father, I have done something terrible," Mirandi said, almost stammering. "I have not only broken my vow of celibacy, I have also caused a young girl, my housekeeper, to become with child. I am at a total loss."

"This IS serious, my son," the Father Visitor said, with officialdom in the tone of his voice. "There must be severe penance, especially since you have taken advantage of a young girl."

"I understand, Father Quiroz. I am not asking for absolution, I am seeking a remedy for the girl and her baby."

"I must think about this matter. I must think about your penance as well as what to do about the girl."

Mirandi had given his bed to the Father Visitor during his stay. He gathered some bedding and left for the ramada but sleep did not come to him easily. He listened to the coyotes howling to each other. He heard the horses moving around in the corral. He heard the distant sound of the river. And all the time he wondered and worried about what conclusions the Father Visitor would come to in the morning.

The Father Visitor spent little thought about the matter except to wonder about the virtue of sending young priests to the hinterlands, into different cultures so foreign that the young priests lose sight of their past and think that isolation is an excuse to act like the natives. Mirandi's case was not the first of its kind that the Father Visitor had been forced to deal with.

Keewa looked forward to the Father Visitor's departure to again talk with Mirandi, and lie next to him in comfort. Her initial feelings of rejection by Alberto had passed, for the most part, but there was a lingering fear from wondering what would happen to them once the Father Visitor left on his rounds of the missions. Mirandi had told her that what the Father Visitor said would have to happen.

The clouds began early. Before sunrise they were racing northward, lower than the day before, and far lower than two weeks before. Ignacio Quiroz pushed himself up to a sitting position with his feet on the floor. He rubbed his eyes, cleared his throat, and began to dress himself for the next leg of his journey.

Keewa had arrived earlier than usual to prepare breakfast so that the Father Visitor would have an early start. Mirandi went to the door of the rectory. "Are you awake, Father?"

"Yes," Quiroz answered gruffly. "I am almost dressed."

They ate breakfast together sitting on the bench. Keewa put more wood on the fire, looked at the sky full of clouds, and wondered if the first storm of summer would bring lightning to set fire to the hills. She then walked back to her hut as Mirandi had told her to do, leaving the two Jesuits to talk.

"That is the girl?" Quiroz inquired, when Keewa had left.

"Yes, Father."

"Well, she is good looking in her Indian way. But that does not excuse your transgressions. I will tell you what I have decided. Obviously you can no longer remain at San Pablo de Guroki. I will have you transferred to San Juan de Loreto in Baja California as assistant to the old man who has been there doing penance for many years. Loreto is not a pleasant place compared to this one, but you are there for penance, not for pleasure. You will be paying for the carnal pleasures that you have, no doubt, enjoyed. I will have a replacement for you here within a month. When he arrives you will leave with his escort to the port of Topolobampo where the supply ship will take you to your new assignment."

Mirandi was stunned by what Quiroz had said, especially the necessity of shipboard travel. "What about the girl, Father?"

"She has done nothing wrong. She has never taken a vow of celibacy. Does anyone else know about her being with child? Her parents?"

"Nobody knows except you, me, and Katarina."

"How will her parents accept her with your child inside her?"

"I have no idea except she has told me that her father had forbidden her to take up with an O'odham. She, like her father, my mayordomo, is Opata."

"There is a convent far to the south. It would be a great expense to send her there. And there is the possibility that she would not go."

"I am really at a loss. I don't know how she will react when she learns that I am to leave without her."

The conversation stopped as Ignacio Quiroz pondered the situation. In spite of what Mirandi had done, the Father Visitor had taken a liking to him. He sympathized with his youth more than most Father Visitors could, because he remembered the time when he was a young priest in Mexico City. He, too, had broken his vow of celibacy, but was sent to Culiacan in Sinaloa before he knew whether or not the girl he had slept with for a month was pregnant or not. Quiroz felt sorry for the young Mirandi, and wondered if the advice he was about to give him was the best.

"Alberto," he began in a far softer tone of voice than before. "You have an opportunity if you choose. The priesthood is not for everyone. Perhaps you were forced by your parents to follow the Society of Jesus. Many are. You obviously love this girl. I can tell because of your concern. Suppose I asked the bishop to defrock you, and give you the freedom to marry this girl and raise your child?"

Mirandi was wide-eyed with surprise. He had not expected anything like that to come from the Father Visitor.

"I have no means to make a living, Father. I am a priest. I don't even know much about the farming here. I leave that up to my mayordomo."

The Father Visitor saw that despite his youth, Mirandi would probably end up in abject poverty if he were to be sent away from the priesthood. The tone of his voice hardened back to the role of Father Visitor. "My son, you will wait here for your replacement, and proceed as I have directed. I have the full backing of the bishop in these matters. Now I must be on my way."

Diego had the Father Visitor's horse and pack mule ready for departure. Mirandi accompanied Quiroz to the corral and bid him farewell. He returned to the rectory with his head bowed, but before he had walked halfway the thunderheads that had converged to form a boiling, black storm sent out a bolt of lightning and an almost simultaneous crash of thunder. Mirandi, startled, stopped to look at the sky. A wisp of smoke rose from the grassy hill behind the rectory, and soon the dry grasses burst into flame. Across the river another fire started after more lightning streaked earthward in front of the storm.

Mirandi hurried for the shelter of the rectory, and closed the door behind him. He was puzzled about how or when to tell Keewa about his future. The thought of duty at

Loreto stymied further contemplation about the possibility of Keewa going south to the convent. He thought about the suggestion Quiroz had given him. But again he dismissed the idea because the world outside the Church had become completely foreign to him. Besides, he would never find work married to an Indian. He felt himself sink into depression, and went to his bed.

The storm came on with full force. The irrigators trotted from the fields before the first clap of thunder, and were safely in their huts when the downpour began. They all hoped for enough rain to spare them the labor of irrigation for at least a few days. Keewa wanted to rush to the rectory to find out what the Father Visitor had said to Alberto, but the rain kept her inside the hut with the rest of her family.

Another, snuffing out the fires in the grasslands, followed the first deluge. The first storm pounced on Tawaki as the second hit Guroki. The thirsty ground soaked up the moisture leaving little to spill into streams.

Mirandi stirred from sleep as Keewa opened the rectory door and walked to his bedside. "What did the Father Visitor say?"

Mirandi hesitated. He finally decided to tell her what their future held, and hoped that she could accept being without him. "Keewa, my dear Keewa," he began. "It is not good news for us. I am to be punished for breaking my vows. I am being sent to another mission far away, and the place is not nice like Guroki."

"I will go with you, Alberto."

"I am afraid that is impossible. I have tried to explain to you that I am married to the Church, and I must go where the Church sends me. I was wrong to be with you, and now I am getting what I deserve. I am sorry, my Keewa."

"What is to happen to me? To my child?"

"You will be fine. Your child will grow up with a good mother, and you can explain about me when it is old enough to understand."

Keewa began to sob. Soon the sobs turned to wails of anguish, and she began pounding her fists against Mirandi's chest. He grabbed her arms, but could barely keep her from beating him. "Stop, Keewa, stop," he said, trying to subdue her and calm her. "I am sorry. There is nothing I can do!"

Keewa eventually dropped to the bed with exhaustion, sobbing with her hands over her eyes. She remained that way for half an hour. Mirandi had risen, and sat at his desk looking into space. The air had cooled from the storm.

As she laid on the bed her feelings toward Mirandi turned to anger. She didn't understand why this man she loved would leave and not take her with him. She didn't understand her anger either. Finally she rose from the bed, and walked out the door without a word to Mirandi. She walked to the river to sit on her log. Alberto Mirandi remained seated. He did not follow. He could think of nothing to say.

Keewa sat on the log until the sun fell below the Sierra Cimarron. She gave no thought to making supper for Mirandi. The thought of talking to him didn't cross her mind. She wanted to go home to her bed and sleep. A deep scowl wrinkled her face as she flipped aside the hide door to the hut, and walked to her bed. "What is wrong, Keewa?" Mumara said.

"I am angry," Keewa replied.

Diego paid little attention as he sat mending some harness.

"What makes you this angry?" Mumara questioned her daughter again. She had never seen Keewa so angry since she was small and was denied walking to the fields with her father.

"I am angry with Padre Mirandi," she said, and began to sob.

Mumara walked over to her daughter's bed and put one arm around her. "What has the padre done to cause you such anger and pain, Keewa?"

"He is leaving," she answered.

"I have not heard of this, have you, Dawa?" Mumara said, turning to Diego.

"It must be something about the Father Visitor," he said.

"What happened with the Father Visitor, Keewa?" Mumara asked, trying to discover why her daughter acted so distraught.

"He broke his vows, and is leaving without me," she said with reticence.

"His leaving without you means nothing. There will be another padre to take his place just like he took the place of Padre Alfonso."

"You don't understand," Keewa said, knowing she must tell the entire story to her parents. "He made me with child, and now he is leaving!"

"What did you say?" Diego shouted across the one room.

"I am with his child. We have been together," she answered, and fell into deeper sobbing.

Diego dropped the harness and stood up. "He is not Opata! What are you doing being with a man who is not Opata! And why do you go with a priest? No Opata man will ever take you now!"

The anger rose in Diego. "We will see to this priest now," he said to his two sons, who were sitting on their beds. "Come with me now, and bring your weapons. Keewa, I will deal with you when we are finished with your priest!"

Keewa had never seen her father this angry. She began sobbing more as Mumara tried to comfort her. The men started toward the rectory at a trot. Keewa suddenly sat up. "What does my father mean by dealing with me later?"

"I am afraid of him when he is this angry," Mumara answered. "Perhaps you should run somewhere and hide until the anger passes from him."

"Where can I go?"

"Anywhere. Somewhere. But stay away for at least the night."

Keewa grabbed a deerskin from her bed and went out the doorway. She paused for a moment wondering which direction she should go to hide. Suddenly she heard a muffled scream coming from the direction of the rectory. *What are they doing to Alberto?* she thought. She ran to a willow thicket on the far side of the corral, and squatted down behind the dense stand of saplings. The next thing she heard was her father giving orders to her brothers. "Get the mule. We will carry the body to the sinkhole. He will never be found after the river has swallowed him."

Felipe trotted to the corral, opened the gate, entered, and caught the mule. He led the animal out the gate, and joined the others as the three headed back to the rectory. *The sinkhole in the river. They must have killed my Alberto.* The thought of her father and brothers killing the man who had given her such pleasure and love almost made her cry out, but she waited silently behind the thicket until the men approached the rectory.

Keewa left her hiding place and ran toward the river. The moon had risen above the Sierra de Piedras giving her enough light to see where she was going. She arrived at the sinkhole, and found another thicket of willows to hide behind. The anger toward Mirandi she had felt shortly before now shifted to her father. She waited behind the thicket with the deerskin covering her blouse.

The sound of the mule on the trail warned her of their approach. She curled herself behind the thicket to be as small as possible, and still see what would happen. Just above the sinkhole the bank of the river was clear of trees and brush. They stopped the mule and lifted the black-robed body from its back. All three men lifted the body and carried it to the riverbank. "Now!" Diego ordered, and they threw the body into the saturated sand of the sinkhole.

Keewa watched in terror under the moonlight as the body of Alberto Mirandi sunk slowly into the sand. "That will take care of the priest," Diego said, with certain finality to his voice. "Now we shall deal with your sister. We will make sure that she does not have the child of the priest."

Keewa couldn't believe the words she had heard from her father. She was glad that she had not waited with her mother, and as soon as she was certain that the three were far enough away, she abandoned the thicket. She found the trail to Tawaki, and decided to travel as fast as she could. She thought that another priest would be her only protection from her father. She sobbed constantly as she saw in her mind, time after time, Alberto's black-robed body sinking into the sand of the sinkhole.

After trotting for an hour her legs felt like they would go no further and her lungs kept gasping for air. She stopped and rested in the middle of a large mesquite bosque, well off the trail. She stretched out on the deerskin, but fought sleep by pinching her cheeks. She sat up and listened intently for any sound of horses, because she knew that her father would be mounted if he chose to come after her. She went back to the trail, continuing her former pace toward Tawaki.

Diego became upset when he arrived home and found Keewa gone. Mumara tried to soothe him, and assured him that Keewa would return in the morning. Diego finally calmed enough to listen to his woman's words, but sleep did not come easily. The anger he felt against the priest had been satisfied, but his anger toward his daughter still burned inside of him.

Keewa arrived at the Tawaki rectory just before sunrise. Krampetz came to the door at her knock. "What is it, child? What are you doing here at this hour?"

Keewa still breathed heavily from both her pace along the trail and the anxiety she felt. It took her a moment to speak. "Father, something terrible has happened at Guroki," she said.

Fritz Krampetz thought that the O'odham had been talking to datura again, but then what was Mirandi's housekeeper doing in Tawaki? "Speak, child!"

"Father Mirandi is dead. They killed him and threw his body into the sinkhole. I watched them." Keewa was close to hysterics.

"Wait just a moment, child. You say Father Mirandi is dead, and his body is in the sinkhole?"

"Yes, Father, I saw them throw in his body. It was terrible!"

"Who did this, child?"

"My father and my brothers, and now they are coming for me. They said they would make sure that I would never have the child of the priest."

"What is this about a child?"

"Father Alberto's. I am carrying Alberto's child, and my father wants to kill it."

Fritz Krampetz led Keewa into the rectory. "Lie down on the bed and rest. I must find Anselmo and Ruth."

Krampetz hobbled faster than he had in years. He first found Anselmo by the corral, and ordered him to ride as fast as he could to Tubaca to summon part of the "Flying Company," the name of a certain cavalry troop, he knew were headquartered there patrolling for Apache raiders. "Send them after Diego and his sons," he said. "They have killed Father Mirandi and thrown his body into the sinkhole. Hurry!"

Ruth had just left her hut when Krampetz hailed her. "Get your son Abelardo, and have him come to the rectory at once," he said to his housekeeper. Panting, Krampetz then hobbled back to the rectory. Ruth and Abelardo arrived at the rectory. Keewa slept. Krampetz sat on the bench outside, waiting. Abelardo trotted up to the rectory.

"I'm glad you came so soon," the priest said. "Abelardo, I want you to take the girl, who is sleeping inside, to the cave in the Cañon de las Tinajas. I want you to make sure she has food, water, and firewood until I tell you differently. Take her to the cave and guard her from anyone who should come up the canyon. Guard her with your life, Abelardo!"

Krampetz then went into the rectory, shook Keewa slightly to bring her into consciousness, and told her to get ready to travel. Keewa blinked her eyes, coming out of a deep sleep, and asked the padre to repeat what he had said.

"Child, you must awaken and go with the son of Ruth to the Cañon de las Tinajas. There is a cave there where you will be safe. Abelardo will make sure of your safety until I send word to him that it is all right for you to return to Tawaki."

Keewa listened, and for the first time since the tragedy at Guroki began, she felt a trust, a trust of her life and the life of her child in the hobbling priest of Tawaki. Abelardo gathered everything he thought he would need to fulfill his duty to the priest whom he admired so much. He felt a deep responsibility. He would make sure that all went well with his task of protecting the beautiful girl he was to lead to the cave in the Cañon de las Tinajas. The canyon of springs that provided water even when other streams went dry. He led the way from Tawaki, and they arrived at the cave before the sun cast its smallest shadows.

Anselmo, charged with summoning the "Flying Company" from Tubaca, had another allegiance. He was Opata, the same as Dawa, or Diego, as the Spanish priests had named him. Anselmo considered Dawa a brother from the same beginnings, and when Krampetz ordered him to alert the Spanish cavalry to go in pursuit of Dawa, Anselmo had no other choice than to alert Dawa of what he had been ordered to do. So instead of heading north to Tubaca, he skirted south to Guroki to warn his tribal brother.

Diego pushed everything from his mind, and readied his family to leave Guroki before the "Flying Company" arrived to try and capture him. No longer was Keewa important for his vengeance. He thought only of escape from the Spaniards. He ordered his sons to saddle the four horses, and to ready the mule with a packsaddle to carry their provisions. "We are returning to our homeland on the Río Sonora to be with our own people," he said.

Anselmo's horse was almost on his last wind when they arrived at Tubaca. He dismounted, and went directly to the lieutenant in command. After relating the message from Father Krampetz, the mayordomo of Tawaki unsaddled his horse, turned him into the corral, and walked to a grove of cottonwood trees. He bunched the carpet of dead leaves into a bed underneath the grove, and went to sleep.

Lieutenant Calavacia mustered his troops, and with six of them, galloped away from Tubaca south toward the

Mission San Pablo de Guroki. He slowed the troop to a trot when they had traveled a mile. The galloping exodus from Tubaca was always for show to live up to the name of the "Flying Company."

When they arrived at Guroki only O'odham women were about. The men were in their favorite mesquite bosque talking with datura. They had been there from the moment Diego left with his family. The O'odham were not aware of the circumstances, but they could tell that they no longer had a mayordomo to look to. The "Flying Company" lost little time before striking out to the south where the fresh tracks of the Guroki horses and mule were plain on the trail.

Abelardo helped Keewa get settled in the cave in Tinaja Canyon. Both carried the provisions up the narrow fissure that gave them a foothold to the cave entrance. He then went about gathering firewood until he had laid in enough for a day or two. After the fire burned brightly he sat down in the cave with Keewa. "You are probably tired from all this, Keewa," he said. "Go to your bed, and I will stay here to watch for any intruders."

"You are right about me being tired," she said. "I could sleep sitting up with my eyes open."

They both chuckled at her humor. Keewa went to her bed of hides, and fell into a deep sleep before Abelardo knew she had closed her eyes. He sat by the fire until he felt comfortable that no intruders were near. Then he too stretched himself out on his deerskins, and thought about the beautiful girl he had been sent to protect.

The following morning Abelardo had the fire burning before Keewa opened her eyes. He looked fondly at her as she slept. He took out a strip of beef from the provisions, laid it on the coals at the edge of the fire, and watched it broil. When the meat was cooked he took his knife and cut the generous strip in half, laying one on the rocks forming the fire circle. The other he ate with relish.

Keewa awoke, as the smell of the roasted meat wafted through the interior of the cave. Abelardo heard her stirring, and carried the strip of roasted beef to her. She looked up at his smiling face. "Thank you, Abelardo," she said sleepily. "You are kind."

Their hunger satisfied, the two began to get acquainted. Abelardo told Keewa how he felt being the youngest of Ruth's children, and why he preferred being a hunter rather than a farm hand. "When you work in the fields there is always someone there to tell you what to do, but hunting is different," he said. "If you are a good hunter they let you go out alone because they know you will bring back some game. I am a good hunter."

Keewa enjoyed listening to Abelardo. She had only heard about farming in her family. Once in a while her brothers would go into the mountains to hunt, but most of the time they worked in the fields.

Abelardo didn't inquire about why Keewa had run away from Guroki. He had only been told to take care of her until the padre sent word otherwise. It was the third day before Keewa volunteered her story about Alberto Mirandi, and the child inside her. She also revealed what had happened at the Guroki rectory and the sinkhole in the river.

The story surprised Abelardo, but didn't shock him. He felt a closeness to Keewa after she had bared her feelings to him. Before sunset he walked slowly and quietly up the Cañon de las Tinajas to hunt. The storms had continued, and the stream flow in the canyon had increased. There were places where he had to wade through the stream in order to reach the section of the canyon that he knew the deer liked to come to for water.

Finally he saw the bend in the canyon that was his destination. It was here that one side of the canyon had a more gradual slope and the deer could traverse it easily compared to the steep sides elsewhere. Abelardo felt the breeze against him, taking his scent away from the watering spot as he slowly and silently crept up to the huge vertical slab of rock that kept him hidden from the gentle slope beyond. He waited.

Thunder rumbled as a storm drenched some of the hills on the other side of the valley. Abelardo strained to hear the sound of deer hooves on the slope as the sun went down behind the Sierra Cimarron. Suddenly he heard a small rock roll. It came from up the slope. He waited.

Carefully, he notched an arrow in his bowstring. Very slowly he moved into position to send the arrow toward his target, a yearling white-tailed deer that looked upstream away from the hunter. Abelardo pulled the bow back, aimed, and released the arrow. The yearling jumped, twisted, and fell with its hindquarters in the stream. Abelardo ran to his fallen game and carefully made sure it was dead.

He was proud of his successful hunt to provide for Keewa. She saw and felt that Abelardo was becoming attracted to her, and she enjoyed his caring for her. But the memories of Mirandi dominated her thoughts. She hoped that her father would accept her again. However, his words at the sinkhole kept returning.

The O'odham at San Pablo de Guroki did not understand why Diego and his family had left in such a hurry. Their dwellings were located at the far end of the mesa, out of sight of the rectory, the corral, and Diego's hut. They did see the Opata overseer leave, and by the way he and his family traveled the O'odham knew it was not a mere day or week's excursion they were on. It was after a group of four men had gone to the rectory to discover the padre missing that they went to the mesquite grove to talk to datura.

It was not a ritual feast, but an impromptu gathering to celebrate their freedom, which none knew how long would last. By the time the "Flying Company" troop thundered through on their way to capture the murderer, Diego, the O'odham had talked so much to the datura that the datura was talking back. They were all completely under its spell.

After a week had passed Krampetz began to wonder if the fugitives had somehow escaped. He felt comfortable that Abelardo would make sure of Keewa's safety, but before sending for them he wanted to be certain that her father was in the custody of the Spanish troopers.

On the tenth day after Keewa had come to Tawaki, Krampetz sat on the bench outside his rectory. He looked up to the storm clouds gathering, and wondered if he would have to go inside. He liked to sit on the bench in the afternoon, but he also liked the storms. The thunder and lightning kept him humble to nature, and the rain pounding on the roof of the rectory soothed his loneliness in this land so distant from his native Bavaria.

Just after the first clap of thunder the troops from the "Flying Company" rode into view. Krampetz looked to see if they had their prisoners. Troopers only, riding at a slow walk. He wondered if they had decided to kill the Opata instead of capturing them. He boosted himself up with his cane as the troopers pulled up their horses in front of him. "You have no prisoners?"

"No, Padre, the Apache found them before we did."

"Aye!" Krampetz exclaimed, and crossed himself. He didn't want to hear the details. "Where did it happen?"

"They must have been traveling fast," the sergeant said. "We found the bodies near the Río Sonora. They almost made it to their homeland."

"Are the Apache acting up again?"

"I think this must have been an isolated raiding party. It did not look like many Apache were involved."

"I hope you are correct, and I hope you are able to keep them away from this valley," Krampetz said. He was always fearful of Apache raids on the mission livestock.

"We do the best we can, Padre. We must continue to Tubaca and report to our commander."

The troopers reined their horses around, and soon headed north along the trail to Tubaca. Krampetz sat back down on his bench and waited for Ruth to come back from her hut. He would have her send a message to Abelardo that it was safe for him to return with Keewa.

Keewa was stunned by the news. She went to the river alone to weep. Abelardo brought her food, but she could not eat. After an attempt to console her he returned to the village. Keewa's imagination threw pictures of her mutilated mother into her mind, and it was mostly for Mumara that she grieved. Abelardo returned the next day with a message from Krampetz that there would be a mass for the dead members of her family if she cared to attend. "I am sorry, Abelardo," she said blankly. "I am not finished here."

She managed to eat some of the venison he brought, and a day later she returned to the village of Tawaki where Ruth gave her shelter. The thought of returning to Guroki did not cross her mind. Gradually she felt comfortable in her new surroundings, especially when the new life within her began moving, and her belly began to swell with its growth.

# PADRE MIRANDI

The replacement priest at Guroki was a veteran missionary from Sonora. During the interim Krampetz had sent Anselmo to Guroki to make sure the work continued, and the crops were cared for properly. In time for the harvest, a new mayordomo came with the new priest. Krampetz asked for and received the two sacks of seed corn that he had lent to Diego the previous spring.

The winter rainy season began in early December with a drizzle lasting three days. More storms came and went to keep the ground moist. One storm produced eight inches of snow overnight, but by the following afternoon the sun had had its way in the valley, while leaving the mountaintops snow-capped for several days.

Cold air swept down from the mountains the morning Keewa's baby boy made his way into the world. She had no trouble with the birth in the hut that Abelardo had helped her build next to Ruth's. Abelardo had waited with patience while Keewa delivered her son. He felt a part of the occasion in spite of not being the father. He did not live in the hut with Keewa. Though she felt close to him, Keewa could not forget Mirandi, especially after the baby arrived. She found nursing and playing with her son delightful. However, she felt a special happiness watching Abelardo talking to Awajalo, the name meaning "white eagle" because of his light complexion.

She refused Krampetz's desire to baptize the child without knowing her reason for not wanting the ceremony. Abelardo agreed with Keewa's decision just because Keewa had made it.

The rains continued intermittently into spring. The valley became a lush garden of flowers. On an afternoon when the valley seemed to be in a climax of color Keewa asked Abelardo to accompany her to Guroki.

They started early the next morning walking southward along the well-worn trail. Keewa had not been on the trail since her flight the night of the murder, but she felt a strong desire to return. She didn't know why, but she did not deny her instincts.

It was where the trail passed close to the sinkhole that she stopped. As a sign for Abelardo to wait on the trail for her, she put her hand gently to his face. With some hesitation she left the trail with Awajalo in her arms, and walked to the edge of the river where she had seen Mirandi disappear in the quicksand. A cluster of orange-yellow poppies with their faces dancing in the sun grew near the riverbank. She reached down and picked a bouquet, showed them to the baby, and tossed the flowers on the souplike sand.

"I will tell you about it someday, and you will understand," she said.

The poppies lay scattered on the sand. She watched them for a long moment, turned around, and walked back to Abelardo.

Awajalo had fallen asleep in her arms. Gently she put him down on a carpet of tiny white flowers. She walked to Abelardo and put her arms around his neck. "I had to do this. I am over it now, and I am once again happy. You have been very patient."

Their lips together sent passion through them both. He put his strong arms around her, and drew her closer. Together with Keewa he felt a particular serenity invade his mind.

Awajalo awakened suddenly, and began to cry. Keewa reached down, took him into her arms, and put her nipple in his mouth. It was not long before he slipped back into sleep. "We should continue to Guroki," Abelardo said.

Keewa released the baby's mouth from her breast, and handed him to Abelardo. "Take your son for a while," she said. "I am through with Guroki, and I would like to go home. I would like to live in the cave in Cañon de las Tinajas. I think that will be a beautiful place to start our new lives together."

# Two
# Gold Coins

**D**ue south from the quay-wall protecting the harbor of Tarifa, Spain, the shores and mountains of North Africa...Morocco...are visible on a clear day. To the west the Atlantic stretches into oblivion. Before Christopher Columbus brought news of the Indies back to Ferdinand and Isabella none of the fishermen of Tarifa speculated what might be beyond the vast western horizon. Maybe the sun, after it had finished splashing the stark white, Moorish walls of the town with the red and orange of its descent below the endless line between sky and sea.

Sebastián Quinteros and Carlos Villanueva, both young sons of fishermen, had become boyhood friends sharing much in common. As with other boys born to Tarifa fishermen, Sebastián and Carlos helped with the sailing and fishing. While the fathers dickered with the housewives of Tarifa for the prices of their catch, the sons were held responsible for cleaning the decks and making sure everything was ready for the next foray to sea in search of tuna, mullet, or bonito. Some days there were no fish. Others the wind was strong enough to keep prudent sailors on their boats repairing equipment or mending nets and sails.

The Moorish influence on Tarifa would remain for centuries, but 260 years (1752) after the expulsion of the Moors from Spain, Tarifa fishermen were Spaniards through and through. Of all the folk in town the fishermen had remained the most Spanish during the Moorish tenure of Spain. The fishermen spurned Moorish women, and most of their daughters managed to retain their virginity until they could give it to a son of a Tarifa fisherman.

Sebastián and Carlos were thus as pure Spanish as could be found in Tarifa. They were admonished never to question their lineage because the fisher folk were a proud lot, not only of their lineage, but also of their work heritage.

But, there was something else that became a strong influence on both lads early in their adolescence. A former soldier had come back to Tarifa to spend his remaining years in the place of his birth. He had fought with the Spanish army in New Spain, and during a skirmish with the recalcitrant Seri, who lived on the shores of the Sea of Cortez, Manuel Cisneros had taken a Seri warrior's poisoned arrow in his left ankle.

Fortunately the battalion surgeon was in the field during the fight, and had been able to amputate Manuel's left leg at the knee before the poison reached the rest of his body. Sergeant Cisneros was eventually sent home to his native Spain and to Tarifa, to live out his life with a wooden peg leg made from the long, strong-grained mahogany from Mexico.

Cisneros established a small bodega in Tarifa, combining the small legacy from his father, who was proud to have sired a soldier in service to the Crown of Spain, and the small pension he received as a disabled veteran from service in New Spain.

The atmosphere, mostly created by Manuel himself, was attractive to many of the fishermen, including the fathers of Sebastián and Carlos. As the two boys grew old enough in their fathers' eyes to accompany the adults for a few glasses of wine after the day's work on the boats, they were allowed their ration in Bodega Cisneros.

That occasion was the same as a quinceañera for their sisters on their fifteenth birthdays, but for the boys it was a plateau for much less parental control than for the girls.

There were days when the catch was better than others and their fathers would put a few more coins in their hands than usual. Sebastián and Carlos would inevitably spend time in the Bodega Cisneros listening to the old soldier's tales of the land beyond the horizon—New Spain. They would sit in silence after the other fishermen left for their siestas, and listen to the descriptions and accounts, which Cisneros told, from his vivid memory. When Manuel told of the Indian girls he had fallen in love with the two lads were especially impressed, because Cisneros left out few details.

"The reason I am not married here in Tarifa, and will live out my life here without a woman is because I had to leave the most beautiful woman in the world in Pitic," he told them. "If you young men ever find your way to New Spain I would hope that you will look in on my family and tell my precious woman that I think of her and my daughter every day of my life."

"New Spain is too far for us to contemplate, Don Manuel," Sebastián said. "We could never save enough reales for passage from the catches of fish."

Both boys had talked about their dreams of traveling to the other shores of the Atlantic Ocean, but neither could see a way in which such aspirations could be accomplished.

"Ay, hombres," Manuel said waving his hand at Sebastián and Carlos as if their doubts were foolish. "There is a way...an easy way...the same way I went to New Spain. You can join the army as I did. In fact, I have heard that if you ask for duty in Pimería Alta you are almost assured an enlistment and even corporal stripes when you get there. My old friends tell me that there has been a rebellion there and we Spaniards are establishing presidios to protect the haciendas, pueblos, and missions in Pimería Alta."

"How can we accomplish all this, Don Manuel?" Sebastián asked. "Where do we go and who do we see to join the army and go to Pimería Alta?"

"It is easy to join the army here in Tarifa as you probably know, but I would suggest you go to Cadiz because it is from Cadiz that the ships leave for New Spain."

"Very well, Don Manuel," Carlos said. "But please do not tell our fathers of our conversations."

"Don't worry," Cisneros said. "What is said between amigos is between amigos."

The old soldier knew well how the fathers of both young men would react to his conversations with their sons if they were to find out. Neither would come to the Bodega Cisneros again, nor would they allow their sons to enter the premises. In fact, the two fathers could probably influence other fishermen to seek their wine at another bodega.

But, in spite of the chance that his conversations could bring an economic gloom over his business, Manuel Cisneros felt strongly that Sebastián Quinteros and Carlos Villanueva held the spirit of adventure stronger than most

Tarifa youth. He felt that to kindle that spirit would do no harm except to rob the young men's fathers of cheap labor on their fishing boats.

Cisneros had seen so many boys follow after their fathers without questioning the direction. He himself had rebelled against his heritage. His father had planned his son's life as a *panadero*, baking bread from early morning until it was ready to sell to the women of Tarifa, but Manuel had joined the army, fallen in love, lost his leg, and returned to Tarifa to tell his stories. He felt lucky.

Another force behind his conversations with Sebastián and Carlos was the separation from the woman and daughter he loved...and his desire for sons. The two boys were what he had wanted all his life. He knew he could never take them in his arms as sons, but he could give them inspiration to adventure, something they would never receive from their blood fathers.

One such day Sebastián and Carlos left the Bodega Cisneros and walked down the narrow, cobblestoned streets toward the port. When they reached the quay-wall they sat down to continue their conversation as dusk settled in.

"I can feel New Spain pulling me toward it," Sebastián said, as he extended his right arm westward where the last of the day's light was fading quickly. "I think I must take charge of my own life and do what I must do to live it as I see fit."

"I feel that New Spain is the place to go to escape the life of a fisherman, but in my family I am the only son to carry on the Villanueva tradition. You are lucky to have not one brother, but two."

"That is true, Carlos, but even so if you feel strong enough to break the tradition, you can. You must do what you must do and I hope you will be at my side on the trip to Cadiz."

When the two young men confronted their fathers with their plans the separate scenes were similar. Both fathers were quick to deny their permission, but both Sebastián and Carlos argued that they should be allowed to serve the Crown in any way they could.

"You can serve the Crown and your family as a fisherman just as I have," the elder Quinteros said stubbornly. "If you go running off to fight the Indians in New Spain, you could come back like old Cisneros, without a leg. And you can't be a fisherman with one leg."

"With all respect to you, my father, I am saying to you that I do not want to be a fisherman," Sebastián said, and he saw the sadness come into the eyes of José Quinteros. For a moment Sebastián felt a rush of sadness himself, and during that moment he was tempted to abandon the entire plan.

José Quinteros derived his sadness not from the idea of losing his oldest son's help, which he had come to depend on, but because he loved Sebastián deeply and enjoyed his companionship at sea. He was also proud to have Sebastián accompany him to the bodega after a day's fishing.

They had been sitting on the front step leading to the doorway of the Quinteros house, which was squeezed into a long line of similar houses along the narrow, steep Calle Columbus, named after the famous navigator.

"Come walk with me as I think, my son," José said after a long silence between them.

Father and son stood up together and walked down the cobblestones toward the old Castillo San Miguel, then turned west to the quay-wall. They walked slower than they were accustomed to when they were heading for their boat and a day's fishing. When they arrived at the place where their boat was tied up behind the wall, they stopped and faced each other. José grasped his son's elbow.

"It is not easy for me to say this to you, my son. I really and truly want to see you in this boat with me until I am no longer able to hold the capstan or pull the halyard to raise the sail."

Tears flooded his blue eyes and rolled down the weathered cheeks into the graying stubble. Sebastián had never seen his father cry, and his own eyes filled quickly.

"But, I give my blessing to your desire for adventure in New Spain."

The two embraced each other, both shaking and sobbing with the intense emotion of the moment.

"Thank you, my father, I love you," Sebastián was finally able to say through his tears.

In that single moment, sadness transformed into the greatest joy either had ever known.

"If I had not decided to break the long tradition of the men in my family," Sebastián thought to himself, "I might never have known how much my father really loves me."

At number 42 Calle Jemez the scene was quite different at the Casa Villanueva. Carlos's father, Alberto, refused to listen to his son's point of view, and when the boy tried to pursue his argument the father turned to his son and spoke sharply.

"You will stop thinking these foolish thoughts, and learn to be a good fisherman just like I did. Now, get yourself to bed so you can open your eyes when I am ready for tomorrow's fishing."

Carlos was silent and felt a wave of depression. He wanted to shout back at his father, and at the same time, he wanted to cry at his own reluctance to rebel against his father's stubborn, adamant stand against him.

# TWO GOLD COINS

Alberto left the house and walked to Bodega Cisneros at Cuatro Esquinas. He walked in the doorway as Manuel was busy cleaning the spilled wine from atop the plank bartop. The last of his fishermen customers had left for bed and Cisneros was ready to close the iron-strapped wooden door and retire to his own bed in the small room to the rear.

Alberto approached the bar and with a small coin between his thumb and index finger, tapped the bar top once, his signal for his usual glass of red port wine from the vineyards of Jerez de la Frontera.

In spite of his plan to retire, Cisneros hobbled to the shelf of glasses, withdrew one, filled it from the wooden cask, and placed it on the bar in front of the fisherman. "You are up and around later than most, Alberto, what's happening?"

"I cannot sleep," Villanueva returned, staring into the crimson-red liquid in the glass he held between his fingertips of both hands.

"Everyone says tomorrow will be a good day for the *pesca*," Cisneros said. He had stopped cleaning and sat down on the stool he kept behind the bar.

"Good day...bad day, what does it matter?" Villanueva muttered and drank half the wine in one swallow.

"Whatever," Cisneros said. "If the fish are running well in the early morning you might be wishing you had had a full night's sleep."

"Another wine," Villanueva said as he returned the empty glass to the bar-top.

Cisneros refilled the glass, and set it down in front of his customer.

"The young people have crazy ideas these days," Villanueva said.

"Our fathers probably thought the same of us when we were young," Cisneros retorted.

"*Quizas*, perhaps, but we were not as crazy...not as crazy." He drained the glass again and set it down firmly on the bar. "Good night," he said to Cisneros, and walked out the doorway. The wine in his stomach and his mind put the fisherman to sleep when he reached his bed.

The next morning, before the sun brought light to land and sea, the Tarifa fishermen were heading their boats under full sails toward the fishing grounds beyond the Straits of Gibraltar where the Atlantic Ocean was known to give forth its bounty of fish for the tables of Tarifa.

To the other fishermen it seemed as if nothing had happened to change things in either the Quinteros boat or that of Villanueva, but there was an unspoken bond of closeness between José and Sebastián. And between the Villanuevas there was an uncommon silence as they proceeded with the Tarifa fleet.

The day proved good for the fishermen and when they returned the word spread quickly through the narrow streets that the day's catch was better than usual. The housewives hurried to the quay-wall hoping for bargains.

When the fishermen reached Bodega Cisneros there were toasts to the day's catch, and Manuel was kept busy filling the glasses from the cask.

José Quinteros put his right arm around his son's shoulders and lifted his glass with his other hand.

"I drink to today's catch, and the hope of tomorrow," he said. "And, I drink to you, my son, and to all your tomorrows."

"And to you, my father, and to all your tomorrows, which will always be in my mind and heart."

They both brought their glasses to their lips and drained the contents.

Sebastián glanced around the crowded room, looking for his friend. At the far end of the bar he made eye contact with Carlos. Sebastián raised his brow and opened the palm of his hand to ask "qué pasa?" without speaking the words.

Carlos, using the same form of communication, tilted his head toward the entrance to the bodega. Sebastián turned to his father. "I will return shortly, father. I must talk with Carlos."

"*Ándele*, go ahead, I'll wait here," the elder Quinteros said, and gave his son an understanding pat on the shoulder.

Sebastián noticed that his father did not accompany Carlos, and when the two friends were free of the crowd, and out on the street, Sebastián asked, "Where is your father? After such a good day's catch I should think he would be celebrating with the rest of us."

"This may have been a good day for the pesca, my friend, but this has been a bad day for both my father and me. After last night when I told him of our plan he didn't offer me one coin from today's catch, and he went straight home."

"As I expected, it started out with difficulty between my father and me," Sebastián said. "But we ended up with an understanding and he gave me his blessing. To tell the truth, I was very surprised."

"It is bad with me," Carlos said as he looked down at the street. "My father refuses to discuss the matter further, and all day he only spoke to me when it was necessary for the sailing of the boat. I do not know what to do, amigo."

"Perhaps in a week or so things will change and your father will be able to listen...I am sorry to hear this, I wish it was different for you, Carlos."

# TWO GOLD COINS

"I wish it was different, but it is not. All I know is that I am miserable with my thoughts. I almost feel like going down to the quay-wall and sinking our boat...It is the boat...Why should a boat cause such misery?"

"It is not a boat that causes misery, it is the stubbornness of the captain...and maybe the reluctance of the crew. Who knows?"

Carlos understood his friend's admonishment only too well. He was very much aware of his reluctance and thoroughly angry with himself for his weakness.

"I will make a decision one way or another," Carlos said, looking his friend straight in the eyes. "I will let you know what happens...and thank you."

Sebastián returned to the bodega and Carlos headed for the cliffs overlooking the sea east of the town.

When Sebastián walked through the doorway into the Bodega Cisneros the heads and eyes of all the fishermen turned toward him. There were smiles on their faces. One of the men raised his glass of red wine and shouted, "To Sebastián Quinteros! Good luck in New Spain!"

There were echoes from the rest of the fishermen packed into the bodega. All the excitement directed toward him surprised Sebastián, because he had been talking with Carlos when his father announced his son's plan to his fellow fishermen.

"Glasses from the bodega!" Manuel Cisneros shouted above the crowded conversations.

Several olés came from the men, who were not only happy with the day's catch and José's announcement, but were always glad to receive a free glass of wine.

"Give me your hat, Sebastián," Cisneros ordered from behind the bar and extended his arm over the plank between two fishermen.

Sebastián removed the somewhat battered cap from his head and passed it to the old soldier. "All right, everybody," Cisneros called out, and the fishermen stopped their conversations to look at the man calling out from behind the bar. "Sebastián will need some coins to make his way in Cadiz," Cisneros said as he took some coins from his cash drawer under the bar. "Loosen up, my friends," he continued. "Today has been a good catch!"

Sebastián's hat went from fisherman to fisherman as the gnarled, weathered, rope-worn fingers reached into pockets to withdraw coins to toss into the cap.

Sebastián was somewhat overcome by this gesture of friendship. When the cap was returned to him his eyes filled with tears of joy. "Gracias," he said.

The men went back to their drinking, but Sebastián Quinteros could only think of his friend Carlos.

Carlos had made his way to the top of the cliffs and sat down on a smooth boulder. He was alone as he wanted to be, to look out over the ocean, and try to put his thoughts in order.

At that moment the elder Villanueva was leaving his house for the Bodega Cisneros. When he had arrived home from his boat he had no desire to mix with his fellow fishermen, but after a while he wanted to forget his thoughts about his son and fill his mind with red Jerez Port.

Most of the fishermen were still in the bodega when Alberto Villanueva walked in and pushed his way to the bar. The room was noisy, and Manuel Cisneros hadn't been able to sit on his stool behind the bar for two hours. But he spotted Villanueva immediately, and without waiting for the tapping coin on the bar top, Cisneros drew a glass full of Jerez Red from the cask, and pushed it toward Alberto.

"This one is from the bodega, old man," Cisneros said. "We are drinking to Sebastián. He is going to New Spain!"

Villanueva scowled. He slammed a coin on the bar. "I will pay for my wine, and I will not drink to New Spain!" He exclaimed in sudden anger. "It is crazy. My son Carlos is filled with the same crazy idea...he is of the sea...he will remain on the sea...and some day he will have the boat...New Spain...loco...absolutely crazy!"

"Calm down, man, calm down," Cisneros said. "Why not let the boy seek adventure in New Spain? I have been there, and I can tell you the women are beautiful."

"Sure you have been to New Spain, and look at you. You came back with a piece of wood for a leg to fill glasses with wine when we come back from the pesca... you are probably the one who gave my son his crazy thoughts... stick your goddam wooden leg up your ass!"

Alberto Villanueva placed his empty glass on the bar and left. The conversations had stopped during the angry man's tirade against the one-legged veteran of New Spain. Cisneros's eyes followed the fisherman to the door. "Poor old man," he said to no one in particular.

The altercation had dulled the merriment in the bodega momentarily, but after another few gulps of Jerez Red the conversations returned, except that José Quinteros could see a sad look in his son's eyes. "I will talk to that stubborn mule when he calms down," he said to Sebastián. "Do not worry yourself with someone else's problem, my son."

"It's not that exactly," Sebastián said. "It is that I wish for my friend Carlos what I have."

The wind came up strong shortly after the bells of the cathedral announced that it was midnight in Tarifa. By morning the sea was a mass of whitecaps and the fishermen spent the day on repairs. The following day was the same. José Quinteros and his son had their boat in order by noon so the father told his son that the rest of the day would be free.

When Sebastián climbed out of the boat to the wall, he looked over to the Villanueva boat where Carlos was still at work under the eye of his father. Sebastián walked away to the narrow street leading to the Bodega Cisneros. "Maybe Carlos will be here later," he thought to himself.

Villanueva wished he could think of something else to do on his boat so he could detain his son the remainder of the day, but he finally had to announce that the day's work was over. Carlos was happy to climb out of the boat he had come to hate, and walked away toward the town. The time he had spent on the cliffs thinking had been valuable. He knew he must wait until his father had calmed himself before attempting any further conversation concerning New Spain, but he had made up his mind that come what may, he was going to join Sebastián when his friend left for Cadiz. He walked quickly to Bodega Cisneros.

José Quinteros waited in his boat until he saw his friend's son leave. He climbed out of his boat and strolled over to meet Alberto as he in turn left his fishing craft.

"Hola, amigo!" José greeted his friend.

"Hola," Alberto returned, but in a subdued, almost embarrassed tone of voice.

"*Oiga*, listen, friend," José continued. "Let's talk together...you and I."

"What is there to talk about? I said it all in the bodega."

"That is what I want to talk about, hombre," José answered.

"Go ahead and talk...all you want to...but don't talk to me...talk to the goddam wind which keeps us from the pesca."

José kept silent. He knew when there was no point in continuing the conversation. "That stubborn mule is worse than I thought," he thought to himself. Alberto Villanueva was already walking toward the town, taking his misery with him.

Sebastián was glad to see his friend enter the bodega and asked Cisneros to serve Carlos a glass of Jerez Red.

"Hola, amigo! ¿Qué pasa?" he greeted Carlos with a handshake.

"I guess everything is about the same except I have made up my mind to be with you when you leave for Cadiz. If my father can't understand me, he will have to live with his own anger. I heard what happened here the night I went to the cliffs to think this all out."

"That was not a pleasant experience for anyone," Sebastián agreed.

"Whenever you plan to leave, my friend, tell me, and I will go with you. Fortunately, I have talked to my mother and she understands, even though she could never disagree with my father openly."

"I am happy with your decision, Carlos. It will be a great adventure for both of us."

Manuel Cisneros could not help but overhear the conversation, because the bodega was empty except for the two young men. He filled their glasses and placed them on the bar. "This one is from the bodega...I am proud of you, Carlos...you have become a man now."

Carlos lifted his glass to Cisneros and drank. He thought to himself that the old veteran was in many ways...important ways...more a father to him than his own....

"The other night they passed my cap," Sebastián said. "My father also gave me the coins from that day's catch, so don't worry about expenses in Cadiz. I will gladly share what I have with you."

"And here is something for you both," Cisneros interrupted. "I have been saving these for the time when they have to bury me. Instead they can take me out to sea and give my body a push toward New Spain."

He had placed two gold coins in front of the two.

"Tell us, Don Manuel," Carlos said. "How will we find your wife and daughter in New Spain?"

Cisneros told them about where he thought his wife and daughter might be located. "Should your search for them be successful, my friends, please tell both that I think of them every day of my life."

Three days later Sebastián Quinteros and Carlos Villanueva were traveling the road from Tarifa to Cadiz. Sebastián's departure had been mixed with joy and sadness, but it had been open. Carlos, on the other hand, was forced to leave his home after his father had fallen asleep, leaving the explanation in the hands of his mother.

The trip to Cadiz was a mixture of walking, riding in ox-carts, and for a twenty-kilometer stretch of the road they were lucky to be offered a ride in a horse-drawn wagon. They arrived at the city, strange to both of them, tired, but exhilarated after the five-day journey.

A week later they were soldiers duly sworn into service to the Crown. Three months hence, they boarded the Spanish galleon, *Esperanza*, headed for the port of Veracruz in New Spain.

Alberto Villanueva never returned to Bodega Cisneros, and remained aloof from the rest of the fishermen, even venturing forth into weather that sent others hurrying to the shelter of the Tarifa quay-wall. It was almost a year from the day of his son's departure in the middle of the night that Alberto ignored the squalls and put to sea as usual. The squalls were on the periphery of a full-fledged storm, and Alberto Villanueva was never seen again. Three days later another fishing boat found the *Estrella* capsized and barely afloat. José Quinteros paid for the rosary in the cathedral, and a hat was passed in the Bodega Cisneros every time there was a good catch and the proceeds were given to the widow Villanueva.

The journey north was slow. The Camino Real, though well traveled, was deeply rutted and traversed many mighty rivers, which were sometimes difficult to ford.

There were three troops involved in the caravan. All three were bound for Pitic for training, after which they would travel further to the newly established presidios of Altar, Tubaca, and Fronteras. It was felt by the Spanish military that these garrisoned towns would thwart further uprisings by the Pima and Seri, and also protect the civilian populations engaged in livestock raising and mining from the fierce raiding Apache.

It was late spring when the caravan arrived at Pitic. The raw-adobe buildings of the city were already baking in the midday heat of May. The officer in charge of the caravan was Lieutenant Carranza, who had aspirations of far more important commands. He halted his men near the wooded banks of the Río Sonora. Before releasing the men he explained that they would bivouac at that point to undergo training for duty on the northern frontier.

"There will be passes for every man once we have established our camp," Carranza announced. "I require one third of this command to be on duty for the next three days. I will muster all three troops at five o'clock in the morning three days hence. Anyone not present at muster will be lashed."

There was a general air of jubilance among the soldiers. The journey north had been relentless, and they were weary and longing for whatever diversions Pitic could provide. The sergeants in charge of the three troops took over their men and divided each troop into three sections. Fortunately for Carlos he was in the first furloughed section. Sebastián would have to stand duty the first day.

"I will try to find the family of Manuel Cisneros," Carlos said to his friend. "If I am successful in finding them, I will take you there tomorrow."

"I hope you can find them, Carlos. It has been many years since old Cisneros was here."

"We owe our best to Manuel Cisneros," Carlos replied. "He was the one who told us about New Spain, and gave us the gold coins. I still have mine."

When the bivouac was made the furloughed one third cleaned up in the river and proceeded to the settlement called Pitic to seek whatever pleasure they could find. Carlos Villanueva had one goal in mind: to find Manuel Cisneros's woman, Etola and her daughter, Manuela. He asked everyone who looked like a local resident until finally, when the burning sun was setting in the west, Carlos entered a small restaurant to appease his hunger. He sat on a roughly hewn bench next to a table with the same texture. He was the only customer.

A young girl appeared shortly, and approached the table with a small earthen cup full of clear liquid. "Buenos noches, Señor," she said, placing the cup in front of him.

"Buenos noches, Señorita," Carlos replied, examining her features: long, black hair hanging in abandon around a face that almost reminded him of the young girls his age in Tarifa.

"We have young goat today," she announced.

"That will be fine, I am sure," Carlos replied without taking his eyes away from the girl.

"Enjoy your mescal, I will bring your meal shortly."

Carlos was surprised to hear the girl speak Spanish in spite of her appearance. She looked like an Indian girl, except there was something about her that was not all Indian. True, she had the coloring, but her facial features were more sharply defined than the Indians Carlos had observed in this part of northern New Spain. When she returned with the meal of baked goat, he asked if she might know of Etola Cisneros.

"She is my mother, Señor. It is she who cooked your supper."

Carlos was excited. "Please tell her I am Carlos Villanueva of Tarifa, Spain, and a friend of Manuel Cisneros, also of Tarifa."

"Manuel Cisneros is my father," the girl replied excitedly. "I am Manuela."

She turned quickly toward the kitchen where a middle-aged woman was tending the fire under the cooking vessels.

As quickly as she left the table where Carlos tasted his meal of *cabrito*, she returned with her mother. Carlos rose from the bench as the girl and her mother approached.

"I am Etola Cisneros, Señor," she said, wiping her brown, pudgy hands on a towel that had once been a flour sack.

Carlos noticed that Etola was shorter in stature and of heavier build than her daughter. Her black hair was heavily sprinkled with gray, but her dark eyes sparkled.

"I am Carlos Villanueva of Tarifa, Spain. Manuel Cisneros is a good friend of mine. He explained where I could find you in Pitic, but there was no one there."

"It is because I have been gone from that house for several years," she said. "Sit down, please, Señor, before your supper is cold."

"Please join me, Señora," he replied.

"Manuela," she said as she pulled out the bench opposite Carlos. "More mescal for the Señor, his cup is empty...and bring me a cup also."

The girl turned and went into the room to the rear. Carlos followed her with his eyes.

"She was just learning to walk when Manuel received his wound," she said.

Carlos quickly returned to his meal, embarrassed that Etola had noticed the intensity of his stare toward her daughter.

Manuela returned with two cups of mescal, and placed them on the table. She then returned to the kitchen. Carlos thanked her without lifting his eyes. Etola sipped at her cup, and continued her story. She told how she had worked for an army officer as cook and housekeeper after Cisneros returned to Spain. And when the officer was transferred she worked for another officer, and so on, until she had saved enough reales to start her small restaurant.

As she talked Carlos noticed a certain sadness to her words.

"Why didn't you go to Spain with Don Manuel?" he asked.

Etola lowered her eyes and looked into her cup that she held with both hands on the table. "We were not man and wife in the eyes of your Church or your government...Only by the words we spoke to each other were we married.

When Manuel was wounded, the army sent him away before we could arrange anything. He told me he would send for me. That was fifteen years ago."

Carlos understood her sadness and saw the years of work and waiting in her hands and face. "Don Manuel asked me to tell you that not a day goes by that he does not think of you and his daughter."

With that he reached into his pocket, and pulled out the gold coin that the peg-legged bodega owner had given him in Tarifa. Carlos handed the coin to Etola. "Don Manuel also asked me to give you this coin," he lied.

"Gracias," she said.

Carlos could see that even though she was grateful for the coin, she had long ago given up hope that Cisneros would send for her.

"It is a hard life for your husband in Tarifa," he tried to explain. "His bodega barely makes him enough reales to live on. And, there are always the taxes."

"You don't have to explain," she replied. "I still love Manuel Cisneros."

More diners arrived. Etola returned to the kitchen. Manuela brought cups of mescal to the newcomers and announced that cabrito was the meal.

Carlos finished eating, and was sipping his mescal, glancing at Manuela as she moved about serving the others. He wondered about what she was like beneath the loose-fitting blouse and skirt. "The mixture of Spanish and Indian is more beautiful than either alone," he thought to himself, remembering that old Cisneros could not be considered handsome.

"More of anything?" Manuela asked.

"Perhaps another mescal," he replied. The strong colorless liquor was beginning to show its sneaking effect, but

Carlos wanted to prolong his stay, and another cup of mescal would be his excuse.

"How much is the meal?" he asked when Manuela returned with his cup.

"My mother says that your messages are enough payment, Señor Villanueva," she replied, smiling.

"Please thank her, and I shall return tomorrow," he said, and finished the drink with one fiery swallow. He placed a few coins on the table, and left the restaurant. The alcohol took full effect when he was halfway back to the camp by the river.

With his brain clouded by the mescal and the picture of Manuela Cisneros, Carlos, half-staggering, arrived at camp to look for his lifelong friend.

Sebastián had finished his guard duty, and was getting ready for sleep when Carlos made his way toward the area occupied by the common troops.

"Hola, amigo!" Sebastián welcomed his friend. "You're not walking too well. You must have found some wine, no?"

"If it had been wine I would not be staggering. It was a bellyful of mescal," Carlos answered.

He sat down carefully across from Sebastián. "I found the wife and daughter of old Cisneros."

"That is good, my friend. What are they like?"

"They are interesting," Carlos said and paused momentarily. "Manuela, the daughter, is beautiful. I could barely keep my eyes from her."

"She must look like her mother," Sebastián said remembering the face of Manuel Cisneros.

"Neither, you will see. I will take you there tomorrow when we are dismissed in the afternoon."

The training exercises the following morning were difficult for Carlos because of his brutal hangover. By late afternoon the raw feeling in his stomach had subsided, and the two friends left the army bivouac for Pitic.

Carlos was anxious to see Manuela again, and quickened his pace as they neared the restaurant. Upon entering Carlos walked to the table he had occupied the previous evening. Sebastián followed.

Manuela entered from the kitchen. "Good afternoon, Señores," she greeted them.

The two friends replied in unison. Then Carlos introduced Sebastián to Manuela and asked to see Etola.

"She will return soon. She went to buy some more mescal because we are not in good supply. We have stew with goat and chile today, did you come to eat?"

"Yes," Carlos answered, looking directly into her eyes.

There was a momentary trance they both shared; then Manuela quickly turned away and went to the kitchen. She returned with two cups. "The *birria* will be ready soon," she said.

Manuela stood by the table as if she was unable to leave. At last she made her request. "I would appreciate hearing about my father," she said. "I only know what my mother has told me."

"Of course," Carlos said. "Please sit down and join us."

"Thank you," Manuela said and sat down.

Carlos and Sebastián took turns telling Manuela about Manuel Cisneros and his life in the bodega, and about life in Tarifa. They explained the importance of her father to the fishermen of their village.

Manuela listened intently, digesting every word, trying to picture her father in her mind as the two soldiers talked. The cups of mescal had been emptied a while when the juice of the birria boiled over and sizzled on the hot coals of the cooking fire.

"Ay, forgive me," Manuela said, and scurried to the kitchen. She returned with two bowls filled with stringy goat meat simmered since morning with red chile, garlic, and onion. "Your tortillas are heating. I will bring them," she said, and returned to the kitchen.

She had refilled the cups, and brought a half-dozen hot, round, corn tortillas wrapped in a cloth. Etola entered carrying an earthen jug full of mescal. After being introduced to Sebastián, she left the former fishermen from Tarifa to eat their meal.

The food in New Spain was strange to the two Spaniards. They had never tasted the hot spicy flavor of red chile, nor the taste and texture of unleavened cornmeal. The tepary beans, cooked into a mushy gruel and fried in lard were also foreign to them. But, the combination of flavors and textures was pleasantly satisfying to their hunger. The fiery, colorless mescal was another matter. It had a far different taste, and a more immediate effect than the robust red wine from Jerez de la Frontera they had once drunk from the wooden casks in Bodega Cisneros.

Sebastián concentrated on the meal as Carlos kept glancing toward the kitchen. Manuela, not unaware of Carlos's attention, came to the table to refill the cups.

"This had better be my last cupful," Carlos said. "I had too much last night. I had best have some coffee."

"The mescal can be deceiving to those who are just becoming acquainted with it," she replied.

When both soldiers had finished eating, Carlos reluctantly agreed with Sebastián to leave the restaurant, and as they walked through the hot, dusty streets of Pitic, they talked only occasionally. It was Carlos who had little to contribute to their conversation, because his thoughts were on Manuela Cisneros.

As the days and weeks of training progressed, Carlos and Sebastián learned the rudiments of horsemanship from Sergeant Bernal, a veteran of the frontier, who had seen service with Captain Manje, the commander of Padre Eusebio Kino's military escort through Pimería Alta.

Carlos spent most of his off-duty hours in Cafe Cisneros talking to Manuela under the ever-watchful eye of Etola, who was concerned that her daughter might follow the same path that she, herself, had taken with Manuel Cisneros.

One day in late July, after the monsoon system had brought the warm moist air masses northward to spill their moisture on the hot, arid land of the northern frontier of New Spain, Sergeant Bernal assembled his charges as dawn was breaking the next morning.

"The governor general has ordered the establishment of three presidios to be located near the northern frontier," he announced. "One month from today you men will proceed to your permanent assignments with the garrisons at these forts."

Sergeant Bernal then introduced three new faces, all carrying the rank of sergeant. They had arrived at the bivouac over the past two days. The announcement of permanent assignments came as no surprise to the men because it was common knowledge that they were training for duty on the frontier. Exactly where each would serve had been the only question.

Each sergeant was assigned a third of the men. For the following month each troop would train separately.

The locations of the three presidios had been determined by what needed protection and from which tribes of

Indians. The Presidio de Altar, located at the confluence of the Río Altar and the Río de la Concepción, was to protect the mines, farms, and livestock ranches against not only the recently rebellious Pimas, but also the recalcitrant Seri to the south and west living on the coast of the Sea of Cortez. Tubaca, the northernmost fortified town, located on the Río Santa María near the mission pueblo of San Cayetano de Tumacacori, was to further control the Pimas and protect the ranches and mines from Apache raiding parties. These raiders made their incursions from their mountain strongholds to the east.

The easternmost garrisoned town, Fronteras, north of Arispe on the Río Sonora, was also to be a buffer against the constant threat of the Apache. Sebastián and Carlos had their hopes to be stationed together fulfilled when Sergeant Bernal assigned them to the Tubaca garrison under Sergeant Velasquez. Velasquez was a veteran of the Pima Rebellion the year before, 1751, and had also fought against Apache raiding parties. He knew the valley of the Río Santa María from his experiences against Luis of Saric, the leader of the Pimas.

As Ruben Velasquez described Tubaca and its surroundings to his men, Carlos thought only about how far from Pitic he would be...how far from Manuela.

When they were dismissed that afternoon, and as Carlos and Sebastián were walking toward Pitic, Carlos was lost in his thoughts. Sebastián broke the silence.

"What do you think about our assignment to Tubaca?" he asked.

"I once thought I would look forward to it, but now all I can think about is the distance between Tubaca and Pitic...and Manuela."

# TWO GOLD COINS

"Ay, hombre," Sebastián replied. "Once you are in Tubaca fighting Apaches you will forget about Manuela."

"I will never forget Manuela, my friend," Carlos said. "I love her, Sebastián, and I don't know what to do. There is only a month left in Pitic."

"Have you spoken your love to her? Has she spoken her love to you?"

"Not exactly," Carlos replied. "You know how it is there in the cafe. Her mother rarely lets Manuela out of her sight."

"Etola is not stupid, and neither am I, amigo." Sebastian laughed. "By the way you look at her daughter, Etola can't help knowing what is going through your head."

"I guess you are right," Carlos said, lowering his head to look at the ground. "When you are with me, Etola is not so vigilant as when I go to the cafe alone. How can I see Manuela alone?"

"That is something you will have to do yourself. I have no idea except to ask her."

"Mother of God!" Carlos exclaimed with exasperation. "I feel like I am hitting my head against a wall of stone."

"Don't feel so frustrated until you have failed." Sebastián advised. "Maybe Manuela does not share your feelings, did you ever think of that?"

"I have thought of that, but I'll never know if I can't talk to her away from her mother."

"Look at it this way, my friend," Sebastián said seriously. "Manuela is half Indian, half Spanish. You are a Spaniard from Tarifa, and men of Tarifa marry only Spanish women, not half-breeds. Wait for a Spanish woman to fall in love with. It is obvious you are too serious about Manuela. Forget her. She is too well watched for your pleasure, and not worthy to be the wife of a fisherman from Tarifa."

The words of his lifelong friend angered Carlos Villanueva.

"When I left Tarifa, I left for good, and I am no longer a fisherman. It makes no difference to me whether Manuela is half Indian, pure Indian, or whatever. I think she is beautiful and I love her."

"She will do you no good as a wife," Sebastián said. "You will be lucky to make the rank of corporal married to her. And besides the way Sergeant Velasquez describes Tubaca, I don't think it's a place for a soldier's wife."

"I don't care about the army, rank, or anything else," Carlos replied. "You are sounding like a damned snob."

"You are sounding like a damned fool! Go to Cafe Cisneros by yourself," Sebastián said, and turned to walk away from his companion.

Carlos stopped and watched his friend for a moment. "My God," he thought. "He doesn't understand."

Cafe Cisneros was empty of customers when Carlos entered. Etola was busy in the kitchen. Manuela was sweeping the dining area.

"Buenas tardes," she said to Carlos.

"Buenas tardes," he replied and returned her smile.

He sat at his usual place and Manuela, after propping the broom against the wall, approached him.

"The food is not quite ready, but I can bring you a mescal," she said.

"Please," Carlos returned. "But, first, I would like to see you alone. I must talk to you alone, Manuela," he said, lowering his voice.

Manuela sensed the urgency in his voice. She had felt Carlos's attraction for some time, and was aware of her own feelings toward him. A plan suddenly came to her mind. She turned and walked toward the kitchen.

"Mama, I am going to the market and buy green corn for tomorrow's tamales. The price should be good for what is left."

She referred to her mother's tactic of waiting to buy produce until the farmers were ready to return home, when they were willing to take less for their corn rather than have to haul it back to their farms.

Etola reached into the pocket of her apron and extracted a few coins. "Make sure you buy the corn at a good price, daughter. Those farmers should be ready to lower their prices by now. And, buy some lard. The jug is nearly empty."

"I will, Mama," she said, taking the brown, glazed crock from the shelf near the stove. As she turned to leave the kitchen, she said in as nonchalant a manner as possible, "Señor Villanueva is going to the market with me to help carry the corn."

Etola had observed the young soldier and had known for weeks that he was attracted to her daughter. She suspected her daughter's mutual attraction to Carlos, but thus far she had had no reason to attempt to confirm the suspicion.

"Be quick about it," she reminded. "The customers will start arriving very soon."

Carlos had risen from his seat, surprised at Manuela's maneuver, and followed her through the doorway. They walked in silence through the narrow dusty streets, keeping to the shady sides until they arrived at the plaza. The mid-afternoon heat nearly emptied the central market of shoppers. The young couple stopped under the shade of one of the cottonwood trees and Manuela turned to face the young man from Tarifa. Carlos felt strangely happy and awkward at the same time to be alone with Manuela. His shyness stifled the words he wanted so much to speak.

"What is it that is so important?" Manuela asked finally.

"We have received our permanent assignments," Carlos said seriously. "In one month I will leave Pitic for Tubaca far to the north."

"I have heard of Tubaca," she said. "The climate there is cooler than here. You will probably enjoy being there."

Carlos fought with himself to speak his mind. Finally, he said, "I will not enjoy being anywhere without you. I love you, Manuela."

She lowered her eyes from his intense stare.

"I want you to be my wife."

It was a long moment before Manuela raised her head to look into his eyes again. She felt herself trembling. Carlos reached for her hands and waited.

"I love you, too, Carlos Villanueva." She spoke slowly. "But, I am afraid."

"What is there to be afraid of?" he asked, relieved to have released his thoughts, and happy that she had confirmed sharing his feelings.

"Mama will object. I know exactly what she will say if I tell her I want to marry you. She has told me many times not to fall in love with a soldier who will leave and return to Spain alone. She is still very bitter about her life without my father."

"But, certainly she will see the difference. I want to marry you now, not someday. Now! And, I will probably never return to Spain. I will talk to your mother."

"No, Carlos. I will speak to her."

Carlos took Manuela into his arms and kissed her willing lips firmly. Passion surged through both their bodies in the embrace.

Manuela broke away. "One of our customers might see us. Hurry. We must buy the corn and lard. Mama is suspicious. I can tell. Come."

# TWO GOLD COINS

They hurried to the marketplace in spite of the heat, and Manuela bargained skillfully for the fresh green ears of corn, after puncturing a few kernels to make sure they were in the "milk" stage. They then went into a small store where the owner filled the crock with lard.

Cafe Cisneros still lacked clientele when they returned, Carlos carrying the sack filled with corn, Manuela with the crock.

"It took you long enough," Etola admonished.

"The farmers were stubborn today, Mama. But, I managed to bring you back some change."

Carlos lowered the sack to the floor of the kitchen and went to his usual table. Manuela filled a cup with mescal and brought it to him, avoiding his eyes, and returned for a bowl filled with steaming birria .

Carlos concentrated on the meal, anxious to leave the restaurant to avoid Etola. Manuela busied herself cleaning the other tables until the next customers arrived. She brought the newcomers mescal and birria, and returned to the kitchen with mixed emotions: the joy of her feelings of love, and the fear of her mother's possible anger in the morning.

When Carlos had finished his second cupful of mescal, he placed the usual number of coins on the table, and left Cafe Cisneros to walk the streets of Pitic. The sun had sunk beneath the far western horizon, but its heat would remain in the still evening air until total darkness brought the relief of a few degrees of lowered temperature.

Carlos walked through the streets aimlessly, trying to recapture every minute he had spent with Manuela in the plaza. He wished that he could be present, but not seen, in the morning when she planned to speak with her mother. It was obvious to him that Manuela shared his own feelings, but he was not sure that she could free herself from the dominating Etola.

The ribald laughter invading the street from the open door of a cantina made him hesitate. He contemplated whether or not to enter for a drink. He entered and walked to a vacant space near the doorway at the rough-hewn plank, which served as a bar.

The barkeep, a short, stocky man, obviously an Indian, placed a bottle of mescal and a cup in front of Carlos. As he filled the cup from the bottle Carlos didn't notice his friend, Sebastián, approach from the rear of the cantina.

"Que pasa?" Sebastián greeted his friend, slapping Carlos on the back.

Carlos, surprised, turned quickly, and saw that Sebastián was drunk.

"How are you, friend?" Carlos returned. "How long have you been here?"

"Too long. Too long," Sebastián slurred. "Why are you here? Why are you not at Cafe Cisneros?"

"I am on my way back to camp. I stopped here for a drink. You look like you've had a bellyful, amigo."

"And, by God, I am going to have more." Sebastián managed to say. He was supporting himself by holding the plank bar.

Carlos had never seen his friend so drunk, and he was concerned that Sebastián would not make it back to the bivouac area by morning muster. "Let's go. You will feel like hell in the morning."

"I feel like hell already," Sebastián said, slurring his words again.

"What is making you this way?" Carlos asked.

"The way things are is not the way I thought things would be," Sebastián said, gazing into his cup.

"I do not understand you, amigo. How did you think things would be here?"

"Hell, I don't know," Sebastián replied. "I thought you and I would be together, and now you are with your half-breed sweetheart every chance you have."

Sebastián's referral to Manuela as a half-breed angered Carlos. At the same time he felt sad that Sebastián could not accept or understand his newly found joy. He decided that further conversation might cause a larger rift in their friendship, especially with Sebastián talking through mescal. Carlos turned toward the door, and walked out of the cantina, leaving his full cup of mescal on the rough plank bar. Instead of returning to the bivouac area, Carlos ambled through the dark, dusty streets of Pitic thinking about his friend, Sebastián, and the love he felt for Manuela. He pondered the words of his friend, and Sebastián's use of "half-breed" with reference to Manuela. "Perhaps Sebastián is jealous of Manuela, because I can think of little else," he thought to himself. His thoughts wandered back and forth with no solution. He found himself walking toward Cafe Cisneros, and as he passed he glanced at the shuttered door. He wondered if Manuela had been able to explain things to her mother, if her mother was adamant against him, and how Manuela would react.

It was after midnight before Carlos arrived at the bivouac area. Sebastián had returned an hour before and slept soundly, much to Carlos's relief. The thought of Sebastián missing morning muster and the trouble it would cause had bothered Carlos because he felt responsible, in part, for the situation.

The following night Carlos had to stand guard duty, and could not leave the encampment. He wanted to know about the conversation between Manuela and Etola. When he was relieved from guard duty at midnight he noticed Sebastián had not yet returned from Pitic.

As soon as his troop was dismissed from afternoon drill the next day, Carlos went straight to Cafe Cisneros. Etola was not in sight, but Manuela seemed distant and cold when she finally came over to his table.

"What happened with your mother?" Carlos inquired with anticipation in the tone of his voice.

"We talked for a long time."

"What was the result?"

"She is still concerned that you are a soldier, and will end up going back to Spain like my father did."

"Did you tell her that I want to marry you?"

"Yes, but she said that would be even worse for me to be left here in Pitic as a married woman with a husband in Spain."

"What is wrong, Manuela?" Carlos asked. "You seem like you agree with your mother. You do not speak to me in your usual manner."

Manuela turned quickly, and went to the kitchen. Carlos, totally confused, rose from his chair, and followed her. "Manuela," he said from the doorway to the kitchen. "What is wrong? What has happened to make you this way? I love you. You told me you loved me. You are not acting like someone who loves me."

Tears filled her eyes as she stood with head bowed looking at the floor. She clasped and unclasped her hands in front of her several times, until the tears flowed down her copper-brown cheeks. Carlos threw away all abandon, and went to her. He took her in his arms to comfort her. He could feel the lurch of sobs in her body close to his. Finally he put one hand under her chin and lifted her head gently. "There is something more than the talk with your mother that is upsetting you," he said. "What is it?"

For a long moment Manuela stayed looking into Carlos's eyes as she continued to sob quietly. "It was Sebastián," she said finally. "He came in last night. He had been drinking for a while, I could tell." She hesitated, afraid to go on.

"What did Sebastián say that has bothered you so much?" Carlos asked.

"He said if I marry you, your career as a soldier would be finished. Ay, Carlos," she said through the sobbing. "He said because I am not only a half-breed, but also a bastard child, you would never be more than a common soldier if we were married. I don't want to be the one to hold you back. I love you too much!"

"Sebastián is a fool!" Carlos said with intense anger in the tone of his voice. "He has been my best friend for all my life, and he does this! He speaks as if he were my father, not my best friend!" He put both hands on Manuela's shoulders, and spoke with sternness. "Sebastián speaks garbage. He is jealous that I have found someone to love and be loved by. It must be clear to you that he is trying to come between us because of his jealousy. I will deal with him when I return to our camp, but right now you must understand that I do not care about being a soldier. I don't know exactly what I want to do, but being a soldier is only for as long as my enlistment lasts. Then I will do something else to support you and me, and all of our children."

Etola walked in the front door, and discovered Carlos and Manuela in their embrace. "Aha!" she said. "I cannot go to the market without wondering what my daughter is doing while I am gone!"

"Señora," Carlos said as he released Manuela quickly. "You must not worry about your daughter. There were things we needed to discuss, and Manuela is upset. I was only trying to comfort her."

"Mama, Carlos and I want to be married, and we would like your permission," Manuela said in a matter-of-fact way that surprised even Carlos.

"I have told you how I feel about you marrying a soldier, Manuela," Etola scolded. "Why do you persist with such a risk?"

"Señora," Carlos interrupted. "I can understand your concern because of what has happened in your life, but I am Carlos Villanueva, not Manuel Cisneros. I am not only planning to stay here in New Spain, I am planning to stay here with Manuela. I am asking for your permission and blessing."

"I have heard promises before," Etola said. "Suppose you are transferred. What then?"

"I will take Manuela with me, and when I am no longer a soldier, we will return to live in New Spain."

"You must also have your commander's permission to marry," Etola replied. "Do you think he will grant permission to one who is going to be stationed on the frontier?"

"I can only try. If Lieutenant Carranza won't grant me his permission, I will go over his head."

"Carlos," Etola said. "I am Opata from the Río Sonora. My people have lived near the Apache, and I knew their fierce nature when I was a young girl. You are going to a fort where Apaches raid frequently. Are you sure you want Manuela in such a dangerous part of the frontier?"

"I will have to discover what Tubaca is like for myself," Carlos replied. "I have never been there, and I have never seen an Apache. Right now, I would like your permission to walk with Manuela so we might be able to talk about these matters."

"You have my permission to walk for an hour. I will need her back here when the diners begin arriving for supper."

"Thank you, Señora," Carlos said. "I respect your trust."

Carlos and Manuela walked out of Cafe Cisneros, turned to the right, and headed for the cottonwood grove along the river. Once mingled with the trees and tall sacaton grass they embraced for a long time before speaking. Manuela was the first to break the spell. "I know she will give us her blessing," she said. "We must be patient with her, but she will relent."

"I hope she doesn't wait long," Carlos replied. "I wish we were married now, I want you so much."

"I know exactly how you feel because I have the same feelings," Manuela said, and sighed from her young passion.

Carlos talked about his thoughts about raising cattle when his army enlistment was up. He enjoyed the horsemanship training he was still undergoing. "I will ask Lieutenant Carranza for his permission tomorrow," he said.

"I want to be with you forever, Carlos," Manuela said, not thinking about the possibility of Carranza's denial.

"We will be together forever, my beautiful one," Carlos said. "Right now I had better get you back to your mother. I don't want her getting angry with either of us."

The happy couple walked slowly back to the cafe, looking at one another all the way. When they arrived, Etola looked up, but said nothing. Last minute preparations for supper occupied her. Carlos sat at his usual table, sipped slowly at the cup of mescal Manuela had brought. He could not take his eyes from her the entire time. When he could see that Etola wanted to close for the evening he left after saying goodnight to both.

As Carlos walked toward the encampment his thoughts turned to Sebastián, and he hoped his friend would be asleep or somewhere else. He dreaded the inevitable confrontation. But Sebastián was waiting. He had returned from Pitic earlier than usual, but still had time to drink enough mescal to be belligerent. Sebastián had waited outside the entrance for his friend to arrive.

Carlos walked toward the camp in blissful thought about Manuela. He didn't see Sebastián leaning on the gatepost. "Hola, Carlos," Sebastián said, slurring his words slightly.

Carlos looked up with surprise. "Hola," Carlos replied. "What are you doing out here?"

"I am waiting for you so we can talk alone," Sebastián said.

"Then talk," Carlos answered. "What do you have to say?"

"I want to talk to you about what you are doing to yourself by chasing after Manuela. You are going to ruin your chances for promotion if you carry this on further."

"Sebastián," Carlos said. "I am going to marry Manuela. Please do not speak against her to me again. Etola has given her blessing to the marriage, and I will seek Lieutenant Carranza's permission tomorrow after the drills are finished for the day."

"You are a fool, my friend," Sebastián said. "The lieutenant will never grant you permission to marry. Wait and see!"

"Good night, Sebastián," Carlos said. "We have nothing further to speak about."

The following morning Sebastián went quickly to Carranza's quarters before muster to discuss the situation. He described Manuela as a half-breed, and carried on

# TWO GOLD COINS

about sons of Tarifa fishermen never marrying a woman who was not pure Spanish. "I request that you deny Carlos Villanueva permission to marry this half-breed bastard child of Manuel Cisneros of Tarifa," Sebastián said in conclusion.

"Thank you for the information, Quinteros," Carranza said. "You are a good soldier, and very good with horses. I am thinking about recommending your promotion to corporal."

"Thank you, Lieutenant."

"By the way, Quinteros, I have noticed that you have been looking poorly these mornings, and there is talk among the troops that you might enjoy mescal too much. That stuff can come to rule you if you are not careful."

"Yes, Lieutenant," Sebastián answered. "I have been upset with my friend Villanueva lately, but that is finished."

"Very good. I don't need drunken corporals on the frontier."

The troop spent the day working on cavalry combat drills, practicing against each other. Carranza kept Carlos in view as much as possible during the exercises. He was pleased to notice that Carlos had become an accomplished horseman under his tutelage. He had the same pride in Sebastián. When the day's drills ended, Carlos hurried more than usual to care for his horse, and put his tack away for the night. He walked to Carranza's quarters without returning to his own. The officer answered Carlos's knock with, "Come in."

Carlos entered the room to find Carranza seated behind his small desk. "Lieutenant," he said standing at attention. "I am here to ask your permission to marry."

"Sit down, Villanueva," Carranza said, pointing to a small chair in front of the desk. "Perhaps you don't realize that we are leaving for the frontier in two weeks. I don't think it wise

235

for you to get married for several reasons. First of all I don't need men who are encumbered with wives at such an outpost where Apache raiding is frequent. I must have men on whom I can depend completely. There are enough women already in Tubaca to get underfoot. And your friend Quinteros was talking with me this morning. From what he tells me, the girl you want to marry is a half-breed, and fatherless."

Carlos sat seething with anger in the chair. He rose, and stood at attention. "Lieutenant, the woman I am going to marry is the daughter of Manuel Cisneros, a close friend and fellow townsman from Tarifa. I find this betrayal of Quinteros distasteful to say the least."

"Villanueva," Carranza said. "Don't be too hard on your friend, Quinteros. I am sure he has your best interests at heart. By the way, as I told him, I am considering recommending both of you for promotions to corporal. You have potential to become a commissioned officer if you marry properly."

"I don't mean to be impudent, Lieutenant, but I would prefer to marry the woman I love than be a general."

"Very well, Villanueva," Carranza said. "Permission to marry denied."

Carlos turned abruptly, and walked outside toward his own quarters. Sebastián had left for town. Carlos changed from his work uniform after hastily washing his face and hands. With no guard duty he was free for the night.

Manuela came to the table immediately after watching Carlos enter Cafe Cisneros scowling. "What is wrong, Carlos?" she asked.

"The lieutenant denied permission for me to marry you, and equally bad, Sebastián has betrayed me. I don't know which is worse, except there must be a way for us to marry without the army's permission."

# TWO GOLD COINS

"My cousin works for a priest at the Mission Santa Rosa del Río," Manuela said. "I will go to see him tomorrow, and find out what we can do."

"Let us go tonight," Carlos replied. "We do not have much time because the troop leaves for Tubaca in two weeks."

Manuela went to the back room where her mother prepared for the evening's work. "I am going to the mission with Carlos, Mama. We are going to see my cousin Federico."

"Why do you need to see Federico?"

"We have questions to ask him, Mama."

"Don't be gone too long, we might have a good business tonight, and I will need your help."

Carlos and Manuela walked quickly across the town to the mission that served mostly Opata people who had come to work in Pitic. Federico was sweeping the sidewalk as they approached. "Hello, cousin Manuela," he greeted. "What brings you here?"

"Hello Federico, I want you to meet Carlos Villanueva."

The two men shook hands, and smiled at each other.

"Carlos and I want to be married," Manuela began. "His lieutenant refuses to grant permission, so I thought maybe your priest would have an idea to help us."

"Come with me," Federico said. "The father is almost ready for evening prayers, but if we hurry, he may be able to see you."

Manuela's cousin led them around the church building to the rear where Father Toribio kept his rudely built quarters. "Father Toribio," Federico called at the rough door made from saguaro cactus ribs.

"Yes, Federico. What is it?"

"My cousin must see you, father. It is very important."

"Come in, then. Come in."

Federico opened the door, and led Manuela and Carlos into the small room. Father Toribio sat up on the edge of the bed. "Forgive me, I was napping a bit before evening prayers. What is it that I can do for you?"

"Father, this is Carlos Villanueva. We want to be married," Manuela said.

"Ah," the priest said. "And your commander will not give you permission. Am I correct?"

"Yes, Father," Carlos replied.

"Well, my children, you are not the first to seek my help in that matter. If I do this, you must keep it a secret from the army. I have done this before, so I am familiar with your problem. I do not like the army or their methods, so I do this as my rebellion against what I don't approve of."

"Then you will do this for us, Father?" Carlos asked hopefully.

"Since you are Federico's cousin, I can trust you to keep it a secret. Otherwise I will get a visit from your commander, and I don't enjoy visits from commanders. When would you like to have your wedding?"

"As soon as possible, Father," Carlos said. "I am due to go north with my troop in two weeks."

"I can do the ceremony now, if you can wait until after evening prayers."

"Let us ask my mother if she will come, Carlos," Manuela said. "Is that all right with you, Father?"

"Certainly. I think I remember your mother."

The young people left the room, and Carlos asked Federico to stay for the wedding to stand up with him. Then Carlos and Manuela hurried to Cafe Cisneros.

Etola was surprised, and hesitated, saying that she should stay to serve her customers. Both Carlos and Manuela insisted that she accompany them to the church. Finally grasping the reality of what was to happen, she accompanied her daughter to the back room to put on their best dresses for the ceremony.

Carlos waited at his table with a small glass of mescal. He hoped he wouldn't see Sebastián on the way to the mission. He thought about what the priest had said. It might be easy to keep the marriage secret in Pitic for two weeks, but he wondered how they could keep the secret in Tubaca. "By that time," he thought to himself, "we will be away from Pitic so the father won't get into any trouble with Carranza."

The father held the ceremony in the privacy of his small room. Etola's eyes filled with tears as she witnessed her daughter fulfilling something she had been unable to do with Manuel Cisneros. The father blessed the couple after he had written out a certificate. Carlos and Manuela thanked both the father and Federico, and the three hurried back to the restaurant.

Two cowboys turned away from the door as Etola approached. She called, let them in, and gave them glasses of mescal to sip while they waited for their meal. Carlos and Manuela followed, glad that Sebastián had not been on the street as they walked back. Manuela went to the back room to change clothes. "This is your wedding night, my daughter," Etola said. "I will take care of the customers. You go with your husband."

"That certainly happened quickly," Carlos said. "Two hours ago I wondered how we would be able to get married, and now you are my wife. I love you, Manuela."

"I love you, Carlos, my husband. Mama seems happy about it all."

"I am glad she is," Carlos said as they walked to the grove of trees by the Río Sonora. "I would not want her to be upset with either of us."

They returned to Cafe Cisneros two hours later, hungry, and smiling at each other. "I will get you some supper," Manuela said.

"Let's eat together," Carlos said. "And bring some mescal for both of us to toast ourselves."

Manuela carried two plates of cabrito and three full glasses on a tray to the table. Etola came out from behind the counter, and sat down. There were no more customers to serve.

She picked up her glass, and said, "To my two children. I wish you happiness forever."

Carlos and Manuela clicked their glasses with Etola's, and sipped at the fiery, clear liquid. Carlos lifted his glass, but Etola interrupted. She reached into her apron pocket, and took out the gold coin that Carlos had brought from Spain. "This gold coin is for you, my children. Be careful with it, but when you need it, let it go."

Carlos and Manuela spent their wedding night in the back room after helping Etola move her straw-filled mattress into the dining area of the restaurant. After muster in the morning Sebastián approached him. "Where were you last night, amigo?"

Carlos looked at Sebastián for a moment, thinking about how the man he had always considered his friend had betrayed him. "Where I spend my nights, and with whom I spend my nights is none of your concern," Carlos said. "I think it is best that you go your way, and I will go mine."

Sebastián began to reply, but Carlos turned quickly, and walked away.

Guard duty prevented Carlos from seeing Manuela that night, and he spent his time wondering how to arrange transportation for her to Tubaca. The following evening he discovered that she too had been thinking about the same problem, and had solved it. "My uncle Anselmo, Federico's father, drives a freight wagon for the army," Manuela said. "He will return in two days or so from hauling supplies to Altar. Federico says he will be going to Tubaca on his next trip, and that he could probably take me with him."

"Suppose the army doesn't allow him to carry passengers?" Carlos asked.

"Federico said that the army has nothing to say about that because Uncle Anselmo drives for the Sanchez Freighting Company."

"I hope that is our solution," Carlos said.

Federico came to Cafe Cisneros as soon as his father arrived from Altar. "I have talked with my father," he said to Manuela. "He wants you and Carlos to come to our house to arrange things."

"Does that mean he wants money?"

"No, cousin, not money. He wants to meet your husband, and talk to you both about when and where you should be ready to leave. He also wants to tell you about where you are going to live. My father is very excited and happy for you."

When Carlos arrived for the evening, Manuela told him of Federico's visit, and they went to see her uncle. Carlos listened intently as Anselmo described Tubaca, the valley, and the road north to Pimería Alta.

Anselmo was scheduled to leave in three days. That would mean Manuela leaving Pitic before Carlos, but Anselmo thought Carlos would probably arrive in Tubaca ahead of her. In any event Anselmo knew some of the civilian residents of Tubaca, and would help Carlos and Manuela find a place to live. "You will find that people are different on the frontier," Anselmo said. "There is more cooperation because of the dangers."

One evening Carlos wrote a letter to Manuel Cisneros, telling him about Manuela becoming his wife, and describing Etola's restaurant. He also told Cisneros that they would both be leaving for Tubaca.

Carlos and his wife spent nights together until the time arrived for Manuela to leave. They rose early, Manuela and Etola said tearful good-byes, and the couple walked through Pitic well before sunrise to the Sanchez warehouse. Anselmo had finished hitching the four mules to the heavy freight wagon, and stood ready to climb aboard. Carlos put Manuela's few belongings behind the seat of the wagon, and turned to her. "It will not be long until we are together again," he said, holding her close. "I will think of you every minute."

"I already miss you, husband," Manuela replied.

They kissed each other, and Carlos helped her board the wagon for the long, arduous journey to their new home on the northern frontier of New Spain.

Three days later the troop assembled before daylight, ready for the ride to their destination duty station. The troop destined for the presidio of Altar remained. The troop assigned to the presidio of Fronteras had left four days before. Now it was Sergeant Velasquez who mounted his horse at the head of the column, and gave the order that began the journey to the presidio of Tubaca, near the banks of the Río Santa María. They would join the advance party that had been sent two months before. Among those already encamped at the new presidio was Captain Ortega, Lieutenant Mendoza, and four troopers. The plan was that as soon as the building phase ended, Ortega had orders to go to Fronteras, which had no buildings as yet. Lieutenant Carranza would then leave Pitic as Captain Carranza to take command of the Tubaca garrison.

# TWO GOLD COINS

As the troop moved away from the bivouac area in Pitic, many in its ranks wondered what they would encounter at their new duty station. Only Sergeant Velasquez had seen action on the frontier as a member of a "Flying Company," a cavalry troop known for its swift reprisals against the Apache raiders. In spite of the stories Velasquez had related, the younger soldiers had little idea what life on the frontier of New Spain would be like.

Sebastián, like the others, rode in silence. He thought about the rift in his friendship with Carlos, and examined his own conscience concerning it. He wanted to find a way to justify his anger toward Carlos. But when he pondered what had happened, and the events that followed, he began questioning these thoughts. He could see that Carlos didn't share his enthusiasm for army life. Finally Sebastián accepted the fact that he must respect his friend's different attitudes and desires or the rift could open into a chasm. He wanted to talk things over with Carlos, but his friend had become more isolated, and Sebastián noticed that Carlos rarely spoke with other troopers either. And after evening meals he watched Carlos wander off in the desert by himself. Sebastián wanted to follow, but could not bring himself to do so.

The troop's arrival in Tubaca, after the ten-day ride, brought the settlers out of their adobe dwellings and in from the fields. Sergeant Bernal brought his men into formation, and saluted the two officers in charge, passing command to them. Work on the presidio had progressed, but much remained to be finished. The commandant's house needed interior work, and the quarters for the garrison, a group of adobe buildings built around a drill area, still needed roofs. Captain Ortega informed the new garrison that they would start cutting mesquite for rafters as soon as the freight wagon arrived with axes.

Anselmo and Manuela, having taken a slightly different road to make a delivery, arrived two days after the troopers. Carlos hurried to meet the wagon before it arrived at the presidio part of the town. Anselmo halted the mules, and Carlos lifted Manuela down to the rutted street. Anselmo handed him her luggage, and yelled at the mules to continue. "I am so happy to see you, Manuela," he said after kissing her in front of the townspeople who had come to their doors to see the freight wagon arrive.

"I missed you, dear husband," she said.

"Come," he said. "Everyone is watching us. I have found us a room, and your helping the family with their household chores can pay the rent. I am hoping to save our money to buy a farm someday, when I get through with my enlistment."

"That sounds perfect," she answered. "I will do anything to help us to that end."

They walked to the far end of the town where a house, larger than the others, dominated a small side street. Carlos introduced Manuela to Señora Orozco, who showed them the one-room building in back. "This is small, but it will do for us when I get it arranged," Manuela said when they were alone.

The Orozco family had been granted a substantial parcel of farm and ranch land north of the town. The barns, stables, and corrals had been built first, but the family house had not been started. The house in town had been built before the land-grant papers had arrived from the governor general. Simon Orozco's influence extended not only throughout New Spain, but also all the way to Madrid.

Manuela had worked in the house for a week when the woman who did the cooking for the family took sick.

Mánuela was sent to the kitchen, and remained there after Simon Orozco sampled her cooking.

The secret between Carlos and Manuela remained. Carlos had explained the situation to the Orozcos, and they kept their knowledge to themselves. The difficult thing was slipping away at night to stay with Manuela.

The presidio buildings had roofs within two weeks after the garrison arrived. First a few of the troopers cut and dragged the rafters to the drill area where others carried them to the structures. Another crew crossed the river to cut and haul ocotillo stems. When the rafters were in place, the ocotillo stems were packed tightly together, and lashed to the mesquite with rawhide. The final process involved finishing the top with adobe mud mixed with the tall, strong-stemmed sacaton grass that grew prolifically in clumps by the river.

Carlos and Sebastián found themselves assigned to the same building when the roofs had been completed. Both felt awkward under the circumstances. Sebastián watched as Carlos left the barracks after dark. He slipped quickly into his clothes, and followed. Just as Carlos turned into the side street, Sebastián hailed him. "Carlos, wait please!"

Carlos stopped, and turned to face the quickly approaching Sebastián. "I must talk to you, amigo," Sebastián said as the two faced each other in the moonlight. "I want to apologize. I have thought about what I said and did, and I realize that it was wrong. I was putting my own feelings first, expecting you to agree. I am truly sorry for what I have caused between us."

"It has bothered me very much too," Carlos replied. "I accept your apology, amigo, but I must wonder what your feelings are about Manuela."

"I realize that it was stupid of me to have said what I did. Obviously you love her. I wish I had kept to my own business, and I certainly should not have gone to Lieutenant Carranza."

"Well, amigo," Carlos said. "Your going to Carranza angered me greatly, but as I have thought all this over, I am sure he would have denied permission for me to marry Manuela whether you went to him or not."

"You are probably correct in that respect," Sebastián replied.

"I hope I can trust you with a secret, amigo," Carlos continued. "Manuela and I are married. She is here in Tubaca."

"For heaven's sake!" Sebastián exclaimed. "How did all this come about?"

Carlos related the story of the kindly priest at Santa Rosa del Río, and the freight wagon. Sebastián stood there in amazement about what had happened, and that Carlos had accomplished everything without being discovered. "I will certainly keep your secret, amigo," Sebastián said. "Carranza should arrive any day. You must make sure he doesn't discover you."

"I am glad I told you, because you are the only one who recognizes Manuela. Now she can walk around without fear of you seeing her."

"Where does she live?"

"In the small room behind the Orozco house. She is their cook. I spend nights with her there."

"Now I know where you were going when I watched you amble out of the compound."

"I must be going now," Carlos said. "I am glad that we talked finally."

"I am too."

The two embraced in renewed friendship.

The first encounter the Tubaca garrison had with Apaches came a month after Captain Carranza arrived to take command of the presidio. A rider had come in from the Hacienda de la Canoa, north of Tubaca, with a message that an Apache raiding party had been seen heading south in the Sierra Santa Rita. Carranza posted a double guard on the grazing horse herd, and sent a three-man scouting party across the river. Carlos took his musket with him when he went to spend the night with Manuela.

The two troopers guarding the horses kept the herd together so that they could be driven to the corral quickly in case the Apaches came. Both Carranza and Sergeant Bernal were out of their beds and dressed before early morning light oozed into the valley, because they knew the Apache raiders usually attacked at dawn.

One of the horse guards happened to look into the foothills across the river, trying to judge when the sun would tell him it was time to gather the horse herd, and drive them to the corral. His eyes caught sight of movement on a distant ridge. He beckoned for the other man to join him, and look in the same direction. "I see movement too," the man said. "We had better get these horses to the corral immediately."

They eased around the herd, and drove them toward the presidio. One of them broke away to gallop in with the news of their sighting. He pulled his horse up in front of the commandant's house, dismounted, and ran to the door. Without knocking, he opened the heavy latch, and stood inside. "Captain! Captain!" he yelled. "Apaches across the river!"

Carranza ran to the trooper. "Where?"

"We saw them coming down the far ridge! The horses are in the corral."

"Alert all the troops, soldier. Tell them to get saddled."

Carranza ran to Bernal's quarters to alert the sergeant, then to the corral, where he caught his horse and led him out to the hitch rack for saddling.

TWO GOLD COINS

Carlos kissed Manuela, and went to the door. As always he opened it slightly to see if anyone might be watching him leave the building in the early morning. He was startled to see three Apache warriors walking straight toward him. "Get down on the floor, Manuela! Apaches!"

In almost one motion Carlos stepped outside, shut the door, and leveled his musket at the first in line. The Apache had brought his own rifle up to aim, but the ball from Carlos's barrel struck him between his eyes, felling him instantly. The other two were armed only with knives, and continued to advance, knowing Carlos would have to reload. Instead, Carlos charged toward them, and surprised the first by a swift upward blow to the chin with the butt of the rifle, and a quick thrust with his bayonet into the Indian's heart. The third Apache turned and fled at seeing the absolute fury in the Spaniard's eyes.

Carranza heard the musket fire, and sent Bernal with two troopers to investigate. They loped their horses over to the Orozco house, arriving just in time to watch Carlos ram his bayonet into the unconscious Indian. "One left running that way!" Carlos said pointing in the direction the third Apache had fled. Bernal and the troopers spurred their horses into a gallop. As Carlos reloaded his musket a shot rang out from the direction Bernal had gone.

Carlos opened the door, and found Manuela crouching on the floor. "Good," he said. "Lock the door from the inside, and stay there until this is over."

Carlos, still in a state of mild shock, glanced at the dead Apaches, and trotted toward the presidio. Sergeant Bernal and the two troopers galloped in just ahead of him. "What was all the shooting, Sergeant?" Carranza asked.

"Villanueva shot one, and bayoneted another. We chased a third devil, and I got him."

# TWO GOLD COINS

Carlos trotted in to the drill area where most of the garrison was ready to mount their horses. He kept trotting toward the corral to get his horse. Carranza gave the order to mount as Carlos entered the corral. "Villanueva, I don't know why you are late, but you will have to follow us when you have your horse saddled," Carranza barked.

Carlos hurried as fast as he could, and caught up to the troop as they assembled near the river. Carranza was splitting the troop into two groups. His tactics were to keep half in reserve under Sergeant Bernal while the other half, under his command, went forward seeking a skirmish with the raiders. Carlos rode up, and stayed with Bernal's group.

Bernal, a seasoned veteran of fighting Apaches, didn't agree with Carranza's tactic because the western flank of the town lay unprotected. They had killed three warriors there, and had not scouted further. "Quinteros," he said to Sebastián when Carranza rode behind the mesquite grove across the river. "You, Villanueva, Garcia, and Jimenez scout to the west, and see if there are any more Apaches in that direction. When you're satisfied, return here."

The four troopers turned their horses away from the rest, and trotted them back toward the town. They rode in the direction that the Apache Bernal killed had been heading. In an arroyo thick with mesquite they found three Apache horses picketed, but left them where they were. "We'll bring them in later if they're still there," Sebastián said.

The four searched every arroyo in the vicinity, and found no sign of more raiders. On their return ride they untied the Apache horses, and led them back to the corral. Bernal and his group still waited. Sebastián reported what they had done. "Good," Bernal said. "Instead of them stealing thirty of our horses, we got three of theirs."

Carranza and his group had been gone for nearly three hours before they crossed the river to join the reserve group. "We picked up some sign on the ridge," Carranza said to Bernal. "But it looks like they must have left. Maybe when they heard the musket fire, or saw how many horses we were driving to the corral, and decided we have more troops than they wanted to confront. The three dead ones were probably a scouting party."

"Next time they might come in earlier on foot to try for a surprise," Bernal commented. "If I might suggest, Captain, they may have gone north to the Canoa. Perhaps the presence of some of us would discourage the raiders from attacking."

"Sergeant," Carranza ordered, "send a detail to put the bodies of the dead Apaches where their horses were found. The Apaches will find them, and take them away. Keep the horse guard doubled, and post guards in all directions. These Apaches may stay around for another chance at us. The thought that they might be going north to the Canoa is pure speculation. Sergeant Bernal, send Villanueva to my office."

Carlos went to the commandant's office as soon as he had unsaddled his horse, and turned him out in the corral. Carranza waited behind his desk. "Villanueva, your personal skirmish this morning was a brave act. To face three Apache warriors and kill two of them single-handedly also shows skill. I must commend you."

"Thank you, Captain," Carlos said.

"However, Villanueva, I want to know why you were away from the garrison at that hour," Carranza continued. "You were not on guard duty."

Carlos hesitated, contemplating a reply. He was tired of sneaking away from the compound to be with Manuela. "I was with my wife, captain. I was leaving to return for muster when I saw the Apaches. I killed them in defense of my wife."

"I don't quite understand, Villanueva," Carranza said, wrinkling his brow. "I recall denying permission for you to marry when we were still in Pitic."

"Yes, Captain," Carlos replied. "We were married in spite of your denial. My wife is more important to me than anything."

"That may be, Villanueva, but you are a soldier, and you must obey your superiors, or face the consequences."

"I am prepared for that," Carlos said stiffly.

"You force me to take measures I do not wish to take. I would like to recommend you for a promotion based on your bravery this morning, but your disobedience should be punished. I tried to explain to you in Pitic that a wife interferes with soldiering, and this morning should prove me correct. Therefore I must order you to spend thirty days in the stockade, and I am recommending your discharge as a soldier of the Crown for disobedience and being away from the garrison without permission. This is not pleasant for me, Villanueva. I am giving you one hour with your wife before reporting to the stockade."

Carlos turned, left the building, and trotted quickly to the Orozco house. Manuela had remained inside their room. Upon hearing her husband's voice she opened the door. Carlos entered, and told her what had happened. He was not happy with his sentence to the stockade, but being discharged from the army couldn't have pleased him more. "I can work at the hacienda, and learn farming," he said. "Someday we will have our own place."

"I will miss you, husband," Manuela said. "I will come to see you every day."

"Thirty days is a short time to spend, and when it's over we will be free. If I hadn't been with you this morning, there is no telling what might have happened."

Carlos took her in his arms to spend the rest of the hour together.

The presidio stockade had been erected along with the other buildings so that the only difference in appearance was the door made from peeled mesquite branches set three inches apart. Should a prisoner have a strong desire to escape, he would have little difficulty, needing only to overpower the one twenty-four-hour guard posted outside. Carlos spent his time thinking about his aspirations to own a farm so he and Manuela could be self-sufficient on the frontier. There would be a market, the army, for grain and meat. The question that continued to plague him was how he could save enough money to be able to purchase land. He contemplated the possibility of applying for a land grant in spite of his lack of political influence. He thought also of Simon Orozco, and asking his advice once he became free from the army.

Later in the day another messenger from the Hacienda de La Canoa galloped in to the compound reporting that the Apache raiding party had attempted to steal horses from the corrals, but the vaqueros were able to drive them away. One Canoa cowboy had been killed, two others slightly wounded. The raiders had lost three of their number to Canoa musket fire, and had two others possibly wounded. The messenger asked for troops to help defend the ranch in case the Apaches returned. Carranza sent a detail of four mounted soldiers.

Sebastián came by to spend a few minutes in visiting, and Carlos shared his thoughts about the farm with his friend. Manuela visited whenever she had time away from the Orozco kitchen.

# TWO GOLD COINS

During Carlos's second day in the stockade, Manuela came quickly to see her husband after finishing with the evening meal. "Carlos, I have good news for us," she said, as they looked at each other between the wooden bars in the door. "I told Señora Orozco about all that has happened. She went to el señor, and when you are out of the army, he will hire you to work on the hacienda with the farming and cattle. He thinks you are a very brave man to have faced the three Apache warriors alone."

"I was scared, Manuela. Thinking of your safety drove away my fear. Keep your door locked from the inside at night, and be sure there are no Apaches around when you leave in the mornings for the kitchen."

The Apache raiding party assembled again at the hot spring at the base of the Sierra Santa Rita. Their leader, an older man who had survived many raids against the Pima, Sobaipuri, and Spanish settlers, sent a small hunting party out for provisions. He was disappointed with the results of this latest foray into the valley of the Spaniards. Not only did he want horses, cattle, and muskets, but he also wanted to discourage further Spanish settlement in the area that had once been lucrative for sporadic raids on Pima villages.

He would hold his raiding party at the spring until joined by another that had ranged further south and east, looking for undefended Spanish ranches. In addition the bodies of their dead warriors, retrieved during the darkness of night, waited for the ceremony of death.

The presence of the garrison at Tubaca had surprised him, and his reason for diverting his warriors to the Canoa was because he knew he needed a larger force to attempt an attack against professional defenders.

The hunting party returned with venison and peccary, enough for several days. The death ceremony sent the spirits of the fallen warriors to the top of the sacred mountain to the northeast. Successful raiding delayed the other band of warriors. They arrived at the hot spring with eight captured horses, twenty head of cattle, and six muskets with a keg of powder and a dozen bars of lead, taken from two ranches. They had lost two warriors, but had killed three Spaniards, and six Opata. They were not certain how many of the defenders had escaped during the night.

The two leaders held a conference away from the others for several hours. When they reached an agreement, they shared the forthcoming battle plans with their sub-chiefs. More discussion. The plan then became known among warriors of both bands so that every man was sure what tactics were to be employed.

The battle plan called for leaving most of the horses picketed at a distance. Eight warriors were assigned to drive the Spanish horse herd away while the warriors on foot provided a distracting force. Scouts had provided information about the horses being pastured at night under two mounted guards. The Apache plan was to strike at first light, before the horse herd had been started toward the corral. The principal goal of the raid was horses, but they also wanted as many muskets as they could come by.

Sergeant Bernal was deeply concerned. He went to the commandant's house to relate those worries to Carranza. Bernal knew Apaches, having battled them many times, but Carranza was new to the frontier and Apache battle strategy. On the one hand Bernal wanted to inform his superior, and on the other he could see that Carranza needed delicate handling from a mere sergeant, regardless of the sergeant's experience with the Indians.

"Captain Carranza," Bernal said. "I can sense that the Apaches are still around, and waiting for a chance at us. We have three of their horses, and all of ours. We also have our weapons, which they need and want. It is my bet that they are waiting for reinforcements before making their move. They will attempt to use surprise tactics, run off with as many of our horses as they can, and if they can grab some of our muskets and powder, they will retreat with a sense of victory."

"I appreciate your concerns, and your speculations, Sergeant Bernal," Carranza answered. "Perhaps some precautions are advisable, but it is my opinion that those savages have left us alone for the time being. Otherwise they would have attacked again before this. They are not a disciplined army as we are."

"Captain," Bernal replied with frustration. "I must disagree. The Apache are disciplined. They don't need uniforms to be disciplined, and they are extremely skillful warriors. They will always have the advantage over us in their knowledge of a vast area of land, and their ability to survive on that land. They are also able to scout our facilities without being seen, and they can approach one of our guard posts without being heard. I think we underestimate the Apache as a military threat."

"Bernal, I think you have been on the frontier too long. You give the savages more credit than they deserve. Send Quinteros to me when you leave, Sergeant."

The soldier left the commandant's house wishing that he was under a different command or that Carranza would be transferred away from the frontier. Bernal felt a strong responsibility for the welfare and safety of his inexperienced garrison. He was determined to influence his men toward precautionary measures without undermining Carranza's authority. He spotted Sebastián across the drill yard cleaning his tack, and sent him to Carranza.

"Quinteros, you are a good soldier, I have watched you closely, and someday you will wear the commission from King Ferdinand VI and Queen Barbara. I have decided to advance you to the rank of corporal. I need someone like you with leadership capability and loyalty. I once thought your friend, Villanueva, had the same potential, but his behavior has told me that I was mistaken. Your friend will never make the military man you are. Congratulations."

"Thank you, Captain Carranza. I will do my best."

Sebastián walked across the drill area to the stockade with mixed emotions. He felt good about the promotion, but he didn't like the manner in which Carranza disdained his friend Carlos. He questioned Carranza's remark about loyalty because he had already questioned himself about his loyalty to Carlos.

Carlos listened as Sebastián told him about his meeting with Carranza, and how he felt about the promotion. "Listen, Corporal Quinteros," Carlos said. "I no longer question your loyalty to the army or me. Perhaps Carranza is correct about me, because my loyalty to Manuela and to you comes long before any loyalty I feel toward the army. Look at me behind these bars because I married the woman I adore, and chose to defend her against the Apaches."

Carranza called an afternoon muster to announce Sebastián's promotion. When he had finished the announcement, he turned the garrison over to Sergeant Bernal, and strode over to the commandant's house.

# TWO GOLD COINS

"Men, we are on Apache alert. This means that the horse guards will graze the horses until midnight, then drive them to the corral. You will remain on guard duty at the corral until relieved. Remember Apaches do not attack in darkness. The perimeter guards will keep moving to cover the entire perimeter, checking with one another at regular intervals. I want the cannon moved inside the corral. If they should try for the horses there, the duty guards will wait until the Apaches are at close range before firing. Load the cannon with iron scrap. Everyone sleeps fully clothed with loaded muskets. Make sure you get enough to eat this evening. It might be a while before you will have time to eat again. Stay alert, everyone. Remember, an Apache can sneak up behind you, and you will never tell the story. Dismissed."

Bernal's talk gave the garrison a lot to think about. Conversation in the barracks after the evening meal centered on the alert and speculation about the Apache presence. Carlos experienced a rapid increase in anxiety to be with Manuela in case Bernal proved correct. He felt angry and helpless behind the wooden barred door.

Sebastián went to his bed early to try and sleep before his turn at horse guard. He would relieve at midnight, riding out to help drive the herd to the corral. Then he and his guard partner would have to stay mounted and ready until after sunrise.

Tension remained with the garrison, especially with those who were guarding the perimeter.

The Apache camp stayed dark. No fires to betray their position by smoke during the day or firelight by night. Four scouting parties returned before midnight and reported to the chiefs. They described the positions of the perimeter guards as well as where the horses were grazing. The chiefs then called for a pre-battle ceremony during which the warriors focused on the success of the upcoming raid on the Spaniards. Then by twos and threes they left the camp on their horses, riding along predetermined routes until the camp was empty of all except four wounded warriors who were left in charge of the stolen cattle.

The eight warriors designated to capture the horse herd remained mounted, taking a wide circle, well away from and outside the perimeter guard positions as described by the scouting parties. The rest picketed their mounts in the canyons of the foothills to avoid any noise that might alert the perimeter guards. They advanced quietly in groups. Each group had at least one member armed with a musket. Others carried spears and knives. They knew the army held a superior position in firepower, but they had an advantage of numbers and skill at surprise.

Sebastián woke up with a start as the compound guard came in the barracks to shake him. He sat for a minute, then grabbed his musket, and walked to the corral. He caught his horse, and had him saddled in minutes. His guard partner arrived as Sebastián finished tightening the cinch around the horse's girth. They rode out together, met those who were there to be relieved, and the four soldiers quietly started the herd toward the corral. Sebastián checked the small cannon aimed through the fence of horizontal mesquite poles. He made sure it had been loaded, and remounted his horse to be ready for anything that might come about. He thought about Carlos and Manuela, their happiness together, and wondered if he would ever meet such a woman to love. He thought about Tarifa, his parents, and when the old man had given him the gold coin, which he now kept safely in a small pocket in his tunic. He thought about being a corporal and what

Carranza had told him about being commissioned by the king and queen. He thought about the chances of someone with humble lineage ever being considered for such a status in an army run by gentry. He thought about Sergeant Bernal with his years on the frontier, and his wisdom about the Apaches and their land.

The first faint light of day, when one is aware that the sun is not far from the eastern horizon, eased its way in from the Sierra Santa Rita. The warriors began moving toward the town, some crawling through grass, others crouched low and silent under and through groves of mesquite. The eight horsemen circled behind the foothill to the west, which would hide them until they were a hundred yards from the grazing horse herd.

The first musket shot came from one of the perimeter guards by the river. He was able to pull the trigger before the Apache, who had jumped at him from behind a large clump of sacaton grass, was able to drag him from his saddle, and slice through his jugular. The horse bolted and ran, but not before the Indian grabbed the musket, and took the trooper's powder and lead shot.

All the men on guard heard the musket shot. In an instant the Apache presence became a scary realization. The compound guard ran swiftly to the cast-iron bell mounted on a post, grabbing the rawhide lanyard, and swinging the clapper. At the sound of the bell the garrison jumped from their beds, and left the barracks. Sergeant Bernal bellowed commands. Captain Carranza came out of the commandant's house to find out what was happening. At that same moment the perimeter guards galloped into the drill yard, led by the riderless horse belonging to the trooper who lay lifeless in the sacaton-covered floodplain by the river.

"Open the stockade, and give Villanueva his musket," Bernal barked at the compound guard. "We're going to need everyone we can get."

The guard took out the large iron key, and opened the lock to the wooden barred door to the stockade. Carlos ran to his barracks to get his musket and ammunition.

Carranza stood in the drill yard wondering what he should do. He walked up to Bernal, who waited for the troopers to fall into formation. "Sergeant Bernal," Carranza said. "What about the horses?"

"There won't be time for saddling," he said. "We have enough men mounted to meet theirs. This battle will be fought mostly on foot."

"How do you know that, sergeant?"

"If they were coming in on horseback they would already be here, Captain." It was obvious to Bernal that he would have to give the commands so he divided the garrison into squads, and dispersed them into defensive positions around the town. "You men with horses!" he shouted. "Go in pairs, and don't be out of sight of each other. If any of them are mounted they'll be going for our horse herd, which is in the corral. Keep the corral in view. And, you two horse guards stay at your posts."

The Apache warriors on foot had advanced on the town. Those on horses came around the hill to find the army horse herd missing from their usual pasture. They stopped for a group discussion about the situation, and decided to advance down an arroyo where they would be partially hidden.

Bernal had positioned the garrison effectively. The small groups of Apaches could not advance within musket range without getting shot. They fired occasionally to maintain their diversionary tactic. Bernal had mounted the dead trooper's horse, and surveyed the battle scene from place to place.

# TWO GOLD COINS

Carlos ran to the Orozco house to make sure Manuela had her door locked from the inside, and then returned quickly to join the squad reinforcing the horse guard. At the moment he entered the compound he saw eight mounted Apaches galloping toward the corral. He saw Sebastián fire his musket at the charging riders, and at the next moment his friend was knocked from his horse to the ground. Carlos leaped into the corral, and ran for the cannon. The barrel was pointed straight at the charging Indians. Carlos grabbed the flint, and ignited the powder in the touchhole. The small cannon roared as it sent its load of assorted scrap iron toward the oncoming warriors. Blood spurted from six of the Apaches as the scrap ripped into their bodies. Four fell from their horses, and the remaining raiders turned quickly to retreat. The Spaniards opened fire on the terrified Indians, dropping two more to writhe on the ground.

Carlos ran to where Sebastián lay on the ground outside the corral. He could see the pain on his friend's face, and the blood staining his tunic near his heart. He dropped to his knees over his friend. "Sebastián," he said. "Can you hear me?"

"Yes, my friend, but I am dying. Listen," Sebastián said in almost a whisper. "Reach into the pocket of my tunic. It is for you and Manuela."

Carlos slipped his fingers into the pocket, and withdrew the gold coin that had traveled so far from Tarifa to Tubaca; from Old Spain to New Spain. Tears flooded his eyes as he gently kissed his friend's forehead. "Thank you, amigo, we will cherish you always."

# The Mines of Magdalena

**C**onfidence artists are found in every city, but small towns are not immune. The Concepción Valley attracted a lot of wealthy people over the years, and where there is wealth there are con artists.

Muriel Edgewater grew up in Lake Forest, Illinois, in a family that was an offshoot of "old money." Somewhere along the line the Edgewaters became estranged from the guardians of the family coffers, and Muriel's father had to work for a salary instead of live on a trust. He made good money because he was competent. His wife preceded him in death after months in the hospital. It took a long while for him to die also, incurring great expense over and above his insurance coverage. Muriel was left with a small legacy and the family tree. As time went on the family tree became more valuable than the legacy. The latter, after being shared with her brother, didn't hold up to Muriel's incessant desire for cars, clothes, and single malt Scotch. She was one of those people who just appeared in La Flor one day, and the next she had put a down payment on a house. Two weeks after taking possession, a stranger to town might get the idea that she had been a lifetime resident.

According to Muriel, she was related to scores of millionaires and people in high places in government and society. She immediately wormed her way into the hearts and some of the pocketbooks of the wealthy folks in the valley. She also enticed a good many of the single, and a couple of married men from La Flor into her bed.

As La Flor grew it became a target for ad salesmen from various media, especially tourist magazines. David Wilton came to town from Rinconada trying to sell advertising space in a magazine published in that city. Dave had tired of winters in Portland, Maine, and landed in Rinconada two months prior to his visit to La Flor. His first day of selling in the village made him question why his boss had suggested the trip. The sum total of his sales was one-quarter page to the festival committee. But he met Muriel! Muriel was chairperson of the advertising committee. At five o'clock, when the shop owners locked up their cash registers, Dave went into El Sombrero, the local saloon, ordered a small pitcher of draft beer, and waited for his drink date with Muriel Edgewater.

He had just poured the second glass from the pitcher when Muriel bounced in the entrance, and took the empty barstool next to him. Within an hour Dave knew all the significant names on Muriel's family tree. He also accepted her invitation to dinner. His little Datsun coupe was parked in Muriel's driveway the following morning.

Dave spent three days trying to sell ads to the shops. That's what he told his boss over the telephone, anyway. All told he was able to convince two shop owners that an ad in his magazine would increase their sales considerably.

Dave Wilton didn't like selling ads. Dave Wilton didn't like to work. He homed in on Muriel after listening to her illustrious background. The return trip to Rinconada was only to pack his meager belongings and jump back into Muriel's bed as soon as possible.

David Wilton and Muriel Edgewater became a significant couple in La Flor and the Concepción Valley. That status didn't bother the bevy of wealthy widows and grass widows whom Muriel counted as best friends. Actually they were delighted to see her beaming from ear to ear over her conquest.

It seemed that David Wilton had done just about everything. In this respect he was much like Jerry Thomas, but the two men rarely spoke. In fact both ridiculed each other whenever the opportunity arose.

Two months after David Wilton first came to the village, he and Muriel went to the county seat and were married by the justice of the peace. Shortly after the honeymoon the mutual con came to light. Dave found that, contrary to his belief, Muriel Edgewater, now Muriel Wilton, Mrs. David Wilton, had little left of her legacy, and a huge balloon payment due on her house in La Flor in two years.

Muriel discovered that David Wilton had absolutely no resources, and a mere three hundred dollars left from a consulting job he had performed in Maine before he went West. Muriel and Dave had to laugh about the dilemma, but decided that if they had been so good at conning each other, together they could con the entire valley!

Dave started a financial consulting business, and Muriel began a bookkeeping service. One of her widow friends lent her enough money to buy the latest, state-of-the-art personal computer, but Muriel found a used one, and put the difference in her dwindling checking account. So the Wiltons made every social event in the valley, some with an invitation; to others they finagled a way in. Together they zoomed in on the valley money. If Dave didn't get their business, Muriel would keep their books. For six months they played a straight hand, but a straight hand wasn't going to pay the balloon payment on the house.

David Wilton sat on his favorite barstool at El Sombrero sipping at his beer, and trying to figure a way to come up with twenty thousand dollars for the balloon payment. It wasn't due for a year, but the thought of it was a tremendous burden for Dave. Muriel rarely thought about it, and had the philosophy that someone would feel sorry for them and pay it. Muriel Wilton had little conception of reality. She conned herself every day! Dave went to El Sombrero when he needed the alone time to think. Otherwise he went to the Golf and Tennis Club where the local gentry could see him. The price of beer was higher, but Dave considered it an investment. After all he was a financial consultant. He probably wouldn't have landed a single account if his potential clients knew how he did his consulting. It wasn't the first time in his life that David Wilton operated a phony scam.

Dave didn't know anything about Wall Street, but he bought a book so that he could learn the jargon of the stock market. He then went to a stock salesman with a firm in Rinconada, went to lunch with the fellow, and when he needed information he would telephone the salesman, get the information, and pass it on to the client.

While Dave pondered the balloon payment dilemma at the bar, a well-dressed Mexican man entered, and took the barstool next to him. "I am Davíd Mendibles, from Magdalena, Sonora. I am looking for a hotel. Can you give me any information?" He said in near perfect pronunciation.

"David Wilton, it's a pleasure."

# THE MINES OF MAGDALENA

"We are tocayos, my friend. That means we each have the same first name. What is your business here? Are you one of the artists?"

"No," Wilton replied. "I have a financial consulting business."

"Really," Mendibles said with more interest. "Perhaps I have found the right person. I have a manganese mine in Magdalena, Sonora, and I am trying to sell shares in the mine to American investors. We should maybe talk, no?"

The two Davids, the *tocayos*, became partners in a con game that shattered some sentiments in the Concepción Valley.

Dave Wilton went around talking up the excellent investment opportunity in Minas de Magdalena. Davíd Mendibles, president of the corporation, furnished a prospectus, written in Spanish, of course, which Dave Wilton passed along to his prospective stock buyers. There were also other legal-looking documents with Mexican notary stamps and fancy signatures scrawled across them. The price of a hundred shares in the manganese mine was five thousand American dollars. For the five grand the buyer received a fancy certificate, also written in Spanish with ornate signatures and scrolled borders appearing almost as if they had come from the king of Spain. Dave Wilton was to receive twenty-five hundred from each sale, and he would charge a hundred-dollar commission to the buyers. Mendibles was to keep the other half. All cashier checks were to be made to the corporation. Mendibles was to send Dave Wilton's cut once the cashier's check cleared the Banco Comercio in Mexico. Dave Wilton believed it all, and was impressed by the legitimate-looking papers and certificates. He had several unpaid bills in the valley, but the largest were his booze and dinner tabs at the Golf and Tennis Club. The real hope for David Wilton was that the Mexican manganese mine looked like a chance to pay the balloon payment on Muriel's house.

The wealthy Concepción Valleyites didn't become rich from investing in Mexican mining ventures, but David and Muriel convinced a few, mostly "Lucky Sperm Club" members, who had little idea about what their trust managers did. Warren Mason bought two hundred shares, and gave Dave a cashier's check for ten grand. Dave sent it to Mendibles's post office box in Robles de Plata, Arizona, and waited two weeks for an answer. He and Muriel were relieved to open the large envelope and find the fancy stock certificates in Mason's name, and a personal check from Mendibles to them for five thousand dollars.

Muriel had borrowed five grand from Aimee Whitlesley two years before, and had never paid the loan back to the accommodating widow. Dave suggested that Muriel take the five thousand to Aimee to pay off the interest-free loan in order to restore their credibility. While at Aimee's house she could sell her two hundred shares of Minas de Magdalena stock, and the Wiltons would get their five grand back without having to borrow it.

Muriel drove over to the Golf and Tennis Club Estates, and Aimee couldn't believe Muriel wanted to repay the loan, especially in crisp one-hundred-dollar bills. When Muriel showed her all the propaganda for the manganese mine "investment," Aimee listened politely, but refused to buy. She explained to Muriel that her now dead husband had lost a hundred grand in a similar-sounding Mexican gold mine deal.

"Dammit," Muriel said, when she returned home to a waiting David. "We just blew five grand, trying to be nice!"

"Don't worry, I'm about to close a couple more," Dave said. "I should know about them at the party this evening over at the Demarests'."

The Demarest party proved a fruitful orchard for Dave and Muriel. The cocktails loosened minds and purse strings, resulting in six solid sales of the mine stock. Dave gathered the cashier checks in the morning after the bank opened, and had them on their way to Mendibles. And by following two more leads he had from the party, he sold two more hundred-share "investments." When he returned from the bank and post office he wore a smug look on his face.

"There's the balloon payment, Mur," he said. "We beat it to the wire. Six more months, and we would have been heading down the road!"

"Just don't get excited until the ink is dry," Muriel said. "I still wonder about that Mendibles character, and remember you've never seen his wonderful manganese mine."

"Hell, Mur," Dave retorted. "I'm a damn good judge of men, and he is A OK in my book. He sent us that five grand, didn't he?"

Warren Mason's motor sailer was due in the harbor at San Carlos Bay, and he wanted to stop and see the Minas Magdalena operation on his way to the monthlong cruise he had planned in the Sea of Cortez. Dave Wilton gave him one of Mendibles's business cards with an address in Magdalena. Two weeks had passed with no checks from Davíd Mendibles. The stock certificates arrived, and Muriel distributed them. With his constant worry about the balloon payment, Dave Wilton became more nervous every day his post office box yielded only bills and "junk mail."

Wilton attempted to telephone Mendibles in Magdalena, but the Mexican operator informed Dave that the Magdalena number had been disconnected.

"I'm going over there and find out what the holdup on our money is, Muriel."

Muriel helped pack a few things in a suitcase, and kissed her husband goodbye, wishing him good luck. Magdalena is not a long drive from La Flor if you don't tarry along the way. Dave Wilton was worried enough not to stop except for gas.

The Wilton telephone rang three times before Muriel staggered out of her bed to answer it. "Warren Mason here. I'm in the middle of the Sea of Cortez on my cellular. Finally got through to you."

"Hi Warren, Muriel. How's the cruise going?"

"The cruise is just fine, but I think your mining stock is as flat as a dead flounder."

"Why are you saying that, Warren?" Muriel slapped her left palm on her forehead.

"Out of curiosity, I stopped in Magdalena on the way down," Mason said, his annoyance showing in the tone of his voice. "The address on that so-called business card turned out to be a goddam bakery, so I looked up the presidente del pueblo, the mayor. He told me that the goddam mine hadn't been worked for years since it played out of ore."

"David is on his way down there right now," Muriel replied. "He should call me from somewhere, and I'll give him your message. Don't worry and spoil your cruise, David will straighten everything out."

"Don't count on it, 'bye!"

Muriel hung up the receiver, and walked to the buffet for a double single-malt Scotch.

"Shit!" she said to the glass. "Why didn't Dave listen to me?"

Dave reached Magdalena, more exhausted from worry than from the trip. He found the bakery, and began to worry more. He realized that Mendibles had never given him a map to the mine, so he went into a bar in the hope someone would give him directions. The bartender spoke no English, but pointed out an old cowboy, with a shot of Tequila in front of him. Dave asked about the mine and directions to it. The cowboy knew the mine, and drew a rough and sketchy map, which Dave hoped he could follow. He left the bar, and found a motel for the remainder of the night.

After an early breakfast the following day Dave began his search for the manganese mine, hoping to find Mendibles. After an hour, bouncing over one of the roughest roads Dave Wilton had ever driven, he came to some mine tailings that had been piled in front of a shaft. A sign, hanging limply from a single post, with letters almost peeled off from weathering, warned of danger. Neither Mendibles nor anyone else had been to Minas de Magdalena in a decade.

David Wilton couldn't believe what he had seen. His stomach pained with the hopelessness of the situation. "How the hell could I get taken like this?" he said out loud, looking at the abandoned shaft.

He drove in an hour to Robles de Plata, hoping to track down the slippery Davíd Mendibles. The bar at the El Toro had few customers at midafternoon. Dave ordered a beer and asked the bartender if he knew Mendibles. "He should be here any minute," the bartender opined. "He comes in every afternoon about now."

Dave felt lucky, and Dave felt smart. He sipped at his beer, and ordered another just as Mendibles entered the room and took his usual seat at the bar. "Hey, Mendibles," Dave said from the end of the bar.

"Hello, Tocayo. ¿Como estás? How are you?"

Dave rose from his stool, and moved over to sit next to Mendibles. "I've been all the way down to Magdalena looking for you."

"I have been in Rinconada trying to buy mine machinery," Mendibles said.

"Where's all the money you were supposed to have sent?"

"Don't worry, Tocayo, it's safe in the bank across the line."

"Why haven't you sent my share? I've got a balloon payment due on my house."

"Don't worry, Tocayo. Meet me at the Banco Comercio at ten tomorrow morning and you'll have all the money coming to you. I have been so busy looking for machinery, I haven't had time to take care of you. I'm sorry if my delay has caused you inconvenience."

The sleepless night was long for David Wilton, and waiting the morning away drinking coffee until ten o'clock gave him the shakes. He decided to walk to the bank to avoid fighting the heavy erratic traffic on the narrow streets of Robles de Plata, Sonora. As the sole gringo, he felt conspicuous standing in the bank waiting for Mendibles. When the mine owner didn't show by ten-thirty, Wilton wondered if it was just "Mexican time" he dealt with, or if Mendibles never intended to meet him. He walked to a desk, and asked to speak to the manager of the bank. "I am the manager," a well-dressed man in his mid-forties said in precise English. "How can I help you?"

"I am supposed to meet a man named Davíd Mendibles here, and he is long overdue," Wilton said. "Would you happen to have his telephone number so I could call him?"

"The name is familiar, but I don't think he is a customer at this bank. Let me check." The manager went behind the tellers to a file, opened a drawer, and fingered

through it. "No, there is no Davíd Mendibles in our customer file," he said when he returned to his desk. "Are
you sure you are at the right bank?"

"I am quite sure," Wilton replied, taking the slip of
paper from his pocket that Mendibles had given him the
night before.

"That's this bank," the manager said. "But like I said,
this Mendibles does not do his banking here."

"Thanks for your help, anyway," Wilton said, and left.

He hurried back across the border, and found a pay
phone. He placed a collect call to Muriel in La Flor.
"We've had it," he said when she answered.

"I know," she replied. "Warren Mason called from his
boat in the middle of the Sea of Cortez."

"I found the mine, which hasn't been visited by anyone in years, and I found that goddam Mendibles here in
Robles de Plata. He told me to meet him at a bank across
the border this morning, and he was to pay me the
money. The sonofabitch never showed, and the manager
told me he doesn't even bank there. We are screwed, Mur.
We are screwed!"

"You should have called last night, I could have told
you. You could have been back by now."

"Muriel, don't give me any shit right now, I'm in no
mood for it. Get off your ass and start packing essentials,
because when I get back we are leaving town, and as quietly as possible."

"Where are we going, David?"

"I have no idea. But we are damn sure getting our
asses out of La Flor before we get lynched."

"David," she said with exasperation. "I think you are
magnifying the entire situation. We have made too many
contacts here to leave."

"And every one of those contacts will be useless now. We are leaving! Goodbye."

As David Wilton placed the receiver back on its cradle, David Mendibles was checking in at Hotel Las Brisas in Puerto Vallarta.

Everyone in La Flor wondered why the Wiltons had left town in the middle of the night, and not taken all their belongings. The wealthy investors in Minas de Magdalena didn't mention the matter at their parties, because none of them wanted to admit their having been duped by David and Muriel Wilton.

# The Last Breakfast

**T**he blue and pink tour bus, with "Heavenly Tours" emblazoned on its sides, zoomed north toward Tombstone, Arizona. It slowed down as it entered the town. Every passenger looked out of the windows.

"Look at that sign in the window, boys," Ike Clanton said. "It says 'The Best Margarita This Side Of The Border.'"

"If she's anything like the Margarita I knew in Juarez, Mexico, we could be in for one helluva good time," Cole Younger remarked.

"All you fellers think about is women," "Doc" Holliday said from the last seat in the back of the bus.

"The Crystal Palace looks to me like our kind of place," Jesse James said.

The bus parked on a side street to discharge its twelve grizzly looking passengers.

Wyatt Earp and Ike Clanton led the way.

Wyatt and Ike stopped so quickly when they reached Allen Street that Morgan Earp and Billy the Kid almost bumped into them. "The sign says Allen Street," Wyatt said, pointing to the street marker. "But it shore don't look like the Allen Street I knew."

"Hell's fire, Wyatt," Ike said. "It's been a helluva while since we was here. Things change with time."

"I know that, Ike, but there used to be saloons, gamblin' halls, and bawdy houses all over town. Now look at it! A bunch of damn tourist shops. I'll bet we'll have a helluva time findin' a poker game."

"I reckon you're the only one hankerin' fer poker, Wyatt," Ike replied. "I'll bet the rest of us would just as soon have breakfast. Let's see if the Crystal Palace is still around."

By this time the rest had formed a sinister-looking group at the corner. Wyatt stepped into the street and started walking north. "There's the *Epitaph* office where Johnny Clum ran the newspaper. I shore had him fooled."

As they were passing the *Epitaph* office a man had come to the door and was scrutinizing the bunch, looking at each one as if he knew them all. As the twelve men entered the Crystal Palace Saloon the same man followed thirty yards behind them.

"Damned if it isn't good to be back," Wyatt said. "The old place looks the same."

"What'll it be, fellers?" the bartender asked.

"We're looking for Margarita," Butch Cassidy said.

"All of you want a margarita?"

"I reckon so, unless you have more girls than her."

"You guys are funnin' me. Margaritas here are the best this side of the border 'cause we use good tequila and fresh lime juice."

"You mean to tell us that margaritas are drinks?" The Sundance Kid asked.

"With or without salt?"

# THE LAST BREAKFAST

One by one the men ordered their margaritas, some with salt, some without.

All the men raised their glasses in a toast, and took tentative sips. Cole Younger said that he would rather drink his tequila straight. Ike Clanton agreed, but lifted his glass for another swallow.

"The movies never had us drinkin' fancy drinks like these," Bob Younger said.

"The movies doin' us?" Billy the Kid said. "Man, they sure got it all wrong, just like them shoot-'em-up novels and stories. Hell's fire, there ain't no man can ride one hundred miles a day, especially on those wore-out nags we used to steal."

"And they always have me with some fancy gun," Ike Clanton said. "Crisakes, I had a bunch of guns, and the one I used was the one that I had stolen ammunition for."

"Another margarita round?" the bartender asked.

"Why not?" Wyatt Earp spoke for the rest.

"Look who's comin' in the door," Jesse James said, as he looked toward the entrance. "If it ain't ole Sittin' Bull hisself comin' in from The Happy Hunting Grounds. Bull, pull up a stool and have a drink."

"They don't allow Native Americans to drink booze," Sitting Bull replied,

"Aw hell, Bull, they haven't had that law around for years," Wyatt Earp said. "Besides, you're an Indian."

Sitting Bull walked to the bar, sat on a barstool. "I'm a Lakota Sioux," he said as the bartender mixed him a margarita.

"Bull," Wyatt said. "Whatever you are you really did a number on ol' George Armstrong Custer. They been writin' about that Little Big Horn Battle for years now and can't seem to get it all straight."

"Well, I'll tell you boys something," Sitting Bull said. "If they had asked me, I would have said the same thing I'll say today, even after one of these drinks. Custer had it coming."

"Any more of you fellers comin' to this breakfast?" Jesse James asked.

"Crazy Horse is right behind, I think. The Border Patrol at that last roadblock stopped him. They think he's an illegal Mexican. He doesn't know what an illegal Mexican is. He told them he was a Native American and had never been to Mexico. He brought his peace pipe along and the officers think it's some sort of drug paraphernalia, whatever that is. I don't know what they are talking about. They said they were looking for pot. Crazy Horse never carries his pots around. His wife always does the cooking."

"Did they stop you, too?" Cole Younger asked.

"When they stopped me they asked me where I was born. I had to think about that one, and finally told them I was born in Fargo, North Dakota. They let me pass through their roadblock. Not old Crazy Horse. Why do you suppose they would let me through and not him?"

"Probably, he told them where he was born is none of their business," Clanton said. "He hasn't said much to the white eyes since those treaties."

"I don't either," Sitting Bull continued. "For one thing I am tired of you white eyes calling us 'Native Americans.' I am a Lakota Sioux, you know, not an American. It used to be that none of you white eyes would ever claim Indian blood. Now all of you claim it to get free medical care, oil royalties, or to get your poetry published."

"But, Bull," Wyatt Earp broke in. "Look at the advantage of being an Indian today. Indian pots sell for more than white eye pots, and there's one publisher I know of that won't publish any poetry unless it's written by a Native American, or Indian, or whatever you call yourselves."

"That's all part of the guilt trip you white eyes are on," Sitting Bull replied, and went back to his margarita.

Frank James turned to speak for the rest. "Reckon we could use somethin' in our bellies about now."

"Do you have reservations at Clanton's?" The bartender asked.

"I have a reservation," Sitting Bull replied.

"Under what name is your reservation, sir?"

"Sioux Nation," Sitting Bull replied. "What does that have to do with breakfast? All we want is some food; do they have any venison or buffalo?"

The bartender looked quizzically at Sitting Bull. "Are you gentlemen here in the valley for a movie?"

"We're here for breakfast," Wyatt Earp said.

"I'm afraid you'll have to wait if you don't have reservations," the bartender said. "They fill up early at Clanton's."

"I just told you I have a reservation," Sitting Bull insisted.

"Just tell us where this eatery is," Earp interjected.

"What did he mean about being here for a movie?" Sitting Bull asked.

"Look at all the photographs on the walls of the movie stars who have played us," Jesse James said. "There's John Wayne, Henry Fonda, and Gary Cooper over there. The Hollywood fellers must make movies around here."

Two sheriff's deputies, badged and armed, swaggered through the swinging doors for a coffee break from patrolling the highway. Billy the Kid, seeing the stars on their uniformed chests, in a lightning-swift movement, reached down to his hip, but found his revolver missing. Wyatt Earp noticed his quick movement. "Don't worry

about those guys, Billy, your wanted poster hasn't been cir-
culated for years. Remember, you're dead, Billy."

"I reckon I was a bit hasty, Wyatt, but every time I see
a badge I get antsy. They didn't seem to recognize any of us,
did ya notice?"

"Yeah," Ike Clanton said. "But, that doesn't surprise
me at all. They think we're them movie stars that have
played us."

"I remember all those wanted posters," Billy the Kid
said. "The pictures never looked like me. I wanted to get a
decent picture taken that showed me better lookin'. Just
think if we was still robbin' stages, banks, and trains, we
could have color photos on our wanted posters."

"Obviously, you never looked in a mirror, Billy. There
ain't a photographer in the world that could make you good
lookin', even in color."

"Speaking of the movies, Wyatt," Holliday said. "That
Kevin Costner sure as hell don't look like you."

"That movie bombed anyway. They should have asked
me before they spent all those millions of dollars."

"Costner did a good job on *Dances With Wolves*,"
Sitting Bull said.

"You're only sayin' that 'cause he was on your side,
Bull," Billy the Kid said.

"Did you come from a broken home or was ya abused as
a child, Billy?" Ike Clanton asked.

"I don't remember nothin'."

"Sounds to me like you must have been abused to turn
out so damned ornery."

"I don't even know what abused means," Billy replied.

"Haven't ya been watchin' television, Billy?" Cole
Younger asked. "Don't you know ya could be absolved of all
your crimes if ya could prove that ya were abused as a child?"

"I ran away when my uncle Joshua told me I had such beady eyes that I could look through a keyhole with both of them at the same time."

"That sounds like abuse to me," Jesse James said. "Maybe we were all abused, and that's why we went to Heaven?"

"From what I hear," Ike Clanton chimed in. "We could have done a lot worse."

"I had a choice," Wyatt Earp said. "I was told to get out of Dodge, or face the consequences. I didn't know what consequences meant, so I left Dodge. By the way, we really should get on with The Last Breakfast or it will be dinnertime soon, and I understand they have a 'happy hour' here at the Crystal Palace, and that means disaster for ole 'Doc' Holliday."

"He's already had five Bloody Marys," Morgan Earp said. "He thinks if he drinks Bloody Marys he won't get a hangover."

"A man with such an illustrious medical background as 'Doc's' should know better than that," Cole Younger added.

"But 'Doc's' a dentist," Ike Clanton said. "Besides learnin' how to yank teeth, they spend four years, these days, learning how much they can charge their patients and get away with it. How about some breakfast, 'Doc'?"

"Breakfast," Holliday said with a definite slur to his speech. "I've already had five stalks of celery for breakfast. That ought to be enough to keep me healthy until we get back." He lifted the tall, narrow glass to his lips for another swallow.

"Butch," Ike Clanton said. "You and Sundance are being awful quiet."

"Haven't anything to say," Cassidy replied.

"Well, I'd sure like to know what you fellers did in South America," Clanton said.

"Who says we went to South America?" Cassidy replied.

"It was all in that movie. You tried to take on the whole durned South American army."

"Sundance can tell you the whole story if he wants to, but I'm sworn to secrecy by the State Department," Cassidy said.

"Well, what about it, Sundance?" Clanton asked.

"I'm takin' the Fifth Amendment, Ike," Sundance said.

"Whatever that is," Clanton said.

"Ya take the Fifth Amendment when you don't want to tell the truth and you're skeered a lyin' 'cause you'll get in trouble," Sundance said. "What if'n I was to ask ya about Hole-in-the-Wall, Ike? What would you have to say?"

"I never could figure all the excitement about that place. We just lived there because there was no rent to pay."

The man who had been following the group entered the bar, staring at the men, trying to figure out who they were. "Bartender, let me buy these gentlemen their drinks," the man said.

The thirteen men turned to see who the drink-buying stranger might be. "Much obliged," Wyatt said.

"My name is Penrod," the man said. "I'm the editor of the Tombstone *Epitaph*, and when I saw you walking down Allen Street I thought you men looked familiar."

"I doubt if you have ever seen any of us before," Cole Younger said.

"You wouldn't be in town for that movie they're shooting would you?" Penrod asked.

"No, sir, we ain't here for no movie," Butch Cassidy said. "We came to town for some breakfast."

"You won't find breakfast here at the Crystal Palace Saloon, gentlemen, but I can recommend Clanton's Cookery down the street a ways. But, you will need a reservation."

"Well, thank you, Penrod," Wyatt said. "And thanks for the drinks."

"You're quite welcome," Penrod said, and a quizzical look spread over his face. "You gentlemen are certainly familiar, but for the life of me I can't place you." He stood next to Billy the Kid. "And you, sir," he said, touching Billy lightly on the shoulder. "What's your name? Do you live in these parts?"

"Name's William, and I don't live anywhere near here, Penrod."

"Well," Penrod said. "Enjoy yourselves in Tombstone, and let me know if there's anything I can do for you. I'll be over at the *Epitaph* office."

The men at the bar said their thanks, and the baffled editor went out the door shaking his head.

"Let's find Clanton's Cookery, fellers," Ike Clanton said. "I could use some breakfast other than tequila."

"Hell's fire, Ike," Cole Younger said. "You just want to see if'n you got kin still around."

"Chances are they just borrowed your name," Morgan Earp said. "I'm for stayin' for a few more tequilas, cause once we have the Breakfast the bus is leavin', and I for one am damned sure goin' to be on it."

"I'm with you, Morgan," Billy Clanton said. "Hey, it would be kinda fun to go have a look-see at the cemetery while we're here in Tombstone."

"Wyatt," Morgan said, turning to his brother. "Billy Clanton wants to visit Boothill Cemetery while we're here. Whadda ya think?"

"Might be fun as long as it's on the way to Clanton's Cookery. Bartender, how do we get to Clanton's Cookery?" Wyatt asked.

"Just past Boothill across the street."

"I guess we might as well have another round, then," Wyatt continued. "Is there a poker game in town?"

"No gamblin' anymore. The city council passed an ordinance against gambling a few years back," the bartender said. "The only place to gamble these days is on the Indian reservations."

"Bull, does your reservation have gamblin'?" Wyatt asked.

"Beats me," Sitting Bull replied. "I haven't been there in years, but if there's money to be made, you can be sure that we'll give it a try. Sounds like a good way to fleece the white eyes."

The bartender poured another round of tequila, and a shot of Jack Daniels for "Doc" Holliday. Wyatt asked for the tab, and the bartender told him it would be $32.50. Earp tossed out a fifty-dollar bill, and turned to Frank and Jesse James. "Did you hear how much this round of tequila cost?"

Both Frank and Jesse shook their heads. "I couldn't believe it," Jesse said. "This stuff ain't worth more than a dime a drink."

"I remember we used to get tequila for a damned nickel right in this very saloon," Wyatt said. "I figured it might cost a fiver at the most for the round. And, they don't even have a poker table in here. Times shore have changed."

"I wonder what breakfast will cost," Frank James said. "We might have to pull another disappearing act like we did back at the Cattle Corral Restaurant and Bar."

"Let's drink up fellers, and head for Clanton's Cookery," Wyatt said to the group.

The bartender brought Wyatt's change and the men lifted the shot glasses to their lips. "You gentlemen can have your breakfast, I'm staying here," "Doc" Holliday announced.

"Now 'Doc,'" Wyatt said. "Remember what Pedro said about stickin' together. We shore don't want you to be missin' the bus."

"You fellows pick me up on your way back to the bus. I already ate my breakfast of celery."

"You'll miss visitin' Boothill, 'Doc,'" Ike Clanton said.

"I really have no other desires except more of this fine-tasting whiskey."

Editor Penrod herded everyone out to the front of the Palace. Wyatt followed and saw his companions being arranged in front of the old building by the editor. Butch Cassidy and The Sundance Kid had "Doc" Holliday propped between them. "Would you find a place among your friends?" Penrod said when he arrived. "I would like a photograph for the front page of the newspaper."

Wyatt joined the others. Penrod fiddled with his camera, getting the lens set for light and focus. "Ready," he said, as he looked through the single lens reflex camera. He pushed the shutter button, and then looked up at the group. "One more, please," he said. "This time please don't smile."

Penrod snapped another photograph. "Thank you very much, gentlemen. If you will give me your names and addresses, I'll make sure you get copies of The Tombstone *Epitaph*, The National Newspaper Of The Old West."

"We'll stop by and pick them up on our next trip, Penrod," Wyatt said. "Just hang on to them until then."

"Fine," Penrod said. "But, would you give me your names for the caption under the photograph?"

"Just put, 'The Gang That Visited Tombstone.' We've got a bus to catch right this minute."

"Thanks again gentlemen, and have a pleasant trip," Penrod said. "I wish you could stay in town longer, I would like to get better acquainted with you. What about your breakfast?"

"I reckon that will have to wait until the next trip. The bus is leaving directly."

The group walked south on Allen Street, turning the corner where the blue and pink tour bus stood with idling motor. The door swung open as they approached, and the twelve men said their good-byes to Sitting Bull. When they had taken their seats the door closed and the bus began moving as Sitting Bull waved at the faces in the windows.

Penrod stood at the street corner watching the departure, and was surprised to suddenly see nothing but an empty street where the bus had been. The bus and the Indian had simply vanished. He returned to his newspaper office shaking his head in disbelief at what he thought he had witnessed.

He went into the room containing the archives of the newspaper, picked up the handful of old pictures he had been looking at, and left for the Crystal Palace Saloon. "George," he said to the bartender. "Look at these old photographs I pulled out of the archives. I knew that some of that bunch looked familiar."

"I thought they were here to audition for the *Shoot Out At The OK Corral* next month, but they weren't carrying any weapons."

"Look at the photographs. This one of Billy the Kid looks just like that short one with the beady eyes. He had a different hat on is all. And, look at this old shot of Wyatt Earp when he was marshal. It's a bit out of focus and yellowed, but it sure looks like the one who was doing most of the talking. And, I'll bet the drunk one was 'Doc' Holliday!"

"Might be, Penrod, but it don't seem possible. Hell, those guys have been dead for over a hundred years. It's

2006. You may have been reading too many back issues of the *Epitaph*."

"Wait until the film is developed and printed. I'll bet my pictures will match up with some of the faces I have in the archives, especially Billy the Kid and the Earps and Clantons."

"When will the film be ready?"

"The drugstore has overnight developing."

Penrod went back to the newspaper office, put the old photographs back in the archive room, sat down in front of his typewriter, and began to write. The following morning he went to the Crystal Palace for a midmorning beer.

The telephone rang. George ambled over, and picked up the receiver. "Crystal Palace," he said. "Okay, Amos, I'll tell him." Penrod left his half-finished beer on the bar, and hurried toward the drugstore across the street. He returned in minutes with the envelope of photographs in his hand. He looked at the prints one by one and handed them to George. Penrod looked closely at the last two from the stack. "I can't figure this out, George," he said, and handed the prints to the bartender. "None of those men are in the pictures, but they are great shots of the Crystal Palace entrance."

"That is strange," George muttered. "I was standing behind the bar watching you take the pictures. But, these are good shots of the Crystal Palace."

"You know, George, I had most of the article written too."